Matriarch

by

J. M. Davis

Matriarch

Cover Art by *Debbie Taylor*

The Wild Rose Press, Inc.
PO Box 708
Adams Basin, NY 14410-0708
Visit us at www.thewildrosepress.com

Publishing History
First Black Rose Edition, 2019
Print ISBN 978-1-5092-2528-6
Digital ISBN 978-1-5092-2529-3

Published in the United States of America

I blinked, finding I was still in the forest. The moon was casting a silvery mist through the trees, and the air was crisp. I gathered what little strength I had and pushed myself up, staggering as I tried to find my footing. I tottered clumsily before collapsing back into the dirt with a thud. Movement to my left caught my attention. I rotated my head and found Roland staring back at me. He swallowed and gave me a slight smile. Again I willed my arms and legs to cooperate, but something felt wrong. Different. I shifted, needing to evaluate my body; take inventory of possible injuries. My head throbbed, but the pain in my limbs was gone.

"Layla, before you do anything crazy," Roland said. I looked at him, confused by his words. His arms were held up in surrender as though he were trying to coax me from jumping off a bridge. "I want you to know that I am here to help. I will guide you through this."

Help me with what? I pushed myself upright but was still unable to stand. My eyes drifted downward. My hands were gone! They were sharp black hooves. I tried to scream, but it came out as something primal, something unhuman.

Dedication

To the little zoo that captured my heart

Chapter 1

For *years* I was clueless. Meandering through life believing I was just like every other boring human being on earth. Then, reality caught up with me. It didn't sneak up and give me a gentle nudge—no—it wasn't that generous. Instead, it reared up angrily and screamed right into my face with teeth bared.

It happened when I was busy making my usual rounds at Greater Hope Medical Hospital, tending to the countless glass cages, full of white mice that lined the wall. As a Tech, it was my responsibility to feed the laboratory animals and clean their soiled cages. I'd seen an assortment of animals come through the lab— various rodents, pigs, rabbits, and even cats.

The mice never bothered me. I actually thought they were kind of cute with their teeny red eyes and twitching noses. Some of the lab's cages were overstocked with them. Fuzzy balls of squirming energy crawling over one another, vying for a morsel of the carefully rationed pelleted food I issued them each day.

Other cages held just one rat or mouse, whose little body was being pumped with an unknown medication. The scientists who concocted the antidote were always hopeful it would cure whatever disease they injected the poor creature with. That's the harsh reality of scientific studies. Trial and error. Then repeat the pattern until you either run out of funding or you finally find success.

Humming to myself, I finished up the last mouse cage, fluffing the bedding and topping off the water bottle when the large metal cage in the far corner of the room rattled. I jerked at the sound, dropping the lid to the cage back into place with a clatter. The steel cage rattled again, raising every hair along both my arms. Shaking off the feeling, I secured the lid, twisting the locks tight before stepping away from the shelf of glass cages.

The animal within the metal cage was going ballistic; screeching and tearing around the small compartment so fanatically the entire cage shuddered across the tile floor. Having been at the laboratory for only a few days now, the creature inside was off-limits to me. No one other than Dr. Moore had been given clearance to tend to him.

But I had to go to it. I had to check to see if it was okay. It could be having a bad reaction to the administered medication.

My paper medical shoes were almost silent on the glossy tile floor as I moved closer. The aroma of bleach was strong in the sterile laboratory, but the distinct trace of feces always evaded the masking effect of the disinfectant. The smell perpetually overwhelmed my senses. I could practically taste the foul scent.

Confined to a small cage made of sturdy sheet metal, a rhesus macaque, a primate no bigger than a toy poodle, bounded about, his body clanging loudly off the bars. With each powerful charge, the cage scratched across the floor.

The door of the cage was designed with cross bars

for ventilation. It looked like a prison. A tiny prison, and the poor felon was an innocent monkey. My heart broke for this animal.

I peered inside the cage.

The monkey screamed in alarm, its mouth stretched wide, baring its razor-sharp incisors as it flung itself against the bars. Startled, I jumped back, clutching at my chest.

After I regained a steady heartbeat, I swallowed hard and took a closer look. The distressed animal retreated to a corner, cowering like a scolded child. The fluorescent lighting overhead barely illuminated his soft pink face, but I could see that its neck had been shaved and tattooed with blue numbers. The code etched into its skin told me that it was a male, and his identification number was 98253.

His nostrils flared wide with each breath he took. It was obvious he was terrified, and I hated that I was the reason. I frowned to myself, watching with a heavy heart as the animal's beady black eyes darted madly around him.

What kind of study is Dr. Moore conducting on him, I wondered as I took a step closer to the cage. The primate peeled his lips back farther, revealing pointed fangs that reminded me of switchblades.

"It's okay," I said gently.

He sat poised, ready to hurl himself against the bars again, his small chest heaving wildly as he panted.

"I'm not going to hurt you. I promise."

As if having a battle of wills, we watched each other carefully for a long while, until finally, his breathing returned to normal. His lips slowly lowered like a closing curtain over his scary sharp teeth. The panic in his eyes receded, and he looked up at me with shining, trustful eyes.

He surprised me by ambling closer. His toes and fingers reminded me of my own. *It's amazing how similar primates are to humans.* The soft skin on his hands and feet were worn from the steel bars, raw and mottled with crusty callouses.

The door to the lab suddenly clicked opened. The monkey's eyes bulged, and the look of complete and total fear spread across his face.

"Afternoon, Layla."

Feeling oddly guilty, I whirled around, my thick braid whipping over my shoulder. Dr. Moore, the head scientist in Greater Hope's laboratory came toward me. I clasped my hands behind my back as if I'd been caught stealing.

"Hello, Dr. Moore." I forced a tight smile.

"Just getting a few supplies," he said as he tucked a handful of latex gloves into the pocket of his medical coat. "Things going well in here?" He lifted a gray brow at me.

"Oh yes. Just checking out the new guy." I turned my gaze to the shivering monkey. His dark eyes were fixated on Dr. Moore. His nostrils flared when the doctor stepped up to his cage.

I turned to stand shoulder to shoulder with the doctor, holding my breath as I waited for something to happen, either for the doctor to speak, or the macaque to rage again.

"His restrictions have been lifted," the doctor mentioned coolly. "So could you please remove his water source before you leave? He's scheduled for testing tomorrow and mustn't have anything in his stomach."

I looked at Dr. Moore sharply. *Testing?* I knew all too well what that could entail. The hospital ran an extensive research laboratory that experimented medicinal drugs on test subjects, such as the small mammals I cared for in the lab. I ground my teeth as I thought again for the hundredth time since I accepted the job, *why the hell do I work here?*

"Testing?" I asked, trying to keep my tone casual.

"Yes. He'll be injected with an experimental drug, called Triplastor. Then, we will simulate an ischemic stroke. With any luck, the drug will counteract the blocked arteries and stop the stroke before it starts."

I swallowed on a painfully dry throat. They were going to force the rhesus macaque to endure a terrifying stroke. Who knew if the drug would work, let alone what side effects it might cause?

My mind swirled in a chaotic windstorm of thoughts. Staring at the doctor, I forced measured breaths deep into my lungs, and out through my mouth. He didn't seem to notice my fraying composure. He gazed almost hungrily at the primate, his weathered face hanging like the folds of a wrinkled shirt. The monkey's shivering image reflected like a mirror against his wire-rimmed glasses. The macaque shrunk into a trembling heap of fur in the corner, and it was difficult to not react. It felt as though my heart was full of lead weights, making it difficult to breathe.

"If the drug proves to be a success," the doctor continued, "it will set the foundation for extraordinary advances."

"And if it fails?" I questioned, my voice low and surprisingly steady.

"Then the project will *rhesus* in peace." He gave a short, snort-like laugh.

I fought against the overwhelming urge to roll my eyes. An overpowering part of me demanded to know the primate's fate, so I pressed him further. "The monkey…will he die?"

"Most likely," he said, turning his back to me. "But we can always get another."

Get another? He acted as though rhesus monkeys were a dime a dozen. Perhaps they were. My throat dried further at the idea.

The doctor went to the nearest cabinet, gathering a few more supplies. Unable to move, I watched him, my feet planted firmly in front of the monkey's cage.

Tucking a final handful of syringes into his coat pocket, he turned to look my way. "Have a good day, Layla," he said with a smile that was too tender for my liking.

I could only muster an acknowledging nod.

His polished loafers clicked loudly on the tile as he walked out of the laboratory. A sigh of relief escaped me as I watched the door sweep close.

I hung my head, my eyes growing misty and my stomach churning with disgust. *What the hell am I doing here? This job is not for me.* I balled my fists tightly, trying to not only dispel my gathering anger, but also collect my composure.

I wanted to strangle the doctor. How could he be so callous? We were talking about a living being, damn it. A creature who felt fear and pain just like the rest of us.

Out of the corner of my eye, I noticed the monkey leaping angrily on the bottom of the cage, clattering the grate with each landing. He seemed to agree with me.

I gazed at him blankly, wondering what to do. Should I quit on the spot? Or perhaps a resignation letter to the president of the hospital, explaining how hypocritical I felt every time I watched one of the animals I cared for die.

The primate let out a shrill scream that sliced right through my skull and rattled my teeth. I clamped my hands over my ears, my eyes wide with fright. *What is wrong with him?* He leaped once more, hurling his body against the door with a sickening *thud.*

A detached voice cut through the air, *"I don't want to die!"*

I spun around, searching the room for the owner of the strange voice. There was no one. With the voice gone, the only sound I could hear was the faint rustling of movement coming from the mouse cages, and my own blood roaring in my eardrums.

Who said that? Trembling, I slowly made my way through the room. "Who's there?" I called. My legs were shaky as I placed one foot in front of the other. Rounding a corner, I gasped when I caught a glimpse of myself in the shiny door of the autoclave machine.

Jesus Layla, get a grip! I smoothed my hair with quaking fingers, tucking the loose pieces back into place as I tried to quell my mounting panic. *Calm down,* I instructed myself. It was probably just one of the interns playing a prank.

"Please help me!"

I stilled. There it was again. A cold, sinking feeling in my gut told me I knew exactly where the voice was coming from.

"I don't want to die!"

It was time to face it. No more denying or ignoring

it. Slowly, I turned. The voice was coming from the primate's cage. With a hard swallow, I met the rhesus macaque's stare. His gaze was relentless as we shared a long, tense-filled moment.

Bristling with unrest, I felt the animal's emotions as my own. His skin was stretched wide across his gaping mouth, his canines gleaming menacingly as he pressed his face against the bars and let out a horrific scream that rang off the barren concrete walls of the laboratory.

Again, I held my palms over my ears, but this time I also shut my eyes tight. If I couldn't see or hear it—it wasn't real. My legs threatened to give out at any moment. *This is not real. This is not happening. This is not real. This is not happening.* I recited the mantra until the shrieking finally ceased.

I waited until a count of five before I finally opened my eyes. The macaque's dark eyes froze me where I stood. *Why is he looking at me like that?* Like he's pleading with me. Begging for help.

"*You have to help me*," the animal said into my mind.

I swayed on my feet, my thoughts crashing into one another as they raced. *This is just a hallucination*, I tried to convince myself. The panic attacks must be getting worse. I'd been plagued with them for as long as I could remember. Sometimes debilitating episodes, that left me spent and wracked with loneliness.

I shook my head violently, determined to get rid of the voice that kept creeping inside the walls of my skull. "This isn't real," I said aloud, hoping the words would anchor me back into reality.

"*Please,*" the primate urged. "*You're the only one*

who can help me."

No matter how hard I tried to rationalize what was happening—I just couldn't. This *was* real, and I knew as much as I stared into the animal's coal-black eyes. Something definite, something almost innate inside of me told me this was truly happening—that this was reality. My *new* reality.

Chapter 2

"Don't leave me here to die."

My stomach lurched. I fumbled to the nearest wastebasket, my lunch barreling its way up my throat. Dropping to my knees, I vomited. Long and hard. When I finally emptied my stomach, I lifted my face from the trashcan feeling exhausted. A sheen of sticky perspiration covered my brow and neck. The lingering taste of bile burned my throat. I needed water to chase away the nasty sting of it.

Wiping my mouth, I rose on unsteady feet. Dimly aware that the primate had disappeared into the shadows of his cage, I stumbled to the sink, and turned the water on full blast. The cool water felt good against my flushed skin. Using my hands, I slurped up mouthful after mouthful of water until I could no longer taste the bitter tang of bile along my tongue.

I shut the water off and looked over at the cage. Taking a deep breath, I inched away from the sink, and walked slowly toward the metal cage. The *prison*. The prison which now held an inmate on death row.

As I drew closer, I braced myself, expecting the animal to fling himself against the bars screeching. Instead, he was curled up on the floor, his back to me and knees pulled up to his chest.

I swallowed. "How is this possible? How can I understand you?" I glanced around the room, suddenly thankful the hospital didn't have security cameras in the laboratory. I didn't need documentation of me having a nervous breakdown right there in the lab.

"You have a gift," he answered, staring at the wall of his cage.

I scoffed. "Gift? More like a curse," I said. "I'm still not sure this is even real. I must be dreaming." I wrapped my arms around myself, wishing I could rouse myself out of the situation as easily as waking from a horrible nightmare.

"I am set to die tomorrow." The animal's tone was harsh, almost cruel. *"Your kind has taken over the role of Mother Nature. Trying to rule what doesn't belong to them."*

I flinched involuntarily. The words were hurled at me like razors. *My kind.* I wanted desperately to deny it. To tell him he was wrong, but the argument fell lifeless at my lips. He was right. Humans overtake anything that is below them on the food chain or on the intellectual scale.

I felt sick inside that I was a part of the same cycle. I took care of the very animals they performed tests on. The innocent animals that endured torture, pain, disease, and the like all in the name of science.

Taking a slow look around the lab at the collection of animals, I said, "Come on. Let's get you out of here."

The primate didn't hesitate. He rolled over and sprang to his feet. I became aware of the low buzzing sound from the overhead lights. I glanced at the clock hanging over the lab door.

"Shit! It's almost five!" I unclipped my keyring full of jangling keys. "Day shift is ending soon. As the next shift comes in, there is going be a lot of activity in the hallways. That can either help us…" I shot a worried glance at him. "Or hurt us."

He didn't seem bothered. He only watched my hands as I took the padlock into my palm.

"Plus, I'm not sure how to sneak you out yet." I bit my lip, trying to steady my shaking hands as I inserted the key into the lock. "We're on the third floor, so sticking you out the window is out of the question." With a quick twist of my wrist, I freed the lock and started to turn the handle of the door.

I hesitated.

It was a well-known fact that primates are ridiculously strong and could be highly dangerous.

His voice echoed in my mind, *"I will not hurt you."*

I lowered my eyes and nodded, ashamed. Then, I steeled myself for what I was about to do. Something that went against everything the hospital instilled in me—allowing an animal to escape. Freeing them.

Swinging the door open, I stepped back, holding my breath as I watched the macaque gaze out across the laboratory—freedom just beyond the walls of his cage. After a moment of quiet regard, he finally looked up at me, his face gentle with something I can only describe as gratitude.

"Thank you, Matriarch," he said.

My mouth parted in surprise. *Matriarch?*

Before I could ponder what that meant, I heard the hallway bustle with activity. The exchange of shifts was happening.

"You're going to have get into my bag," I told him. "It's the only way to get you out of the hospital without anyone seeing you. It's in the workroom. Stay here and I'll go get it."

"Don't leave me." The macaque's eyes were wide with worry.

"You can't come with me. Someone will see you." I tossed a nervous glance over my shoulder.

"Please don't leave me here alone." He touched my hand, the contact took me by surprise. I glanced down at him, noticing the heart-wrenching attack of shivers that wracked his tiny body. He was terrified. Fearful to be alone in the room that had tormented him for the past several days.

I gnawed at my lip again. How could I force him to stay behind? He was scared, and desperate. A combination that was not only tragic, but dangerous. If I left him alone and someone came in as he raged, they would make an easy target for a very pissed off primate. "Okay," I relented. "but on second thought, let's wait until the hallway clears. Hide in one of the cabinets until it does."

He blinked those shiny obsidian eyes at me, then climbed down from the cage, landing lightly on the tile floor. His feet padded tenderly, like slippers, as he ambled alongside me toward the laboratory door. I opened the door to one of the cabinets and waited for him to climb in. After the last of his tail slipped inside, I gently closed the door.

Dozens of different voices buzzed like a swarm of bees on the other side of the laboratory door. Technicians, doctors, nurses, and interns were flooding the hallway as the shift change began. I felt jittery in my own skin, adrenaline kicking my heartrate up several notches.

After a few endlessly slow minutes, the noise outside the lab faded. I risked a quick peek, opening the door and taking an assessment of the hall. With most of the day-shift staff gone, and the night-shift staff already starting their duties, the space had almost cleared out. Just a few straggling technicians were exiting the workroom. They packed into the elevator, the doors pressing together just before they were carried down to the first floor of the hospital.

"The coast is clear," I said, knocking lightly on the cabinet door. The monkey poked his head out. "We have to hurry," I told him. "You ready for this?"

His glossy eyes went hard. *"Yes."*

He climbed out of the cabinet and kept close to my heels as I swung the lab door open.

As soon as the macaque and I stepped out into the hall, my legs felt like water beneath me. *Someone is going to see us,* I thought, panic flaring in my breast. Hurrying faster, I broke out into what wasn't exactly a run, but it was definitely faster than walking. Glancing down to my right, I noticed that the macaque was keeping pretty good pace with me. We were a few feet from the workroom when I heard voices. I took in a sharp intake of air and froze.

"Hide," I whispered, gesturing to the potted plant beside us. The primate pressed himself against the ceramic pot and tucked his furry head into the cascading hibiscus leaves.

"Hey, Layla."

"Oh, hi, Cheryl," I said through a tight smile.

"You're here later than normal. You're usually the first in line at the time clock." She smiled to show she was kidding, but what she said rang true. It wasn't because I was lazy—it was because I didn't like my job. My heart simply wasn't in it.

I had always wanted to be a zookeeper. As a little girl, I played with stuffed animals, not dolls. Dirt, outdoors, bugs, and nature were my playground. While some girls played "house", I would play "zoo" where I'd pretend to care for my toy animals and give grand speeches to invisible zoo patrons.

However, my father quickly shot down my dream to work at a zoo. He wanted me to follow in his footsteps. Go to med school, and someday work at Greater Hope as a physician. I vehemently objected. Layla Carson was no doctor. Refusing to totally give up on my dream to work with animals, Father and I came to a compromise. I agreed to accept the position as a laboratory technician at Greater Hope, and I've cursed myself ever since for allowing my father such control of my life. Over *me*.

Cheryl elbowed me playfully. "You high on energy drinks or something?"

I tried to laugh, but my fraying nerves diluted it into an awkward gulp. *Damn it,* I scolded myself. *How could I forget about Cheryl 'the work horse' Mitchell?* She was always the first tech in and the last tech out.

"Oh, no. I'm actually on my way out now." I tried to keep my tone casual, but my voice came out small, and strained. "How about you?" My eyes darted around the hallway as I rubbed my damp palms along my cotton scrubs. My feet itched to keep moving.

"Just clocking out," she answered as she started away.

I moved to go with her, but then halted. "Oh, darn," I said, snapping my fingers. "I can't remember if

I locked the lab. I better go check." I turned away from her, as if going back down the hall. "I guess I'll just see you tomorrow."

"Okay," Cheryl said. "Have a good night."

I gave her a small wave, watching as she padded away in her clunky clogs and disappeared into the work room. I held my breath as I waited for her to emerge again, and then at last, step into the elevator. As the doors closed, I let out a sigh, my shoulders sagging with relief.

"Okay. Let's go," I said to the primate, clenching my hands at my sides. The potted plant rustled, and the macaque was at my feet again. He shambled along beside me, his long tail curled over his body as he moved. When I stepped through the threshold of the work room, I felt as though I crossed a marathon finish line. I snatched my tote bag from my locker, thankful for my taste for oversized purses.

"Climb in." I lowered the bag, watching him scramble inside. I slipped my arm through the strap and hoisted it over my shoulder. It was heavy. Luckily, he was a young monkey, not reaching maturity or it would have been impossible to stow him away in my bag. Hastily, I clocked myself out and peeked down the hallway. It was empty.

I felt awkward as I moved through the hospital corridor, my balance thrown off by the extra weight hanging from my shoulder. I glimpsed up at the elevator light. The elevator was three floors up, slowly descending its way to my floor. I hit the button, watching the light blink as it changed from the eighth floor, then the seventh…

"Come on," I muttered, tapping the button in quick

repetition. The door at the end of the hall opened. My already pounding heart picked up speed. I looked over my shoulder, praying it wasn't Dr. Moore. And of course, it was.

He moved quickly through the hallway, his dull reflection cast out at his feet on the shiny tile floor. Scratching his chin thoughtfully, he scrutinized a medical chart. He walked briskly, as if he were on a mission, but suddenly halted at the laboratory doors.

I closed my eyes, trying to will the elevator doors to open. My skin flushed with uncomfortable warmth as the space around me warped and tilted. *Please no! I can't have a panic attack right now.* I took in several deep breaths, forcing myself to focus on the intake of air coming in through my nose, and going out through my mouth. Slowly, my pulse stopped banging, and I was able to gather my composure.

I looked down the hospital corridor, expecting Dr. Moore to be there, but the only thing glaring back at me was the harsh lighting. Dr. Moore was gone. *Good God, he's in the lab! He'll find the empty cage!*

The elevator finally dinged, and I shot inside, punching the first-floor button frantically. My heart hammered violently, as if it were trying to beat its way out of my chest.

When the elevator doors closed, the primate shifted in the bag, sensing the brief sanctuary the elevator provided.

I pressed my hand against the fabric of the bag, and whispered, "We're almost there." I leaned my head against the wall and clung to the railing as the elevator descended. Aware my palms were still sticky, I scrubbed them on my pants once more before stepping out. Quickly scanning the lobby, I was relieved to find it empty except for the security guard at the information desk. He was talking into a walkie-talkie, his back to me as I hustled past him. I couldn't help but wonder: *Is he talking to Dr. Moore? Have they issued a code AE?*

Code AE stands for animal escape, issued by any personnel who discovered an empty cage. They were rare, but occasionally it happened in the lab. Usually the animal was easily contained and returned to their cage, but sometimes the staff was outwitted and outran. Once, a pig got out and somehow ended up in the children's ward of the hospital. Running amok, he crashed into wheelchairs, and chewed the paper shoes off the feet of squealing nurses. The kids loved it. He was definitely the highlight of their day.

Walking with clipped steps, I kept my head down as I made my way through the lobby. The exit door was only a few feet away when the feedback from the security guard's walkie-talkie startled me. I chanced a quick look to the security guard. He was listening intently to the message coming through the static. My heart thudded painfully, propelling me faster toward the exit door. When my hand finally rested on the cold metal handle, I gave it a hard shove, swinging it wide open.

Glad to be out of the suffocating walls of the hospital, I felt a refreshing sense of freedom course through me as I walked away from the building. An evening breeze wafted across my face like silk. I inhaled deeply, reveling in the sweet smell of the outdoors. That delicious first breath of clean air after being cooped up in a sterile building all day. My hollow chest felt as though it was suddenly blooming with wildflowers.

Feeling charged from the crisp air around me, I picked up speed, weaving through lines of parked cars. I took care to steer clear of incoming traffic, glancing over my shoulder as I went. No one came after me. No one even seemed to notice me. Still, I kept a hurried pace. When I finally reached my truck, I was winded. Panting, I sat my bag on the ground.

"We made it." I tucked a loose strand of hair behind my ear and surveyed the parking lot. There were a good number of cars, but the macaque and I were the only ones around. "You can come out now."

He surfaced from the folds of my tote bag, his movements slow as he tested the spread of asphalt before him. When he seemed satisfied it was safe, he crawled out of the bag, and ambled closer to my truck. He stared at his reflection on the silver metal, again lost in the knowledge of being free. The moment was tender, misting my eyes before I took time to stop it.

Inclining his head, he looked up at me. The skin around his mouth quirked, as if he was about to smile.

"I can finally fall asleep in the arms of Mother Nature."

I smiled at his words, touched by the sincerity of his tone, and gentle face.

"Thank you, Matriarch. Because of you, I am free."

"Where will you go?" I asked.

"I will survive in the shadows until I can find more of my kind."

That shouldn't be hard. Lucky for him, Yemassee, South Carolina, is home to commercially bred primates. They're shipped off to research facilities, much like

Greater Hope Medical Hospital. There's even an island of free-ranging macaques close by. Weird, but absolutely true.

I knelt to his level. "You take care."

The primate laid his hand on mine. *"You as well, Matriarch."*

He withdrew his touch but held my gaze in the clutches of his dark, knowing eyes. It was an intense exchange, and though we did not speak, he clearly communicated something with me that night. It was gratitude, and genuine concern for my wellbeing.

And then, as quick as a lightning flash, he was off and running. With a body buoyant with excitement and energy, he scampered off toward the patch of trees that flanked the parking lot. Just before he entered the forest line, he paused and looked in my direction. I nodded approvingly, then watched as he disappeared into the brush and tangled thicket.

Chapter 3

After sliding into my truck, I slouched low into the seat, suddenly exhausted. *Did I really just release a rhesus macaque into the wooded lot of the hospital?* Shaking my head at what I'd done, I straightened and cranked up the engine. *What has gotten into me?* I flicked a glance at the rearview mirror and jolted upright.

The set of bold jade eyes staring back at me were not my own, yet somehow they were. Deeper and richer, they were almost primal. I rubbed them furiously with the heels of my palms, then leaned closer to the mirror for a better look. Blinking several times, I stared dumbfounded at the dark emerald eyes.

What is happening to me? Have I totally lost my freaking mind? I slumped forward, banging my forehead against the steering wheel. *That must be it,* I thought. *I've lost it. Not only am I talking to animals, but now my eyes are changing colors.*

My cellphone suddenly trilled, causing me to nearly jump out of my skin. "Jesus!" I cried, whacking my elbow on the console. Ignoring the sharp pain, I retrieved my cellphone from my bag, quickly glimpsing the caller ID screen. I groaned. *Not now.* The phone rang in my hand, almost shouting this time.

Reluctantly, I answered it. "Hi Dad," I said, slapping a hand across my face.

"Layla Faye, what did you do?" His tone was cutting and gruff, like a blade on a whetstone.

I straightened at the use of my middle name. *Oh shit.*

"What do you mean?" I asked, my dry throat constricting my breathing to an unbearable degree.

"I just got off the phone with Dr. Moore. You are responsible for an animal escape."

My body went still, but my mind was anything but. A full-blown panic attack was rearing up on me.

"Layla? Are you listening to me?"

"Yes," I choked out, wrapping my fingers around the steering wheel to steady myself and the whirlwind of possibilities bounding through my head. How far will they go to find him? What will they do once they do?

Father continued, "You failed to secure the macaque cage and now he's missing. A Code AE has been issued. The animal has yet to be recovered." Then his voice grew grim as he said, "Layla, it is common practice to dismiss personnel who fail to practice hospital protocol."

I barely registered what he was saying, my only worry was the primate. I had to know he was going to be okay. *Will Moore send security officers out into the forest to search for him?* Somehow, I know he won't. Why bother when they can just have another monkey shipped in to take his place.

"What happens if the monkey isn't recovered?"

"What happens if the monkey isn't recovered?" he scoffed mockingly into the phone. "Layla, who in the hell cares? Did you hear what I just said? The hospital fires anyone who fails to follow protocol. And damn it, *you* didn't follow protocol."

His anger exuded through the phone receiver like toxic fumes. With irritation spiking through me, I realized he was just like the rest of the laboratory scientists. He didn't give a damn about animals. Never did.

"So what?" I countered. "What about the macaque? What will happen if they don't find him?"

He grunted. "You just fucked up a million-dollar testing that was taking place tomorrow, and all you care about is some stupid animal?"

I gripped the steering wheel, watching my knuckles go white. "He isn't a stupid animal."

My anxiety suddenly diminished, along with my interest in the escalating conversation. Practically growling, I sneered into the phone, "I'm going to hang up now before I say something I'll regret."

"Layla." His voice boomed. "You will not hang up on me. In fact, this conversation is far from over. What you did tonight was careless. Forgetting to secure that cage proved how irresponsible you are. And you wanted to be a...a *zookeeper?"*

I wanted to reach through the phone and strangle him. Don't get me wrong, I loved my father, but it was like he and I were from completely different worlds. He was a well-respected surgeon and benefactor of the hospital, and I was...well, *me.* I often felt out of place at his charity banquets, so I'd sneak away and feed caviar to the stray cats at the back door.

Hob-knobbing with the pillars of the community just wasn't my thing. I enjoyed the simplicity of life. The feel of the autumn wind, the smell of wisteria in the summer. I felt more connected, more *alive* when I was outside. Father on the other hand, poured over countless books in his library and meandered around art museums for fun. *Bo-ring.*

"With you around there'll be elephants and lions walking down Main Street. You are lucky I started you down the path that suits you better than being some shit-shoveler. Now, show a little god-damn respect and thank me."

Lava raged in my veins. My vision suddenly tunneled, allowing me to see past the tree line before me, and through the thick of the forest. Though it was dozens of yards away, I could clearly see an owl, sitting hunched on the branch of an old oak tree. At the ground below it, scurried a swift-footed rodent.

Mesmerized, I grew lost in the experience. The owl's bright yellow eyes blinked once before it spread its wings and launched into a silent flight, swooping down effortlessly and snatching the rodent with its talons.

I gasped, covering my mouth with my fingers as the great owl lifted into the breeze, and took off into the crowded forest, diving deeper into the darkness.

"I saved your ass at work today, the least you can do is thank me," Father barked.

I startled, my mind still reeling from what I just saw. "What?"

"You could have been fired right on the spot tonight, Layla. If you weren't a Carson, you'd be jobless right now," he said.

The line went silent as I thought about that. *If I weren't a Carson, I wouldn't be working in that dreadful place in the first place.* I gritted my teeth, feeling the muscles in my jaw tick with annoyance.

Gathering my nerves, I took a deep breath and said, "Fine. I accept their dismissal."

"You *what*?" His voice was slick as oil.

"I think you heard me." I threw the truck in gear and backed out of the parking spot.

"Don't be ridiculous. That job is your stepping stone to becoming a research scientist." There was the tiniest trace of panic edging into his tone, and I relished it, letting it fuel me into becoming bolder.

I laughed without humor. "Research scientist? Please. I'll never be a Dr. Moore."

"Moore is a great man, and one of the best damn doctors I've ever met. You could only wish to be a shadow of him."

"Dr. Moore is nothing but a man full of greed. He's willing to sacrifice animals in the name of money."

"In the name of science," he corrected. "And since when are you so righteous? Animal testing has proven some practices and medicines that have been life-saving. If it weren't for men like Dr. Moore more people would be dead and dying."

"There are other means," I said. "There has to be."

"Layla." For the first time ever, his dominating voice wavered. I couldn't believe it. He was losing control over his ever-calculated confidence. I had him grasping in desperation like the rope of command had been yanked from his fingers. "Don't let pride foul up your future," he added.

I stomped on the gas pedal, growing more irate by the minute. "It's not the future I want. It's what *you* want. I didn't get a biology degree to become a research scientist."

"You will not embarrass me," he interjected, tone

harsh. "You will apologize to Dr. Moore and continue down the path I have paved for you."

I scoffed, completely ablaze with anger as I pictured my father's pinched face. If we were in the same room, he'd be looking down his nose at me. His arms crossed stiffly over his chest. I had seen that pose more times in my childhood than I cared to remember.

"I'm creating my own path, *Father*. So, tell them I quit. Hell, tell them whatever will make *you* look good. That's all you care about anyway." I ended the call and tossed the cellphone on the passenger seat.

As I sped down the road, I glanced back at Greater Hope Medical Hospital in the rearview mirror. That was my past. Never again would I yield to my father. Never again would I settle, or compromise just to shield myself from his wrath. As the hospital grew smaller, and the more distance I put between it and me, the more peaceful I became.

Smiling, I let the old me wane and disappear completely, never to return. I thought to myself with a newfound steeled spine, and tough-as-nails attitude: *Tomorrow is a new day for Layla Faye Carson. Tomorrow, I will find myself.*

Chapter 4

And that's exactly what I did. I decided it was time to pursue my dream of being a zookeeper. During college, I volunteered at Preston Park Zoo, and absolutely loved it. I hated to leave, but I'd stupidly accepted the job at the hospital after I graduated from Bluffton University four years ago.

After a surprisingly restful night's sleep, I awoke the next morning feeling refreshed and hopeful. Sitting at the edge of my bed, I dialed the phone number of the zoo's mammal curator.

"It's the purrrfect day to visit Preston Park Zoo. This is Rachael, how can I help you?"

I smiled at the familiar greeting.

"Rach? It's Layla. Layla Carson," I said.

"Oh hey, Layla. How have you been?"

"Pretty good." I felt a twinge of guilt and shook my head. *Pretty good?* I can hear animals talk. I released a lab monkey into the wild...*and* I quit my job. Life is freaking dandy. "Well, actually that's a lie," I admitted. "Since I left the zoo, things have been crap." I flopped back against the mattress, sprawling myself out across the comforter.

"Crap, eh? Well, the zoo is full of crap, so it looks like you left one type of crap for another."

I could practically hear her smile, which made me grin in return. God, how I missed the zoo...and the staff. Rachael Thorn was an awesome boss and an even better zookeeper. What I loved most about her was she didn't apologize for putting animals above people. She felt that their feelings were just as valid as humans' and she'd debate anyone who said otherwise.

"Yeah, I guess you can say that." I ran my fingers through my hair, suddenly realizing how much of a tangled mess it was. "I'm not cut out to work with research animals. It's monotonous and a lot harder mentally than I could have ever imagined."

"I bet," she sympathized. "I know I couldn't do it. I'd probably sneak mice out in my pockets on my first day." Her breathy laugh blew into the receiver. Stilling at her words, my voice snagged in my throat, causing me choke into the receiver.

"Layla? Are you all right? I was just kidding," she said. "Or maybe I wasn't…you know how I am."

I tried hard to laugh, but it came out as an awkward squeak. I cleared my throat. "Anyway, I just wanted to see if there were any volunteer positions available. I'd love to come back to the zoo. I've really missed it."

"There's a waiting list for volunteering," she replied shortly.

My heart sank. I may have found myself, but my new start will have to wait until a volunteer position opened up.

"However," she continued, her tone picking up energetically.

I bolted upright, hopeful and eager to hear more.

"We have a keeper position available. It's yours if you want it."

"Oh, my God, yes! Of course I do!"

"I hated to see you leave, Layla."

Rachael's sudden serious tone caused me to take pause. "You were a promising zookeeper, whose heart was truly in her work. I told you back then, if you ever wanted to come back, a job would be waiting for you and I meant it."

My heart warmed. "Thanks, I appreciate that."

"Come on down to the office to fill out your paperwork and be sure to bring a copy of your resume just so we have it on file."

"I'll be there in an hour. And Rachael?"

"Yeah?"

"Thanks."

"No need to thank me, Layla. Zoo keeping is what you're meant to do. It's in your blood. I'm just glad you finally realized it."

I didn't know what to say. Emotion welled heavily in my eyes and throat.

Rachael bid me good-bye and hung up. For a long while I just stared at the phone in my hand, reliving what Rachael had said. *Zoo keeping was what I was meant to do. It was in my blood.* After my experience with the rhesus macaque I had never been surer of it.

I had a unique gift. Whether it worked on any other animals besides the monkey, I wasn't sure, but if I could truly talk to animals, it would absolutely give me an upper hand in the competitive field of zoo keeping.

The clock on the wall chimed a jarring *bong*, stirring me out of my stupor. Blinking a few times to ground myself back into the here and now, I couldn't help but smile. I needed to get going if I was going to be at the zoo in an hour.

Tossing my phone on the bed, I leapt up and skipped across the room to my vanity mirror. God, I was grinning like an idiot. An idiot with a snarled head of black hair. I made quick work of the knots and wove my hair into my ever-present braid.

Catching a glimpse of my eyes, I swallowed hard, bracing myself squarely before leaning in close to the mirror. The deep green hue had not faded, in fact, I was surprised to find flecks of gold now sparkling from within the jade. They were not natural—not human. They were animalistic.

Feeling shaken, I reached for my contacts out of pure habit, drenching them with solution before slipping them in. I'd been wearing contact lenses for a few years to help my near-sighted vison, so the routine of inserting them was as simple as tying my shoes.

The lenses were cool, like normal, and laid against my eye with a familiar, gentle weight. I blinked several times ensuring they were in place before peering cautiously at my reflection. It was like looking through a glass bottle, all distorted and blurry. I stumbled backward, clumsily falling against my vanity, knocking my perfume bottles onto the floor. The smell of floral mingled with the warm air of my bedroom. *What the hell?*

I couldn't get them out fast enough, practically clawing them out like a wild animal. I flicked the tiny discs to the floor, not giving a damn where they ended up. Frantically, I searched for something small to read. Something I normally could not see if not for the corrective lenses. A knowing in my gut told me my eyesight was now perfect, but I had to see for myself.

A romance novel lay on the nightstand. I scrambled over to it, picked it up and took a measured breath. Slowly, I opened it to the first chapter. My gaze fell on the page, skipping across the words with ease. I dropped the book with a gasp, feeling light-headed. Clambering into bed, I dove under the comforter and buried my head under the pillows. I clamped my eyes tight, trying to control my spinning head. *What is going on with me?* This was unexplainable. How could my vision be perfect?

Before I could give it another thought, the doorbell rang. *Go away,* I thought with a groan. I had to figure out was going on with me, or I'd go crazy. I had no time for a door-to-door salesman or uninvited guests.

I curled up into a tight ball, ignoring the stifling air the pile of the pillows atop me brought. I wanted to go back in time. Go back to the Layla I was before. Before I had crazy, primal eyes. Before I could talk to animals. Before I was a freak of nature.

I inhaled sharply in alarm as footsteps entered the bedroom. A twinge of fear crept like ice cold fingers up my spine as I drew the pillows away from my face.

I flung one angrily at the approaching figure. "Damn it, Gwen, you scared the shit out of me."

"I'm sorry," Gwen said with a laugh. "You should have never given me a key if you didn't want me to let myself in."

I glared at her, but she was oblivious to it, too busy checking her hair in my mirror. She looked great, as usual. Clad in slim jeans, her athletic body looked tone, and lean. She always looked pretty, no matter what she wore.

Turning from the mirror, she asked, "What's going on with you?"

I scowled at her. Gwen was my best friend, and I loved her like a sister, but she knew little of personal space or privacy.

"Nothing." I folded my arms over my chest.

"Liar." She inspected her polished nails for a second, then shifted her gaze to me. "What is it? Men issues? Period problems? You are looking a little bloated, and there's a monster zit on your forehead."

I touched my forehead, searching for the so-called monster pimple.

She chuckled. "I was kidding, Layla." She walked to the bed. The look of sudden shock spread across her face when our eyes met. Her mouth parted to speak.

"Yes, they're different," I said, answering her question before she could even ask. "And no, they're not contacts." I bit my lip, wondering if I should continue. I needed to tell someone. I didn't know what was happening to me, but I knew I didn't want to go through it alone. But how do you tell someone you can talk to animals without sounding like a mental case?

She kept staring. I couldn't blame her. It's not every day someone's eyes go from simple green to a startling jade.

"Layla, this is crazy." She leaned in closer. "I mean, really. It's like you have those costume contacts in. You know, the kind you can buy at a Halloween shop?"

I rolled my eyes. "I know," I said with a sigh.

Gwen kept staring, and it made me feel small. I wanted to duck beneath the covers and never come back out. Instead of doing that, I pushed myself to tell her more.

"It gets weirder," I continued carefully, my voice shaky. "I put my contacts in this morning, and they made my vision blurry. It's like I don't need them anymore." I studied her face, waiting for her reaction.

With her eyebrows drawn tight, she looked just as confused as I felt.

"But that's impossible." I toyed with the silver ring on my thumb feeling as though I was losing my mind. "Right?"

"Are you screwing with me right now, Layla?" She gave me a little shove.

"No." I felt panic rising in my stomach. If I didn't figure out what was going on with me—quick—I'd lose my mind.

"It's a stretch, but maybe your near-sightedness was due to some sort of vitamin deficiency? And now it's finally regulated?" She lifted a shoulder. "Or maybe eating all those carrots finally paid off." She winked and smiled, trying to lighten the mood.

I returned her smile and decided not to tell her about my other newfound ability: how I can communicate with animals. "Yeah, that's probably it." I picked at a loose thread on the comforter, my stomach a bundle of raw nerves.

"Ask your dad. He is a doctor after all."

I stiffened at the thought of it. There was no way in hell I was going to ask him.

"Layla? Are you okay?" she asked, cocking her head at me as she sized me up.

I nodded, pushing the thought of my father away. "So, anyway, what's up? Is there a particular reason you came barging into my house?"

"Since when do I need a reason?" She played with the tassels on the end of her purple scarf. Her blue eyes shifted to mine. "But…actually, I do have an agenda." The corners of her full lips quirked upward.

"I figured as much." I untangled myself from the comforter and went to my closet to dress. "So what is it?" I called over my shoulder as I slipped into a soft cotton T-shirt and jeans.

"There's this guy…" she drawled as a sly smile broke across her face.

I rolled my eyes. "Isn't there always?" When it came to Gwen Gibb, there was *always* a guy involved. I stepped into my ballet flats, then went to my vanity to pick up my fallen perfume bottles from the floor.

"Oh, shut up," she said, flinging a pillow at me. It fell short, landing quietly in the middle of the floor. "Anyway, there's this guy, James. He's taking me to the Monster Bash at Zbornie's."

"And?" I kept working, arranging the perfume bottles back into place on the vanity.

"And…he has a friend…"

I stiffened.

"I kind of volunteered you to be his date."

I whirled around, glaring at Gwen and her sickening sweet smile.

She winced, and added, "He sounds nice."

"*Sounds* nice?" I snapped. "Have you even met him?"

She looked at the floor.

I threw my hands in the air. "Even better!" I stalked toward her and snatched my phone off the bed. Gripping it tightly, I faced her and said, "This is so typical of you."

"What?" She stood up, planting her hands on her hips. "It will be fun. Zbornie's goes all out for Halloween. There will be plenty of people there, so if he ends up being a loser, you can ditch him."

I shot her a dark look before marching out of the bedroom.

With her boots tapping across the hardwood floor, she caught up with me by the time I made it the living room. "Please Layla. I *really* like James."

"So go with James," I replied curtly. "But, tell him that his buddy will have to find his own date." I retrieved my messenger bag from the coat rack by the front door and looped it over my head. I put my hand on the door knob and looked back at her. *Ah hell.* She was giving me her best pouty face.

"I am not going," I said firmly, opening the door.

"Please please please Layla." She lunged forward and hugged my neck. I tried to pull free, but she held fast.

"James is super cute. And I already have my costume," she said. "Come on. I swore I'd bring a hot friend."

"You did what?"

She pulled back, her face serious. "Be my hot friend, Layla." Then, her face broke out into a goofy grin.

"You are a complete ass."

"We established that when we were thirteen, remember? When I convinced you to break up with Robbie Jones because he smelled like moldy cheese."

"He didn't smell like moldy cheese. And I didn't break up with him just because you told me to."

She finally let go of my neck and lifted a blond brow. "Oh really? Then why did you break it off with him?"

"Because he said Lance Bass was gay." I stuck out my chin stubbornly.

She burst out laughing, filling the room with her infectious giggles and snorts. "I guess that still ended up being a pointless break up after all."

I cut my eyes at her and scowled.

"Oh, sorry. My bad. If you had actually made it backstage way back when, you probably could have turned him straight."

Gwen was referring to the *Nsync concert we went to in Raleigh, North Carolina, in 1998. I tried (unsuccessfully) to sneak backstage so I could confess my undying love to Lance. I even wore a shirt that read: *'Mr. Bass, Lance get married!'* A part of my soul died the day Lance revealed he was gay.

"I've got to go," I said, not interested in reliving the day my teenage dream of marrying Lance came to a screeching halt.

"Where ya headed?" she asked, following me out the door.

"The zoo. They offered me a job." I couldn't keep from smiling.

"The zoo? Wait, what about the hospital?"

"They fired me. Or I quit, I'm not sure which one." I bit my lip. I wondered which one it was. Either way, I'm sure as the tides come in each day, Father ensured it was amicable.

"Hold up," Gwen said, catching my elbow. "What do you mean, you're not sure which one?"

There was no use in lying to Gwen. She could always see right through any bullshit I tried to hand her. I exhaled, resigned that I had to come clean with what I did to *someone.* Might as well be her. "I'm sort of responsible for a monkey getting loose. I was supposed to be fired on the spot…"

"But with your Dad being the head honcho, you got off with a slap on the wrist?" Gwen knew how much influence my father had at the hospital, so guessing the outcome of the incident was as clear as crystal to her.

I shrugged. "I guess. I told him to do whatever would make him look good. Either way, I'm not working there anymore." I unlocked my truck and slid inside.

Gwen shut the truck door and waited for me to roll down the window.

She rested her elbows on the door, every bit as lithely and casual as a cat. "You seem happy about it."

"I am." I tossed my messenger bag in the passenger seat. "I didn't belong there."

"Your dad is going to shit bricks if you don't go back."

The mention of him and his anger made me bristle. "I don't care," I ground out. "It's my life. I'm the one living it, so it's on me if I screw it up."

"Preach it, girl," she said, giving me a small smile. "I'll call you about Saturday," she said, slapping the door before stepping away from the truck.

I groaned. *Damn it, she's relentless.* I was in too much of a hurry to resist her anymore. "You're lucky I love you," I said as I started the engine and slowly backed out of the driveway.

She gave me a wink.

As I drove away, I thought about blind dates and how much I despised them. Then, I thought about the zoo, and how happy I was at the way things had turned out. In a matter of twenty-four hours, my life had changed drastically.

I lost my job at the hospital but gained my dream job at the zoo. And then of course, the freaky ability to talk to animals. *A handy gift if my date ends up being a dog,* I thought, laughing at myself as I stomped on the gas, roaring down the road toward my destiny.

Or so I thought. On my way to the Preston Park Zoo, a crow dive-bombed my windshield. Startled, I yanked on the steering wheel, swerving my truck into the other lane. Thankfully I was alone on the road or I would have slammed into another vehicle.

My eyes darted to the rearview mirror but couldn't find the suicidal bird. Surely it was killed upon impact? For a split second I wondered if I should turn around and look for it. *No. It's dead. There's no way it could survive that.*

Feeling shaken, I decided to pull over anyway, just until I got ahold of my frazzled nerves. *Poor bird,* I thought, as I put the truck into park. I blew out a ragged breath, relieved to let my foot off the gas pedal. I needed a few moments to collect myself. A few moments to pull myself together enough to fake the confidence I needed to walk into the zoo and begin my new life.

Enjoying the quiet, I took one last measured breath, and began to steer my truck back onto the road when something crashed into the driver's side window. I jumped, simultaneously gripping the steering wheel with all of my might and stomping on the brake.

The crow was back. It was hovering outside my window, its wings beating wildly around him. *It's still alive?* I felt a rush of relief flood through me. *I didn't kill it.* The bird flew to the front of the truck, and landed on the hood, its talons scraping across the metal as it hopped closer. I cringed at the sound. The crow moved like a mechanical toy, its movements erratic and jerky. It stood just on the other side of the windshield, staring at me with eyes black as an endless pit.

My pulse pounded faster as its beady black eyes searched my face. He was so close, I could see his chest fluttering with each breath it took. We stared at each other for a long time through the windshield glass, then it cocked its head at me. *Ah hell. It's going to talk.*

Chapter 5

I closed my eyes and covered my ears, steeling myself for what it would say.

I was met with silence.

The seconds stretched on, so finally, but hesitantly, I opened my eyes. The crow was gone. Mystified, I sat alone, wondering in that moment, had I completely lost my mind?

I don't remember turning on to Clifton Drive or following the winding road to Preston Park Zoo Boulevard. I don't even recall parking and walking through Rachael's office door, but I found myself sitting, wooden-like, in a cushioned chair, filling out paperwork.

"Layla, is everything okay?" Rachael asked, concerned, leaning across her desk to retrieve the completed forms. She scrutinized my face and I knew she could tell something was wrong. She read the body language of animals all the time, so my blank expression and trembling hands were a dead giveaway.

"Yeah," I answered. "Had a bird dive bomb my truck on the way here, so I guess I'm still a little shaken up." I tucked a stray piece of hair behind my ear.

"Oh, wow. Is the bird okay?"

I nodded. *At least I think so anyway...*

"Well that's good." She sat back in her office chair, scanning the papers quickly before slipping them into a folder. "Got your resume?" She looked at me, her brown eyes expectant.

Oh no. I forgot it. Damn Gwen and her stupid blind date. "Uh, can I just email it to you? I still need to update it." I wrung my hands nervously.

"Oh sure, that will be fine." She studied me. "What's different about you?"

I swallowed. "Different?"

"Yeah, something is different." Her eyes tightened further, searching my face. "Is it your hair…or?" Then she brightened. "No! I know. You don't have your glasses."

Oh right. I wore glasses back when I volunteered. Rachael isn't used to seeing me without them. I laughed nervously. "That's it. Went to contacts."

She nodded, "I knew something was different." She smiled at me warmly. "So, when can you start?"

"Today," I answered quickly.

Her eyebrows lifted. "What about the hospital?"

"What about it?"

"No two-week notice?"

"No," I said, my voice surprisingly steadier than I expected. *What if she asks me why I left? How can I tell the curator of the zoo that I let a monkey escape…on purpose!*

A smile slowly filled her expression. "The shifts are covered this week, so how about making a fresh start on Monday?"

I breathed a quiet sigh of relief, thankful she didn't ask anything further about the hospital. "That sounds great."

"Wonderful." She turned in her chair and dug through a pile of blue T-shirts. "What size are you?

Small?"

Without letting me answer, Rachael tossed three shirts at me. I clumsily caught them, but not before they hit me square in the face.

"Still got khakis and boots?" she questioned.

"Of course," I answered, stuffing the shirts into my messenger bag.

"Well then, you are all set. I'll see you Monday."

I smiled and stood up. "I can't wait."

"The zoo is lucky to have you back, Layla. If they could tell you themselves, I bet the animals would say 'welcome back'."

I felt myself go rigid, but I forced a smile and a polite wave. As I made my way back to my truck, I wondered about my upcoming first day. *Will the animals speak? Will I be able to hide the fact that I can hear them?* Thinking about the crow and the eerie silence that came with him, I thought, *can I even still hear them?*

I got in my truck and turned the key. The low rumbling from the motor drowned out my musing until my phone beeped. I rifled through my bag and finally located my cellphone. It was a text from Gwen:

[Start text set off]

Pick u up @ 9 on Sat. Kurt is ur date

[End text set off]

"Damn you, Gwen," I said out loud.

[Start text set off]

The phone beeped again: He's a fox

[End text set off]

I groaned at her choice of words and proceeded to crank up the radio until the point of being too loud, drowning out all other sounds. As I backed out of the parking spot and made my way back home, I couldn't stop myself from processing the last twenty-four hours of my life. How much I had strayed from the neat little path my father had blazed for me, and surprisingly still, just how much I didn't care.

I was creating a life of my own—how I envisioned it should be—not his idea of what suited me. I thought about the macaque, and the bizarre exchange that transpired between us. I said that I wanted to find myself but learning that I was a real-life Doctor Doo Little was a little more than I bargained for.

Chapter 6

Ugh. I can't believe I let Gwen talk me into this. I slid on a headband and adjusted the fuzzy faux cat ears attached to it. I peered at my reflection in the mirror. *Actually, I look kind of cute.* I penciled in whiskers with eyeliner and smudged black paint on my nose. I stood back and examined myself. My cashmere sweater was clingy, and my black leggings were form-fitting, but not to the point of being obscene. I turned slightly and pinned a long cat tail into place. Shaking my backside, I couldn't help but giggle as the tail swished side to side.

The doorbell rang. Gwen and the guys were right on time. I took one last glimpse in the mirror before snatching my messenger bag off the bed. I hustled to the door and took a deep breath before opening it. *Here we go.* When I swung it open, I had a hard time hiding my shock.

Gwen stood grinning, looking like a devilish vixen beneath the dull porch light. She wore a tight, low-cut red dress and sparkly panty hose. Her killer stilettos made her at least four inches taller. Her blond locks were teased into a sexy bouffant with two tiny horns peeking out. I looked down at myself and swallowed. Gwen looked incredible as a she-devil, completely overshadowing my lame cat costume.

"You look adorable!" Gwen said, taking in the length of me. "What do you think of my costume?" She spun around. "Is it a whole lot of *oh la la?*"

"It's definitely…"

"Hot?"

"I was going to say, *revealing.*"

"That too," she said, winking at me. "So, let me introduce you to James." She gestured to the bulky man beside her. He was wearing an aviator flight suit and dark sunglasses.

He nodded and said, "Tonight, you can call me Maverick."

Gwen giggled and looped her arm through his. I made a clumsy attempt at a wave and swung my gaze to the pirate beside him. He was cute, even with the eye patch and scraggly wig. His cheek bones were to die for and he had a cute dimple in his chin.

"Hey, I'm Layla." I shifted nervously from one foot to the other. *He's not the dog I was imagining,* I thought, suddenly feeling awkward. The whole time I thought he was going to be a loser. It never occurred to me that there was a chance he'd be a babe, and that I might actually *like* him.

"Kurt," the pirate replied. "Cool contacts, by the way. Very cat-like."

I opened my mouth to speak, but I was too stunned to find the words. *My eyes,* I thought. *He noticed my freakish eyes.*

Gwen thankfully cut into the conversation. "All right. That's enough small talk. Move your asses because I am ready to shake mine!" She playfully smacked James' butt as I yanked the front door closed.

Forcing my feet to move, I followed the trio to James' small SUV and squeezed myself into the backseat. My stomach churned anxiously as Kurt slid in beside me. Since James was over six feet tall, the back seat was cramped. My knee brushed against Kurt's. I gave him a sideways glance, and he just smiled.

Gwen and James climbed in the front and off we went. Thankfully, they chatted about nonsense and didn't seem to notice how little I contributed to the conversation. I was too freaked out about the cat eye comment to even pay attention.

Was I turning into a cat? I recalled my reflection in the mirror. The searing, bold jade color my eyes had turned, and the savageness that came with it. *No, that's ridiculous,* I thought. *It's not only ridiculous—it's impossible.*

After James parked, we piled out of the SUV, each one of us anxious for different reasons. Gwen was eager to dance. James seemed stoked to be parading around as an Airforce pilot and Kurt seemed to be nervously gauging whether I was worth the trouble.

My gut twisted into a heavy knot as I faced the dance club. Zbornie's was a massive brick building, designed to appear aged, giving it a mobster vibe. Its bright neon sign lit up the night sky. The smell of alcohol wafted through the air, not helping my already roiling stomach at all. Not being one for parties, or large crowds, I was beginning to curse Gwen for roping me into this stupid double date.

After our ID's were checked, we made our way to the bar. The room was crowded and hazy with smoke. I coughed and sputtered, shielding my eyes from the flashing strobe lights.

Pushing our way through the mingling bodies, I bumped into a broad chested Spartan warrior, nearly knocking his beer from his hand. "I'm so sorry," I stammered. My cheeks flushed with embarrassment, but he only glared at me before turning back to the Greek goddess he was with.

"Four beers," James called to the bartender, his head bobbing to the beat of the music.

"Ah, just three," I said, holding up coordinating fingers. To me, drinking beer was like gargling Alka-Seltzer and pennies. "I'll have a Mudslide."

As the bartender worked on our drinks, Gwen flirted relentlessly with James. Kurt removed his eye patch and leaned against the bar. He looked about as uncomfortable as I felt. His eyes flickered around the room briefly before settling onto me. He winked, but I could only muster a weak smile, suddenly feeling like a complete kill joy. *I'm so lame,* I thought. I'd never been much of a party girl. I preferred to stay home, curled with a cozy comforter and a good book. Gwen, on the other hand, reveled in being the center of attention. If she could hire someone to shine a spotlight on her all day—every day—she would.

The bartender returned, setting three bottles down in front of James and then placed my Mudslide on a napkin and pushed it toward me. I smiled and thanked him, taking a long sip of the thick drink, inhaling the rich smell of Kahlua as it worked its way to my belly.

With beer in hand, Gwen led James to the dance floor. I watched them disappear into the crowd of swaying bodies before turning back to my drink.

"So, Layla..." Kurt started, his brows lifting in question. "Want to dance?" He appeared reluctant, almost as if he was asking solely out of obligation. I felt a stab of annoyance at Gwen for forcing this blind date on me, and also for my not being the *fun* girl. *Damn it,*

47

just loosen up!

I forced an enthusiastic smile and said, "Sure." I took another sip of my drink and followed him to the dance floor. We pushed through the crowd. The strong smell of perspiration, cologne, alcohol and blaring techno music created a nauseating combination.

Thankfully, the music faded into a pulsating pop song. It was light and catchy. An easy tune to dance to. I liked to dance, so working my body into a smooth rhythm came easy. Kurt smiled and took my hand in his. We danced together for a while, enjoying the moment and letting the music envelope us in our own little world.

Kurt twirled me. I laughed out of delight, allowing my inhabitations to fall back as I danced. He twirled me again, but this time, like a ballerina with two left feet, I stumbled into his arms. Chuckling, he righted me, and together we started moving to the music once again. He was a great dancer, which made it easy to get lost in the moment. The string of songs blurred into one another, and before long, an hour had passed.

Unfortunately, the longer we danced, the more comfortable Kurt got with me. His hands crept like spiders into private areas. Pursing my lips, I looked up into his face, surprised by the undeniable hunger in his eyes. I tried putting some space between us, but he caught my wrists with two strong hands. He leaned close to my ear and said, "Enough dancing. I'm ready for you sink those cat claws into my back."

I gasped, jerking away from him. "What did you just say?"

He gave me an almost angry smirk. "Gwen promised me a good time, and you're going to give me one." He grabbed me by the elbow, and I nearly buckled under the pressure of his iron grip. My heart thumped wildly, knocking with continuous one-two-punches to my ribcage like a boxer in a ring. I tried to wrench myself free, but Kurt easily pulled me through the throng of dancers. Confused, furious, and down-right scared, I fumbled along beside him, my mind spinning. Why is he doing this? What happened? We were having a good time.

He shoved me toward the back of the bar, the bright lights blinding me as they twirled and throbbed to the music. I struggled against him. "No," I said. "Stop it."

No one seemed to notice the struggle. Everyone was either too busy dancing or too wasted to care.

"Help," I called over my shoulder, trying to free my wrists from his grip. "Someone!" The music swallowed my voice as if I never spoke. Kurt reached for the door of men's restroom. "No, please, Kurt. Just stop now and we can go our separate ways. I'll never mention this."

He was like a wall of unforgiving, uncaring stone. He flung me inside. My shoes slid across the tile floor, and I frantically looked around. I was alone. Alone with a mad man.

I backed away from him as far as I could, until my back became flush with the far back wall. "What are you doing?" My chest heaved and compressed my heart until I thought it would pop. Why was Kurt doing this?

He took his time sauntering toward me, *stalking* me. When he was standing before me, Kurt snatched his eyepatch off and dropped it to the floor. With his hungry eyes boring into me, he crushed the patch beneath his boot. The sound ominous in the otherwise silent room. Then, like a snake striking prey, he grabbed me, and shoved me into a stall. I bucked and fought, but he was too strong. Too determined. He pushed me onto the commode, forcing me to sit down. The toilet seat was cold, even through my thick leggings, chilling me to the bone.

"Help me!" I shouted up to the ceiling. My voice only echoed off the tiles, falling upon the deaf ears of the party-goers outside.

Kurt shushed me, tracing a finger down my cheek. Bile rose in the back of my throat. "Calm down. You got me so horny right now, this won't take long. I promise. In and out. Just like that." His sick smile never left his face, in fact, it only curved further, like he was really enjoying seeing me squirm, and resist.

I swatted his hand away, infuriated that he had the nerve to touch me. To attempt to force himself on me. "Don't touch me," I hissed through locked teeth.

Unaffected, he just gazed at me with that cocky smile, the fluorescent light flickering above his head. His frame filled most of the stall, acting like a human shield, blocking my only way out. I looked down at the dingy tile floor. *I could crawl out.* I lurched forward, landing hard on my knees. I ignored the bits of torn toilet paper, and old gum, tucking my head under the stall partition.

Nearly on my belly, I tried desperately to shimmy beneath the partition. I didn't make it far before Kurt wretched me up by my shirt, knocking my head on the partition as he yanked me back into the stall.

"Where the hell do you think you're going?" He flung me back onto the toilet. My heart hammered against my ribcage, begging to be set free.

"Please, don't do this." Everything started to blur, Kurt's silhouette became dark and hazy as tears flooded my eyes.

He grunted, the corner of his mouth lifting into a sneer as he unzipped his pants. Panic flared within me. He raked his fingers through my hair, fisting a handful before snatching my head back. I winced. It felt like hundreds of needles were digging into my scalp.

"Open up that pretty little mouth of yours," he snarled.

My thoughts swirled frantically as I tried to find a way out of the horrific situation. Then, my eyes caught his. They held no sympathy. No remorse. No feeling. Kurt gazed down at me with that arrogant smirk, which only infuriated me. With his grip still tight, he reached out with his other hand and grazed my wet cheeks with his fingers. The touch made me shudder. Shame ate at me. *Why am I crying? Fight, damn it!*

"Be a good girl and do what you're told." He patted my head like I was a child. "Go on."

My bloodstream coursed with adrenaline, then something within me literally *snapped*. A crackle of ferociousness tore free from my very core, barreling through me like raging bull in a pit.

"No!" I roared. The sound vibrated my vocal cords as I shoved him with all of my might. Kurt stumbled backward and slammed into the far wall. The tile cracked and flaked all around him. For a split second I looked down at my hands, surprised at my own strength.

Kurt's eyes flashed with anger before lunging at me with open arms. "You little bitch!" His hands tore at my shirt. "So you wanna play rough, huh?" He wrapped me in an embrace that was nothing short of a viper's squeeze around my waist. I tried calling for help again. He cranked tighter, stealing my breath. He spun me around, so my back was against his chest.

"Kitty is a wild cat. I like that," he said against my ear. I writhed beneath him, disgusted by his breath being so near. He dragged me back into the stall, even though I flailed and resisted the entire way.

I threw back my head, and was able to call out, "Someone help me!"

Kurt's hand slip across the fabric of my leggings. He found the elastic band at my waist, and before I could scream again, his fingers dipped inside, clumsily searching for my panties.

Distantly, I thought I heard the soft click of the door opening, but with Kurt's hands in intimate areas, I couldn't focus on anything else. I had to get away, and it had to be *now*.

Then, with an ear-numbing crack, the stall door came off its hinges. Startled, Kurt stilled, his hand frozen between my legs. I looked up at the stranger, my pulse hammering painfully within me as he surveyed the situation with a dark expression. His piercing golden eyes held me captive, demanding to focus on him and *only* him. I obliged, completely terrified to do otherwise.

Kurt's grip never slipped. Instead he tightened, and sneered, "Fuck off."

Still gripping the stall door, the man's stormy gaze slowly drifted off me, and settled menacingly on Kurt. Before I could register the movement, his hand lashed out, and clamped down on my arm, yanking me out of

Kurt's hold. He shoved me away just as quickly. I stumbled to the corner of the room, my chest heaving frantically with panic.

Kurt hurled himself at the man but was easily deflected. The stranger allowed Kurt's own momentum to crash him into the bathroom wall. Kurt's face bounced off the now visible sheetrock—thanks to my moment of brute strength—sending a gentle dusting of powder into the air around him. Furious, Kurt grunted a curse and spun around, ready to pounce again.

The stranger swung the stall door, cracking it against Kurt's body in a sickening blow. Kurt dropped like an anvil, wailing as he clutched his arm.

"You broke my arm!" he screamed in anger. "Mother fucker, I'll kill you for that!" He clumsily, almost drunkenly, staggered to his feet. With his good arm, he reached into his pocket and withdrew a switchblade. Flipping the blade open, he held it before him in a tight fist, ready to slash it across anything in his path.

The stranger just stood there like a loaded weapon, silent and deadly.

Kurt lunged forward, the knife poised for the man's gut.

I gasped, horrified and scared for the intimidating stranger who came to my rescue. For a split second his eyes lighted on mine. Kurt took advantage of that moment, thrusting the switchblade at the man's torso. The two men engaged in hand-to-hand combat, wrestling and taking turns delivering blows to one another's face, and body.

Not sure what to do, I held back, frozen in fear.

The stranger shouted at me, instructing me to lock

myself in the far stall, away from the fighting, away from the blood and violence.

Dashing into the stall, I swung the door closed and latched it. Looking around at the stifling partitions around me, I cursed myself for putting myself back in the confinements of the stall again.

Outside of the stall came cursing, grunts, and snarls. I wondered what was happening. Who had the upper hand? If it was Kurt, what was I going to do? The sound of struggle tapered off into silence, an eerie silence that sent a cold chill through my bones. My chest compressed with dread as I inched closer to the stall door. Who stood victorious behind it? Was it Kurt or the dark stranger?

My legs refused to move any closer to find out, they remained rooted in place, my brain only able to channel enough energy to keep me upright. After what felt like an eternity, heavy footfalls stalked toward the stall, then stopped just outside the door.

A light knock startled me.

"You all right in there?"

The man's gruff voice came as a relief. I unlocked the door, and slowly opened it.

The man, with tousled dark hair and smooth, tanned skin stood staring at me. He wore a gray flannel shirt, pushed over his elbows. His eyes, intense and alarming, pinned me into place.

"You okay?" His voice caressed me like smooth silk, though the tough gravel in it was throaty and sensual. His square jaw was prominent, dusted with stubble that only enhanced his rugged good-looks.

I forced a slight nod, my breathing hitching on a painfully dry throat.

"He's been disarmed." His gaze flicked down to the floor, hands clenched at his sides. I watched him, weary and cautious. Though he helped me, the man radiated danger and power.

His fists relaxed, slowly flexing and revealing creepy, elongated fingers. Each were tipped with curved, blackened claws. I drew in a sharp, surprised breath, fascinated, and repulsed at the same time. I blinked, gaping at his hands, realizing with each shutter of my eyelids, his nails shrank back into his skin, morphing into perfectly normal fingers.

"Don't be afraid," he said, his tone now as tender as an embrace, drawing my eyes from his hands to his handsome face. He was watching me with those feral, transfixed topaz eyes. His nostrils were still flaring and his chest heaving, almost panting. It was as though I was staring at a vicious jungle creature who had just maimed its prey.

"I don't know what I just saw," I said, withdrawing until my back hit the tile wall. "But I'm praying that you have some majorly high-tech nail extensions, cause if not, then I may need to be fitted for a straitjacket."

He cocked his head, studying me, slowly lifting his hands in the air. No claws. Just normal, human hands. Had I imagined the awful claws? I licked my lips and swallowed hard. "Please, I just want to find my friend and get out of here."

Kurt groaned.

The man's gaze swung to the sound. His jaw tightened before facing me again. "Come with me, allow me to—"

"What? No!" I could feel the hysteria began to build in my stomach and work its way up my throat.

My head ached, and I squinted against the blaring fluorescent lights overhead. "Thank you for helping me, but please, I just want to get away from here." The stall was suddenly stifling, and I felt as though I were drowning. Needing air and space, I tried to move my feet, but instead I wavered and fell into his strong arms.

"I've got you," he said. "I won't let go until you're ready. You say when."

He smelled of campfire and musky spice, an intoxicating elixir of maleness and nature. I gazed up at him, trying to read his face, but then the restroom door swung open. I withdrew from the stranger's arms, almost regretting it as soon as I stepped back.

A drunken boy, no doubt celebrating his twenty-first birthday, staggered in, carrying with him the strong scent of booze. He took one look around, then said, "Awesome, they even decorated the john." He stepped over Kurt, who was moaning into the floor.

Stumbling to the urinal, the boy unzipped his jailbird costume and proceeded to relieve himself. I wrinkled my nose in distaste, wishing I could plug my ears. I turned my head away, only to catch a glimpse of him in the mirror as he adjusted himself, then proceeded to make his way through his drunken fog out the restroom. The thump of bass rose momentarily as the door swung open, and then muffled as it shut again.

I looked back to the stranger. He seemed to bristle with alertness, taking in every sound, and every movement with sharpened awareness. Our gazes met, and I wanted to break away, but his almond shaped eyes held firm. He was a total contrast of emotion. His body seemed coiled with restlessness, like a caged panther ready to either break loose or shred the bars with his very teeth, but the tenderness he had shown was almost comforting, if not for the fact that he was a total stranger. An intensely scary, and massive stranger.

He cleared his throat. "We better go before someone sober comes in," he said.

I nodded, taking one last glance at Kurt as he groaned and felt blindly at his busted lip.

"Is he going to be okay?" I asked. *Why should I care?* I thought, as I shuddered, recalling those fearful moments I experienced before all hell broke loose. *That asshole deserves what he got.*

"He'll hurt for a while. But it will be a good reminder for the punk." His tone was harsh and held a frightening edge to it.

He pushed open the door and I grimaced against the bright neon laser lights that flickered back and forth across the room. My head pounded with each beat of the thumping music. *I just want to go home and forget everything about this horrible night.* I glimpsed the stranger again. *Everything, but him.*

"Layla! Where have you been?" Gwen was padding toward me, her stiletto's dangling from her fingers. "What happened to Kurt?" She looked from me to the mystery man beside me. "Who are you?"

"Roland," he answered simply.

"So you ditched Kurt for Roland, here?" She took in the length of him without shame. "Not that I blame you." She raised an eyebrow and shot him a sexy smirk.

"And you are?" he asked with an air of indifference.

"Aside from single?" She flipped her hair and reached for his hand. "I'm Gwen."

Roland's lips twitched in amusement as they shook

hands.

I felt jealousy pang in my gut. *Why? This man's a total stranger. A stranger who just beat the shit out of a man for me.*

"Where's James?" I questioned, surprised by how irritated I sounded.

Her gaze shifted back to me. "At the bar getting us some more drinks. You want something?"

I shook my head and wrung my hands. "I have to tell you something about Kurt," I said, my voice faltering as I stared at the floor. "He...he's..." *An asshole? A rapist?* My mouth wouldn't form the words. Tears welled in my eyes, and I wrapped my arms around myself, suddenly feeling weak and cold.

"Layla? What's wrong?" Gwen asked as she touched my arm, searching my face with her wide blue eyes.

"Your friend was lucky tonight," Roland answered.

"Got lucky tonight?" Her face broke out in a stupid grin and she waggled her eyebrows at me. "Do tell."

"No." I rolled my eyes. "I didn't *get* lucky, I *was* lucky," I snapped. "Because of you and your overzealous sex drive, you stuck me with a major sleaze." I no longer felt chilled, in fact, it felt as though lava surged through my veins. "He assaulted me in the men's bathroom. He said you promised him a good time." I glared at her, with anger rising up in me.

"I didn't mean it like that," she said, shaking her head. "Layla, I swear. If I had known what kind of guy he was, I wouldn't have set you two up." She took a step toward me and tried to embrace me.

I ducked away. Gwen's empty arms dropped to her sides.

"That's the thing, Gwen. You didn't even *know* him." I balled my fists and fought the urge to strangle her with my cat tail.

"Come on," she urged. "Let's go find James and we'll take you home."

"I'm not getting in a car with him. I can't, Gwen. He's friends with Kurt. I just can't."

Her lips quivered, and her face was colored with guilt. "Then we'll call a cab. I'll go with you."

"Well," I began, hesitant to go with Gwen. I wasn't in the mood to rehash the details of my night, nor was I interested in hearing about hers.

"I can give you a ride," Roland offered.

I looked up at him, shocked at his offer. "But I don't—"

"Know me?" he finished. His lips curved into a wicked smile before leaning in and whispering, "Perhaps not, but I know you, Matriarch."

My eyes widened at his words. *Matriarch?*

He leaned in even closer, his strong smell of fire and spice nearly intoxicating me. I could feel his warm breath on my neck as he spoke. "And I know *what* you are."

Chapter 7

I didn't hesitate. "I'll ride home with Roland," I said, the words tumbling out of my mouth before I could think better of it. Gwen blinked in surprise. She knows me all too well. I would never agree to ride home with a man who I had just met at a bar. I was always careful, always the designated driver in the group. So why was I willing to toss caution to the wind and hitch a ride with a complete stranger? Maybe it was the connection I felt to him for coming to my rescue, or the unexplainable comfort he brought to me, just by being near. Or maybe it was the fact that he called me, Matriarch. Was it possible Roland knew what was happening to me?

Gwen's brows shot up. "Are you sure, Layla? You just met him."

I wanted to say something hurtful, like how she's gone home with countless guys she'd just met. Or how she didn't know Kurt at all, yet she paired me with a pervert. But, the agony in her face was too much to bear, so I sucked in all my bitterness, all my anger, and muttered, "I'm sure," as I closed the space between us. I wrapped my arms around her, giving her a tight squeeze.

"I'm so sorry, Layla. I really had no idea."

I hugged her again and forced a smile. "Are you going to be okay with James?"

"Oh sure, you don't need to worry about him. His uncle knows Daddy."

That said it all. Anyone who knew Mr. Gibb knew how much he adored his baby girl. It wouldn't be surprising to learn that he ran criminal reports on all her dates. Unfortunately my date was the one who needed it.

Before I dwelled on that thought, Roland said, "I'll be waiting outside."

Gwen and I watched him as he walked away. He moved with such confidence, it was almost intimidating. People parted for him, like a wake from a speedboat as he wove his way through the crowd.

"Wow, Layla. He's beyond gorgeous." Gwen fanned herself.

"I know." For Gwen to say a man was attractive was so common, it was hardly a compliment anymore. Her taste in men ranged from silver foxes to young bucks fresh from the playing field to everything in between. But for me to take notice, to truly say with honesty that a man is handsome came a lot less frequent.

It wasn't because I didn't appreciate the male species, it was just that they required the total package to catch my eye. Gwen could overlook intellect, humor, or ambition. I couldn't. Though I didn't know the first thing about Roland, somehow his mysterious demeanor intrigued me. He exuded ferocity, danger, tenderness, and poise. A bundle of contradictions, and I wanted— no, I *needed*—to know more.

Gwen and I giggled like teenagers until I caught sight of two bouncers stepping out of the restroom. They seemed to be searching for something. Or someone. My stomach dropped into my toes. *Roland.*

"Have fun, and be careful," I said, eager to get outside to warn him.

"Ditto," she replied.

I hurried across the room, my heart pounding as I pushed through the crowd. When I flung the bar door open, I was thankful to have the crisp night air wash over my skin. It cleared my head. I had to find Roland and figure out what he knew about me. It was dark outside, but my eyes adjusted quickly. The night sky was pitch black, the crescent shape of the moon barely visible behind a dusting of gray clouds. I turned around myself, searching for Roland. The parking lot security lights glowed dimly, but somehow I was able to see him in the shadows.

"Roland?" I called, stepping off the asphalt and into the wooded area that lined the parking lot. My feet crunched across the scattered leaves and twigs. "The bouncers are looking for you."

He materialized out of the depths of the woods. "Then they had better be part bloodhound."

I stiffened at his odd choice of words. I really needed to stop reading into everything, but since the discovery of my weird ability it was proving to be difficult not to.

"What if he presses charges?" I asked.

"He won't." He jammed his hands into his pockets, flicking his gaze in the direction of the club. He spat on the ground, the angles of his face severe in the moonlight.

I rubbed my slick palms on my leggings, suddenly aware that I was still in my cat costume. I removed the headband hastily and scrubbed my face with my sleeve, removing my black nose, and silly whiskers.

His gaze moved back to me, the corner of his mouth curled, and I thought for a moment he was going to smile.

"What?" I demanded.

"Very fitting," he said, his lips twitching as his eyes roamed over me, pausing at my swaying tail.

Heat crept across my cheeks. "What is that supposed to mean?"

He arched an eyebrow at me. "You really have no idea, do you?"

"Idea about what?"

"About what you are." He sauntered over to an oak tree and leaned against it.

"Well, since you seem to know, please feel free to enlighten me." I crossed my arms over my chest.

He let out a long, unamused breath, before unhitching himself from the tree. "Come on."

"Where are we going?" I hesitated, watching him disappear into the depths of the woods. I chewed my lip, weighing my options. *Follow a complete stranger into a secluded area or turn around and take my ass home.* I turned on my heel. *Home it is.* As I walked, his words, '*I know who you are, Matriarch. And I know what you are.*' played in my head.

I closed my eyes, took a deep breath and listened to my gut. It told me that I was safe, and that Roland wasn't a threat. Sighing, I headed back into the woods, pushing back the low-lying branches as I made my way deeper.

A gentle breeze carrying a hint of crocus blossoms blew past me. I tucked my hair behind my ears and peered into the darkness.

"Roland?"

I heard a rustle of movement.

"We're not playing hide and seek," I called, ignoring the uneasy feeling that was blooming in my gut. I looked up at the night sky. The clouds had dissipated, allowing the sliver of moon to glow faintly in the distance. It was spooky, and unfortunately my imagination was starting to get the better of me. Fear began its arresting, and all-consuming crawl until it took complete hold of my senses. My pulse rose, my palms slickened, my breathing grew shallow. I had to get out of there.

Before I could take a single step, I felt a presence near me. I looked around, searching the shadows, my chest heaving as I struggled to reign in my mounting panic.

"Roland?" I said into the night, my voice broken and scared. A few feet away, a black panther slowly crept out of the darkness, the moon shining its silvery rays on its sleek black coat. Its steps were sure and steady, its eyes firm as it held me in the cross-hairs of its keen vision.

I took in a sharp intake of air and froze. My chest instantly tightened, capturing the scream that bubbled in my throat. The panther padded closer, those golden eyes locked upon me. Its footfalls surprisingly silent as it moved easily, and swiftly.

My heart pounded in my chest as if trying to escape—with or without me. Understanding that if I moved, the panther would surely give chase and I'd be dead before I could take three steps, I closed my eyes, bracing myself for an attack.

It was hard to be still, I had to press my lips

together to keep myself from screaming. *Please go away,* I begged silently. My mind hitched with a bumbling thought, and I scurried to hatch a plan. I opened my eyes, focusing my gaze on the animal, imploring it with unspoken trust and understanding. The panther was so close I could see the silvery thread of whiskers on its chin.

"I am not a threat," I said, my voice shaky but clear.

The panther hesitated, its great paw lifted in mid-step. The cat stared at me with golden eyes so intense I felt violated, as if this animal could see down into my very soul.

"Allow me to leave in peace." I took a small and timid step backward, not noticing the collection of loose stones at my heels. My footing wavered, and I stumbled, my arms flailing outward as I tried to catch myself. The panther was a blur of motion as it leaped into the air. I braced myself for the piercing sink of teeth, and agonizing tearing of flesh, but it never came. Instead, the carnivore landed gracefully behind me, intercepting my fall. The animal barely grunted under my weight. I slipped to the ground with just a pitiful thud, sitting upright as I caught my breath. The panther saved me. If it hadn't had caught me, I would have likely cracked my head open on a rock.

Ever so slowly, I shifted my gaze to look at the animal. It was regarding me with kind, golden eyes, an air of calm encompassing us as its body began rippling with gentle purring.

"Don't be afraid, Matriarch."

My chest cinched. The ability to hear animals' thoughts still jolting and strange. The panther's body began to tremble violently. I scrambled away from it, my eyes wide as a weird gurgling sound cut through the still of the forest. It was an odd combination of noises. Like tree limbs snapping and a landslide of sloshing mud and boulders.

With a howl, its black fur shrank and sucked inward. I gaped in awe as smooth, tanned skin took its place. The panther's massive canines retracted and transformed into a human jawline, its whiskers withdrew until they were merely stubble on a chiseled chin.

Roland!

I covered my mouth with both hands, completely shocked

and mesmerized. My gaze drifted down the length of him. He was completely nude, his lean muscles flexing as he tested his human body.

I breathed through parted fingers, "Roland?"

He rotated his head and lifted his shoulders. A chorus of crackling of bones filling the air. He sighed deeply. "Ah. That's better. Those tiny vertebras in the neck can be tricky to get back into place sometimes."

"What? What just..." I couldn't find the right words, my thoughts a jumbled mess in my head. "What the hell are you?"

"I'm exactly what you are."

Dumbfounded, I stood there speechless.

Roland worked at a few kinks in his muscles, rolling

and adjusting his prime body. "You have Shifter blood in you, Layla. You've been denied knowledge of it, because it was thought that you didn't possess the gene."

"I don't understand." I began to pace. "This has got to
be some sort of joke. Some sort of…misunderstanding." I knew I was rambling, but I couldn't help it. I just watched a panther shift into a human being. I felt unsteady on my feet. "Or maybe there was something in my drink. That's it. That's why I'm seeing things. That asshole Kurt spiked my drink when I wasn't looking."

"How do you explain the voices?"

"Voices?" I mimicked, stopping in my tracks.

"You heard me when I was in panther form, did you not?"

I stared at him for a long moment before swallowing the
lump that was forming in my throat.

"Have you had the gift long?" he asked, regarding me with fierce eyes.

I looked down at my trembling hands, knotting them
anxiously, before saying, "No."

"Your gifts are manifesting because of your fertility."

My head snapped up at that. "Excuse me?"

"When a female Shifter approaches her peak fertility cycle, the gene manifests itself by Turning them into the animal of their true nature."

I grew dizzy, struggling to fit the pieces together, but it all seemed implausible.

"You should have Turned," Roland continued, oblivious to the inner turmoil raging deep within me. "Instead your ability to communicate was revealed."

"Turned? Like a werewolf?"

He snorted. "No. Not at all like werewolves. There are wolf-Shifters, but rest assured Little Matriarch, there aren't any wolf-men running around, howling at the moon in torn jeans."

"You say that like it's impossible."

"It is," he said with absolute certainty.

"Seems like all things are possible now," I murmured, wrapping my arms protectively around myself. "And speaking of jeans, where are yours?"

His lips twitched. "Are you uncomfortable? I'm sorry, nudity is common practice among Shifters." He strolled leisurely to a cluster of bushes. I watched the firm muscles in his buttocks work as he moved. He caught me looking and shot me a wink as he bent to retrieve his clothes.

I felt my face flush. "Aren't you cold?" I asked as I averted my eyes, catching his movements in my peripheral vision.

"Shifters have higher body temperatures than humans. Especially Shifters who Turn into mammals."

Suddenly, I became utterly exhausted. The night's events caught up with me all at once. My eyelids and feet felt heavy and my body yearned for a hot bath and a soft bed. I glanced over at Roland, who was buttoning up his shirt as he walked up beside me.

"I know this is all overwhelming for you, Layla. There is much that you need to know. But first, you need rest. Let me take you home."

I stood there, lost in thought, and lost in a pocket of shadows, barely illuminated by the soft rays of the moon. I had vowed to find myself, but instead, there I was, more lost than ever.

Chapter 8

As I followed Roland through the parking lot, my thoughts turned as dark as the sky above us. *If what he says is true…that I indeed have Shifter bloodlines flowing through my veins, then that means I am going to Turn.* I shuddered. *And I don't have a choice in what I'll become.* I swallowed and suddenly felt uncomfortable in my own skin. In fact, I wished I could crawl out of it, leaving it behind as I disappeared into the night to start anew. *My life is still not my own,* I thought. My breathing became shallow and quick, and I soon felt the familiar wash of panic trail its way up my spine. I scowled. *Fine time for an attack.*

"Layla are you all right?" Roland asked.

I pursed my lips and nodded, slapping on the mask I often wore. My 'normal Layla' mask. The mask that hid my fears, the stress, and the panic attacks that consumed me. Being the perfect daughter was daunting—draining—and I often felt as though I were drowning. Drowning in my own sea of expectations and not one person could spare the time, nor the compassion to toss me a life ring.

Fighting back the tears, and willing my heartbeat to steady, I concentrated on putting one foot in front of the other. The ground slanted beneath my feet and I struggled to ignore the mounting need to scream.

Roland stopped at an oversized SUV, whose paint

job was more rust and gray bondo than it was red. He lifted a brow at me. "Quit judging her. She'll look good once she's painted," he said with a smile as he unlocked the door.

I climbed in, grateful to sit down. It always helped to ward off the vertigo. Roland slid into the driver's seat, his gaze sweeping over me before he started the engine. "Are you sure you are all right?" He studied me for a moment.

I grew self-conscious, shifting nervously in my seat. He started the engine. "Yes," I murmured, and turned my head to look out the window. The rumbling from the motor drowned out my weak voice, but he seemed content to read my body language, which clearly read 'leave me alone'.

As we pulled out of Zbornie's parking lot, my thoughts tormented me all over again. Being Doctor Harvey Carson's daughter, meant living a life carefully crafted by him. A life I did not want. My stomach rolled with disgust and anger. My father's domineering nature had always taken lead in the Carson home. Mom's passive personality allowed him to carve the perfect family from a cloth he had sewn. Father tried to control me my entire life, and now my own blood is turning against me. I clenched my hands into fists, gnashing my teeth together to keep from sobbing. *I will not allow it. This life is mine.*

I stared out into the night, blindly, not really seeing much more than the quick clip of tree line zip past my window. *How'd this happen to me?* I thought about my family; my grandparents and cousins. *Who among them is like me?* Roland was surprisingly quiet, allowing me to muddle through my thoughts in peace. It wasn't until he pulled into my driveway did I realize, with a gasp, that I had not given him directions.

My eyes darted to him. "How did you know where I lived?" I put a shaky hand on the door handle.

"The Clan's eyes have been on you." He spoke low as he stared straight ahead.

"The Clan?"

"It's an alliance of Shifters. There are many Clans around the world, but their laws remain the same. Governed by Shifters, it ensures that our kind stays undetected by humans." He adjusted his grip on the steering wheel, then shifted his eyes to mine. They sparkled like golden champagne in a flute. Under different circumstances, I would have been drawn into them, but instead, I wanted to flee.

"Why have they been watching me?" I demanded, my chest cinching tight around my heart, suffocating it.

"You were born Unmarked, which led them to believe that you did not possess the Shifter gene. But, to be sure..." He paused, his eyes firmly on mine as he framed his next words. "you have been sought and have been watched closely."

"By you?" I shot, glaring at him.

He nodded stiffly and licked his lips before saying, "They just want to help you through the Turning process. It's not easy. No one should endure it alone."

"I'll take my chances," I said, climbing out of the vehicle. "Tell the Clan they can stop watching me now." I slammed the door closed and stalked across the front lawn.

"Layla, wait," he called, sliding out of the SUV and catching up with me quickly. "I know this is overwhelming. Too much to process at once, but you cannot ignore the call of your true nature."

"I can, and I will," I said through gritted teeth as white-hot anger burned my veins. Would I ever have complete control over my own life? First my father, and now the Clan? It was all too much. Too much pressure, too much restraint.

"Shifting is like the moon," he continued. "You can't hide from it. And you can't outrun it." His intrusive, honey-hued eyes warmed, and for a moment I allowed myself to be captivated. "It's innate within you, Layla. You are a part of this world." He touched his heart. "*My* world. Whether you like it or not."

His gaze held firm, unrelenting, as he waited for my response. Although Roland was intriguing, and his eyes nearly left me spellbound, I forced myself to ignore my attraction to him, and walk away.

He didn't follow, but I felt his stare follow me across the lawn, and all the way up my porch steps. I placed my hand on the door knob and said over my shoulder, "I won't be a part of your Clan."

And with that, I turned my back on my bloodline, refusing to let anyone or anything control me again.

****

The alarm clock blared, rattling through my head as I swatted the air blindly. Finally quieting it, I yawned and rubbed the sleep from my tired eyes. Inhaling deeply, I forced myself to get out of bed. I drew back the window curtains, squinting against the brilliant sunlight. In an exhausted daze, I somehow brewed a cup of coffee and brushed my teeth.

Once dressed, I stood in front of the mirror, admiring my Preston Park Zoo uniform. Grinning like an idiot at my reflection, I took the time to acknowledge the day as a triumphant achievement. Not only was I starting my career in the field that I loved, but I was making my own decisions. Choosing my own path.

I combed my hair into a ponytail and tucked a blue headband into place. Then, the butterflies hit. Though I was excited about my first day, I was also anxious. I had always dreamed of being a zookeeper, but that was before I could talk to animals. And before I could turn into one.

Shaking the thought away, I grabbed my messenger bag and headed out the door. Slipping into the driver's seat, I gave myself a quick pep talk. "All right, Layla, this is it. You are on your way to a new beginning. You are in charge of your own destiny."

As I merged onto the main road, my hands grew clammy on the steering wheel as images of the strange crow crawled back into my head. Just recalling its beady eyes and wicked stare, sent a shiver up my spine. I cranked up the radio, trying my best to drown out the memories of that day. I found myself repeatedly checking the mirrors for signs of the peculiar bird. Thankfully, I was alone on the road and my drive was uneventful.

I pulled into the zoo's parking lot and quickly found a spot close to the office. Jogging across the asphalt, I checked over my shoulder once more. No crow. Before I entered the office building, I took in a big breath, collected myself and squared my shoulders. *Here I go...*

I made my way through the halls and found the employee lounge. Cramming my bag into an empty locker, I headed out to find Rachael. She was sitting behind her desk, a broken walkie talkie laid out in front of her. Her brows were pulled in concentration and her hands steady as she worked.

"Ready for your first day?" she said, not even looking up.

"Absolutely," I answered. "Am I shadowing you today?"

"Sorry, no. I have a board meeting today. I'm putting you with Ashley. She's really good. You'll like her." She snapped the battery in place and looked up at me. "Josie got a hold of my radio. Stole it right off my hip and smashed it. Damn pesky monkey." She smiled and shook her head before setting to work on the mangled antenna. The radio soon crackled and garbled voices and static filled the air. Rachael rolled her eyes.

I chuckled. "Sometimes I bet you feel like smashing the radio yourself."

"Damn right," she agreed. "Josie was just doing me a favor I suppose."

I heard footsteps coming up behind me. They stopped right outside Rachael's office door. I turned, finding a petite brunette peering through the doorway.

"Hi," I said, giving a small wave.

"You must be Layla." She said this more like a statement, rather than a question. "Let's roll."

I threw a look at Rachael, who just smiled.

I had to hurry to keep up with Ashley as she wove her way through the building. This girl seemed to have a motor throttle for feet, darting quickly around corners, and through hallways.

"You used to volunteer here, right?" she asked as she shoved the exit doors open.

"That's right." I said, shielding my eyes from the

blinding sunlight.

It was an unnaturally warm November day, but I relished in the pleasantness of it. Tiny wrens skittered across the winding pathways, disappearing into the bushes whenever we drew too close. There was a faint waft of pretzels and hotdogs in the breeze, and a distant whoop of a Gibbon ape ringing through the air.

I felt winded from keeping pace with her as she made her way to the Mammal House that was clear across park grounds.

"So have you always wanted to shovel shit for a living?" she questioned.

Ashley didn't hold back, or even look back. I watched her buzz along, her short bob bouncing as she moved. The walkie-talkie on her belt crackled every so often with feedback and unfamiliar voices.

"For as long as I can remember," I answered. *Until my father found out anyway,* I thought. I could still hear him. *'No daughter of mine is going to be a zookeeper. What prestige comes with that?'* I pursed my lips together to keep from answering him out loud: *Prestige is irrelevant when you're happy with yourself.*

I recognized the Mammal House in the distance. It still looked the same. The dome roof and mottled façade of mortar and clay gave it a primitive appearance. Vines snaked their way up and over the building, reminding me of a giant ball of leafy yarn. We followed the sidewalk to a backdoor that read: Zoo Staff Only. Ashley yanked it open and stepped aside, allowing me to enter first. The smell of bleach and wet hay instantly overwhelmed my senses.

"Things probably haven't changed much since you were here," she said.

I took a look around at the familiar rows of holding cages that stretched along the length of the room. The floor was as I remembered. A damp concrete slab punctuated with drains. Several zookeepers were busy mucking cages, dumping clumps of soiled bedding into trash bins before spraying them clean with water hoses.

"No, not really," I said. "Looks pretty much the same."

"We will start you with the North American small mammals, which are located in Block Two. But before we do, let me introduce to everyone." She gestured for me to follow and led me to the middle of the room.

"Hey everyone," Ashley called. "I want to introduce you to our new keeper, Layla."

The low chattering quit, as everyone turned around to look at me. I waved, recognizing a couple of familiar faces in the crowd.

Emmanuel, a guy I remembered as hardworking and friendly came up to me. "Good to have you back, Layla." He rubbed his hand along his khakis before sticking it out to me. His palms were smudged with dirt.

The folks at the hospital would be scrambling for their hand sanitizer right about now, I thought with a smile. I shook his hand firmly.

The zookeepers I didn't know made their way over and introduced themselves, all appearing genuine and friendly.

After a few minutes of small talk, everyone went back to their work. Ashley led me through the room, toward Block Two, where the small mammals were housed. That's when we passed Jack, a man in his mid-sixties, who has been working at Preston Park Zoo longer than anyone else. He hasn't changed since I was a volunteer, except now he leans heavily upon a cane. He stood near the African lion cage, completely ignoring us. His pinched face and hooked nose always reminded me of a vulture. From what I remembered of him, Jack didn't particularly like volunteers. He thought we were nuisances, and had no issue telling us so. I did my best to steer clear of him, not just because he didn't like me, but because of the uneasy feeling I'd get whenever I was around him.

"Hi Jack." I gave a tight smile. He only grunted. His deep-set eyes followed me briefly. His scowl seemed permanently etched into his weathered skin.

I looked past Jack, finally noticing the lion behind the strong steel bars. He was pacing the length of his enclosure, his golden eyes wide as he snarled at the man.

"I don't think the lion likes him much," I noted.

"I think the feeling is mutual." Ashley chuckled, but it was without much amusement. "Sergio swiped at him several years ago. Practically shredded his left hand."

I was surprised to hear that. Jack had been working with that lion forever. What had caused the animal to turn on him?

Ashley removed a shovel from the tool rack and handed it to me. "Let's see if you remember how to shovel poop." She proceeded to instruct me on the protocols of properly servicing the bobcat's holding cage, but my mind was elsewhere.

I glanced back at Jack. He was staring at the lion. A look of loathing colored his wrinkled face. I tried to ignore the tight ball of unease that was unfurling in my gut. Something was not right with Jack and Sergio.

What, I didn't know, but I was determined to find out.

Ashley and I worked our way through Block Two until all the animals had been observed briefly to ensure they were healthy, and each enclosure had been thoroughly cleaned.

"Well done, Layla. Take a fifteen-minute break, then meet me at the Misty Falls Exhibit. I'll introduce you to the primate keepers. They are a pack of oddballs, but then ya got to be to work with primates." She jabbed at me with her elbow. "Am I right?" She chuckled. "Hey. I'm going to the vending machines. Want anything?"

I shook my head. "No, thanks. Is it all right if I just stay in here? I want to look around and re-familiarize myself with the work stations again."

"That's not much of a break," she said, frowning at me. "But I guess so."

"I'll see you in fifteen." I started to browse the hanging racks of tools, memorizing where the bleach was stored and where to find the first-aid kit. When I heard the Mammal House door slam shut, I scanned the room. It was empty now except for Jack and me. Now was my chance. I hurried across the room, back toward the lion enclosure, slinking along the wall, trying to keep my footsteps light.

The male lion was standing, his posture guarded as he kept a close watch on Jack. I didn't realize I had been holding my breath until my chest felt as though it were filling with hot coals. I blew out a quiet breath, steadying my quaking hands by clutching them into fists. *I have a bad feeling about this…*

"Are you going to move, or am I gonna have to make ya?" Jack said, his haggard voice echoing off the concrete floors. He held a water hose tight in his hand. "Move, beast!" He aimed the nozzle straight at the lion's face and sprayed. The strong stream of water hit between the eyes, splashing across the lion's muzzle.

The lion snarled and pawed at his face. "Move!" Jack shouted. The massive cat didn't budge. "Fine. Sit in your own filth for all I care." He turned and cracked his cane across the bars of the cage. *CLANG!* I cringed as the sound rattled through my teeth. Jack's boots clomped across the wet concrete floor as he trudged away, disappearing through the exit doors, taking with him the sickening scent of perspiration and day-old coffee.

Taking small steps, I hesitantly approached the lion's cage. My heart sank when I saw him. His face was sodden, the droplets of water sparkling like diamonds against his black mane. He watched me carefully, his amber eyes sad, but proud. I took in a deep intake of breath, and cleared my mind, readying myself for a conversation with him.

"Does he hurt you?" I asked.

We studied each other for a long time. Feral, golden eyes, much like Roland's, watched me intently, gauging my sincerity. Several tense minutes stretched past, so many so that I thought that my so-called gift had disappeared, until I heard the familiar whisper within my mind.

"He tries to break me, but his efforts only fuel my hatred for him."

"How does he do it, Sergio?"

"His stick strikes like lightning."

His stick? *He's talking about his cane*, I concluded. *It strikes like lightning? What does that mean?* Emotion collected in my throat, and I fought to swallow it before I said, "I won't let it continue."

"How, Matriarch? His brutality has gone undetected for years."

"I promise you. It ends now." The rage I felt was fierce, and unsettling. Only once before did I remember feeling that protective, that passionate over something. It was when I rescued the rhesus macaque. His freedom and safety were the most important things to me in that moment, and now in this moment, the only thing that mattered was revenge for the lion.

The doors suddenly clicked open, causing me to snap my head in the direction of the sound. Sunrays streamed in through the opened door, blanketing the person entering in a blinding white light. Once the door swung closed, extinguishing the sunlight, there stood Jack. He moved slowly and haggardly, leaning on his cane as if it were a third appendage.

He eyed me suspiciously from across the room, the air between us turning tense as I glared at him, unable and unwilling to hide my revulsion and anger. He drew closer, his boots scuffling across the floor, and the steady *tap-tap* of his cane jabbing the concrete. He was a few feet from Sergio's cage when my gaze dropped from his pinched face to his right hand. Deep scars ran like silvery ribbons from his wrist to his fingernails, and he was missing his pinky entirely.

My gut churned as I envisioned what he had done to Sergio to warrant those hideous wounds. What torture had the great cat been through? What abuse did Jack dish out to him, and the other animals entrusted to his care?

"I know you hurt him," I said, squaring my

shoulders. The lion was at my back, stalking the length of his enclosure anxiously.

Jack stopped short. "What are you talking about?" His gray brows rumpled, deepening the creases in his forehead. His guilty eyes darted to Sergio, and I noted a falter in his grip on the cane.

I gestured to it. "The cattle prod. You use it on him, don't you?"

He snorted and straightened himself as if he were trying to intimidate me. "What cattle prod?"

My lips twitched, and I nearly laughed at him. *Nice try, Jack, but you're dealing with the mother of all animal lovers. Layla, 'the Matriarch' Carson.* My chest swelled with a flurry of emotions: pride, confidence, and triumph. It was in that moment that I felt like roaring. Roaring like a lioness overlooking her pride.

"You can fool the others," I said. "but I see you for what you are. A pathetic, weak old man who tortures animals. You disgust me."

"You don't know shit." He spat on the ground.

I lifted a brow at him and rushed him, snatching the cane out of his hand. He staggered and clung to the wall for support.

Surprised by the weight of the cane, I unsheathed a cattle prod, expertly hidden within its carefully constructed case. I looked at Jack, who stared at me, dumbfounded.

Internally, I was torn in two. On one hand, I was thrilled my instincts were dead on, but on the other, my heart felt heavy knowing Sergio was subjected to years of abuse by this man.

I switched the cattle prod on. A gentle hum of electricity zipped down the length of it until the charge of raw voltage flickered along the forked tip. Anger spiked further, and darker within my gut. "I'm telling Rachael what you've done."

Jack grabbed at the cane, but my reflexes were quicker. I swung the prod on him, pressing it deep into the tender flesh above his wrist. His hand jolted and twitched, his eyes wide in fear.

I withdrew the prod, shocked by my actions. Jack's hand trembled, the scars bright against the white in his knuckles. His eyes flashed as turned his gaze on me.

"You stupid little bitch. You'll be fired and charged with assault for this!"

My stomach turned with worry, but I wouldn't allow Jack to intimidate me. "It's well worth it for what you've been inflicting on Sergio all these years." I lifted the cattle prod again, aiming it like a spear straight toward his chest. Jack swallowed nervously, his eyes flickered to the prod.

"Easy there," he said, raising both hands in the air.

Sergio paced the length of his cage. His ears were perked to attention, his jowls pulled back, revealing a set of impressive canines. As he paced, I noticed the slash of a healing scar across his shoulder blade. Sergio's eyes met mine, and I knew. That scar was caused by Jack. Fury blanketed my vision. Steady with my grip, I inched the forked tip closer.

"I should open up his cage, and throw you in." I crowded his space, causing him to stumble backward, unaware of how close he was to the lion's cage. My gaze jumped to Sergio. His ears were pinned to his head, his mane bristled with excitement. In a flurry of motion, he charged the bars and snagged his abuser's shirt with his claws.

Jack howled in pain. Sergio snarled, and snapped at him, unable to get his huge muzzle through the cage bars. Everything within me suddenly halted.

The veil of anger that clouded my thoughts lifted, and I was able to process the entire situation with one hurried glance. Sergio had sliced the skin along Jack's bicep to elbow into bloody ribbons. His claws were still embedded deep within the muscle, keeping Jack a prisoner in his grasp.

As much as I despised Jack, I didn't want him dead.

"Sergio! Don't!" My tone came out strangled and panicked. The great cat ignored me, answering back with just a menacing growl. "Sergio," I tried again, doing my best to talk calmly, careful not to excite the four hundred plus pound feline any further. "I know it's hard, but you must release him." I walked closer, keeping my movements slow and deliberate.

The lion's eyes were glazed with rage, and the instinctual need to still the squirming prey in his grip. "He will not hurt you anymore. I give you my word." I took Jack's arm, there was no fight in the old man. He hung there, limp and losing blood. I was going to lose him if Sergio didn't relent. I gave the stern command, "Release him!" and the massive lion stilled.

"Good boy," I said, aware of the sudden shift of the power. Sergio awaited instructions, daring not to move even the slightest muscle. I peeked over Jack's shoulder. Trails of bloody gashes stretched along his thin arm, exposing shredded muscles and skin. The tips of Sergio's claws were still sunk deep into Jack. I reached around the seemingly frail man, and carefully unhooked Sergio's claws, feeling the resistance of one being rooted into the bone.

My stomach heaved, but I had to keep my focus. Jack's life depended on it. Bracing myself for Jack's screams, I pried the claw out of the bone with a quick yank. I winced as he let out an agonized cry before collapsing into me, his slight frame not much more than feeble muscle and brittle bones. Jack's breathing was extremely shallow, but at least he was alive.

"You must erase his memory."

I snapped my head upward, staring into the golden eyes of the lion. "What?"

"You can't let him go without scrubbing his memory. It's too dangerous. As the Matriarch, you can tamper with the memories of humans."

"I can't," I mumbled, shocked to hear such a revelation. The thought was almost too much to bear. My legs felt like water, but I firmly kept ahold of Jack, knowing full well that if I fell, he'd go down with me. "I don't know how."

"Follow your instincts."

I looked into Jack's eyes, they were distant, and I knew that he was going into shock. Gently, I sank to the floor, taking Jack with me. Jack's legs were sprawled out on the concrete, his bleeding arm hanging uselessly at his side.

Inhaling a cleansing breath, I cupped his face with my palms and closed my eyes. Reaching deep, I searched my instincts for what to do, some sort of nudge or whisper that I have come to rely on. I leaned in close to Jack, ignoring the smell of salty copper and sweat that wafted off him.

"This incident was completely initiated by your actions," I whispered into Jack's ear. "You will not remember me or my involvement, except that I found you injured and called for help."

A whimper escaped his lips, and my heart sank. Only moments ago I stabbed an electric-charged cattle prod into his wrist, and here I am, cradling the feeble man in my arms.

I grabbed the two-way radio from his belt, and screamed into the receiver, "I need an ambulance at the Mammal House!"

I glanced back at Sergio. He paced the length of his enclosure just as he had before, but instead of bristling with fear, he radiated satisfaction.

"Are you pleased?" I asked.

His long tail whipped through the air with superiority. *"I would have taken delight in destroying his jugular, but that would have been too quick for the vile man. The wounds on his arm will mirror those on his hands. Perhaps this time, he will recall the strength behind these claws."*

I opened my mouth to speak, but the double doors flew open and in filed a herd of chaos. Rachael was in the forefront, directing the zoo's first-responders through the building. Her eyes scanned me briefly, before falling on Jack. Her lips pursed slightly before speaking to a man beside her.

A stout EMS worker rushed to my side, taking Jack's body from me. "I've got it from here, ma'am," he said. The emergency workers worked swiftly, securing Jack onto a gurney.

I blinked in quiet shock. What had I done? Suddenly Rachael was there, offering to help me to my feet. I gladly took her hand, allowing her to pull me up from the floor. She wrapped an arm around my shaking shoulders.

"You okay?" she asked.

The weight of what had transpired made me heavy on my feet and light in the head. The room suddenly seemed too dark and too crowded. "I need some air," I gasped, shrugging out of Rachael's grip.

I ran past the stretch of mammal holdings, the animals within them scrabbling out of sight in surprise.

Rachael called after me, "Layla!" just before the steady pace of clomping boots crunching on the concrete echoed behind me.

I kept running, shoving the building doors apart and stumbling to a stop out in the bright sunlight. I breathed in the fresh air, allowing it to cleanse me as it always had. I closed my eyes and lifted my face to the sun, letting its warmth seep through my skin and caress my very soul.

I contributed to Jack's injuries. If I hadn't turned the cattle prod on him, he wouldn't have fell against Sergio's cage bars, and he wouldn't have sustained those horrible lacerations. He'd still be all right. He'd still be able to use his arm. Like railroad cars slowly hitching to one another, my thoughts bumped along in a row until crashing into the inevitable, bitter truth. *He'd still be tormenting Sergio.* My throat dried to an uncomfortable scratch.

"Layla," Rachael said gently. "I know it's been a shitty first day, but can you tell me what happened?"

The memory of it rushed up on me like a tidal wave. Sergio's pained expression, the genuine fear in his eyes when Jack entered the room.

I nodded, feeling my stomach knot with apprehension. *Forgive me, Rach, for lying...*

The doors of the Mammal House swung open, eclipsing anything I had to say. EMS workers gingerly maneuvered Jack through the doorway. He was awake, but still lost in a fog of shock. His gaze was glassy, and he stared out at nothing as they pushed the gurney along.

Rachael and I watched in silence as they loaded him carefully into an ambulance. One man climbed inside with Jack while the other slammed the doors tight, stealing our view inside.

Rachael hung her head.

Sirens trilled, drilling deep within my already pounding head. The obnoxious sound grew fainter and fainter until finally, all was quiet.

Rachael sighed, and turned to face me. "Layla, what the hell happened in there?"

"Jack…" My voice cracked. I cleared my throat and tried again. "Jack was trying to get Sergio to move, but when he wouldn't…Jack used a cattle prod on him."

Rachael inhaled a sharp, shocked intake of breath.

"Sergio turned on him," I continued, searching her face for some sort of sign on whether she believed me or not. Could she see through my lie—though it technically wasn't a lie. Jack may not have used the prod on Sergio today, but he had many, many times before according to the big cat.

Rachael took to pacing, her hands drawn in tight fists at her side. "Damn it. I can't believe this!"

I watched her walk a determined line back and forth in front of me, her head clearly overwhelmed with information. She paused for a second, thinking. "How did no one know about the cattle prod? Where did he keep it?"

"Within his cane," I answered, my tone solemn and sad.

"Shit, shit, shit," she repeated, massaging her temples with her fingertips. "I wanted to pull him from working with Sergio a few years ago." When she lifted her eyes to look at me, they appeared full of regret and frustration. "But he insisted that he didn't want to *punish* the lion by taking away its longtime keeper." She let out an exasperated huff. "That was a load of shit and my dumbass fell for it. Hook, line and sinker."

Zoo employees swarmed like busy bees, erecting blockades around the Mammal House to keep unwanted people out. It was officially a crime scene that needed to be examined by authorities.

"You can't blame yourself for this, Rachael," I offered, ignoring the sounds of hurried voices, and their labored task of assembling barricades. "Jack did this. And now he's paying for it."

She looked thoughtfully for a moment, then muttered, "Karma's a bitch." She turned, aiming her clipped steps for the Mammal House. I watched her yank the door open, and go inside, anger roiling off her like hot lava.

A moment later, she remerged from the building, carrying Jack's cane. She walked up to me, her brows knitted bitterly over her stormy gaze. "I'm pressing charges against Jack."

I nodded, unable to offer anything useful. My attention was far too focused on the cattle prod. I stared at it, lost in the memory of switching it on, and pressing it to Jack's wrist. How easily I discarded Jack as just a vile man who needed to be taught a lesson. How easily

I forgot he was capable of feeling pain. Was I forgetting what it meant to be human? Was I becoming too animalistic? Was my rationality yielding to my urges? I quelled the need to shiver at the thought.

Rachael unsheathed the cattle prod, her eyes sad as they traveled down the length of it. "Sick son of a bitch." She turned it on, and together we watched the forked tip flicker with electricity. She expelled a long, defeated breath. "I failed Sergio."

"Rachael," I said, touching her shoulder lightly. "There was no way for you to have known."

She pulled her gaze away from the cattle prod and looked squarely into my eyes. "Oh yeah? Well, you've been here less than six hours and you figured it out."

I withdrew my hand. Obviously I couldn't tell her about my ability—how easily I could hear the thoughts, and fears, of animals.

I swallowed down the truth, and said, "Jack's injuries are bad, Rachael, but they're not fatal."

"They could have been," she whispered. "and knowing that Sergio has been abused for so long without me even noticing is salt in the damn wound." She pinched her eyes tight, and for a moment I thought she was going to cry. Instead she seemed to be steeling herself, readying herself like a soldier preparing for battle.

She opened her eyes and glanced toward the gathering horde of spectators. Zoo-goers, fellow employees and even the Press were clamoring around— all seeking information on what happened. She was preparing herself for the onslaught of questions, accusations and beratement that ensues after such an incident.

"What will happen to Jack…once he recovers?" I asked over the din of the crowd.

"He'll be forced to retire. This is the second incident for him and Sergio. Management will be forced to take action." She clasped her hands in front of her, visibly stepping back into her professional role.

"And Sergio?" I watched her expectedly, anxious fear wringing me inside like suffocating vice.

Her expression wavered momentarily, her eyes grim as she said, "Well, luckily for Sergio, this incident was obviously prompted by the use of brute force. As long as Jack's wounds are considered minor, he'll be granted a reprieve."

"Reprieve as in…he won't be euthanized?"

Her nod of assurance sent a dizzying spiral of relief through me. I was so happy Sergio would not be punished for something I clearly instigated. If I hadn't let my anger overtake my senses, none of this would have happened.

"Miss Thorn," someone from the crowd shouted. "Miss Thorn, can we get a statement?"

Rachael's face withered slightly, but she didn't lose a bit of that hardened backbone. She was always tough as nails, and just as sharp. Whether it was a brash member of the Press, or a respected dignitary, Rachael Thorn didn't flinch away from anyone. She tilted her chin skyward, and called back, "No comment at this time." She turned to me, and said, "Why don't you take the rest of the day off, Layla? This has been one hell of a first day."

She placed a hand on my shoulder. The gesture comforted me, and for a quick moment, I actually almost agreed to it. But I wasn't about to abandon her,

Sergio or the zoo. This incident was partly my fault, and I was going to see to it that I made things right again. "Thanks, but I'd like to stay, if that's okay?"

She gave me a feeble smile, and together we went into the Mammal House.

Police officers were chatting quietly to one another, jotting things down in tiny notepads. Staff members were already disbanding, each going back to their usual duties. Ashley lingered around Sergio's cage, looking bleak as we approached her.

"You okay?" The question was directed to both Rachael and me, but Rachael was the one who spoke up first.

"No. That son of a bitch provoked Sergio." She held up the cattle prod.

Ashley covered her mouth with both hands, gasping between her fingers. "Oh my God. Poor Sergio!"

Rachael's eyes trailed over the pool of Jack's blood, and over to the police officers. "Look, I have an incident report to write and news reporters to deflect," Rachael said. "You guys get back to work and I'll let everyone know about Jack's condition as soon as I hear something."

We watched her as she walked away, lost in our own thoughts and not sure what to do next.

"Are you all right, Layla?" Ashley questioned with genuine concern. "I mean, dang, what a thing to witness on your first day!"

"I'm fine," I assured her, walking away to pluck a rake from the tool rack.

"This isn't going to scare you away, is it? I mean, you will be coming back tomorrow, right?"

Knowing full well my anger caused the horrific scene to unfold in the first place, I told her, "Accidents happen. This one just happened to take place on my first day. It's unfortunate, but I still want to be a zookeeper. It's who I am."

Ashley smiled. "Spoken like a true zookeeper. Come on girl, let's go. We've got more shit to shovel."

Chapter 9

I somehow made it through the rest of the day without dwelling on the horrible incident in the Mammal House. Ashley and I mucked stalls and disinfected den boxes until our nostrils burned from the bleach fumes. Before the end of my shift, Rachael informed me that Jack was conscious and recovering well, which was actually a relief to hear. She also said his story collaborated with mine, which meant he agreed to the forced resignation and wouldn't be returning to the zoo.

That night I collapsed into bed utterly exhausted—mentally and physically. Although I should have fallen asleep as soon as my head hit the pillow, my thoughts wouldn't allow it. I relived my encounter with Jack and Sergio over and over, each memory bloodier than the first. The most unsettling realization was how I had become a scary, almost primal, version of myself. How did I allow my rage to take the reins on my actions? I acted completely on impulse when I turned the cattle prod on Jack, allowing my instincts to cloud all rationality.

I shuddered and pulled the comforter to my chin. On top of all that—I learned I could alter the memories of humans. *Humans.* Had I really just called them humans, as though I wasn't one anymore?

My thoughts snapped back to my discussion with

Roland. *'You have Shifter blood in you, Layla. You've been denied knowledge of it, because it was thought that you didn't possess the gene.'*

Did that mean one of my parents was a Shifter? I tried to dredge up a memory, *any* memory of either of them acting peculiar, or *different.* I came up empty. They were both so normal, they could be considered boring.

I laid in bed for hours, tossing and turning, unable to find a comfortable position, until finally, my body gave out and my mind gave in to the exhaustion. Of course, I didn't have a peaceful rest. That night I dreamt I was locked in a cage. My hands—hideous claws— were gripped around the bars. My ankles tethered to the ground with silver chains ached from the weight of the metal. I growled at the guards, shredding my shirt angrily, revealing matted fur instead of skin. I was a snarling, dangerous beast, thirsting for the taste of blood.

I awoke with a jerk, sweaty and panicked. My chest heaved as my heart raced. I swung my legs over the side of the bed and pressed my face into my hands. I couldn't hold back the tears even if I wanted to. Hot tears ran until they were cold over my cheeks. *What is happening to me?* I found myself wishing I could go back, back to when things were simple. When things were *normal.*

My phone chimed. I wiped my face with the back of my hand, ignoring it. Then, it chimed again. Sighing, I reached across the nightstand, flipping it open to find a text message from Gwen.

—Morning miss zookeeper how was ur first day?—

I quickly punched in an answer:

—Eventful—

—Do tell—

—No time. Got 2 b at work @ 8. Text u later—

—K. xoxo—

I smiled. Texting Gwen was the most normal thing I had done all week. I got dressed and headed out for work, losing myself in the mundane details of the day. Driving, clocking in, working, eating, and clocking out. It was all normal and non-eventful, and I was relieved.

As I unlocked my truck, I heard a flapping in the tree above me. Squinting against the glow of the fading sunset, I saw a small shadowed body, darting limb to limb. The sound of beating wings sent a shiver down my spine. It was the crow. Swallowing, I steeled myself. "What do you want?" I called up to the tree.

The sun suddenly winked out of sight. The tree became nothing but a cluster of shadows and whispered movement.

"Why are you following me?" I demanded. Again, I was met with a cold silence. "I know that was you the other day."

The frantic fluttering of wings startled me, but I stood firm. The crow landed on the hood of my truck, its talons scraping across the metal as it skittered toward me. I caught the faint trace of cigar in the air, which was unusual, but then, what wasn't unusual anymore?

The bird seemed to be measuring me, its piercing eyes unwavering and unfeeling. We studied each other for a long moment. I admired its sleek, oil-slick features and strong talons. I'm not sure what it saw when looking at me. I hoped it didn't notice the tremble in my hands, or the uncertainty in my face.

It cocked its head ever so slowly, then leapt! Claws like needles dug across my face, sinking deep into my cheek. Panic welled through me as I swatted wildly at it, my swings never connecting with the damn thing. The crow cawed loudly, the echoes haunting and jarring.

There was a rustle of leaves behind me. The bird shrieked as a paw swiped at it, missing by mere centimeters. I clambered backward, watching in awe as a spotted cat vaulted itself at the crow. I quickly identified the cat, with its small stature and short tail: a bobcat. With talons bared, the bird slashed at the cat's face. Bright red blood oozed from his tanned muzzle. The crow screeched as though victorious, then circled one full loop around us before disappearing into the darkness.

The bobcat's pale-yellow eyes settled on me. They were familiar eyes, comforting and intense all at once. *Roland?* The cat turned and trotted into the sparse woods that ran along the highway. I wanted to follow, but I couldn't make my legs work. I stood there in a stupor, staring blankly into the night.

Only seconds later, footfalls roused me from my daze. Instinctively, I tilted my head and listened, absorbing the sound, feeling it through the soles of my feet. I sniffed the air, catching the faintest trace of him. Smoldering campfire and s'mores. I exhaled through my mouth, my shoulders sagging with relief when I saw him emerge from the shroud of shadowed trees. He wore a black thermal shirt, pushed up to his elbows and dark jeans. Roland's gaze was fixated on me as he walked toward me.

"What are you doing here?" I asked.

"That's some greeting," he said, tapping his fingers to the still bleeding scratches left by the crow. "You'd think you'd be nicer to the guy who keeps saving your ass." He inspected his fingertips, which were tinged with blood, before wiping them on his jeans.

"You're still following me." It wasn't a question. I somehow already knew the answer. Our eyes locked as he closed the space between us. He stood in front of me. His scent was strong; distracting and enticing.

He ignored that entirely, his eyes tracing the wound on my cheek. "You're bleeding." He reached out to touch my face.

I slapped at him, furrowing my brows and frowning. "Are you still watching me?" I demanded.

"Are you always this thick-headed or are you just that way to me?"

"Answer me," I said through clenched teeth.

"Yes, I've been watching you and by the looks of things, you need to be watched."

"Why? Because of a damn *bird*?"

He laughed mockingly, infuriating me further. I could feel the heat creep its way from my neck to my ears. I balled my fists at my sides, squaring my shoulders and lifting my chin defiantly.

"That *damn bird...*" His brows pinched tighter. "is Sid McCarty," he said. "He's Victor Rizzo's second in command. If Victor's sending his henchman after you, then you got yourself an enemy."

"Sid McCarty? Victor Rizzo?" I shook my head. "I don't know either of those names. What would they want with me?"

"I can think of two reasons. They either want your

bloodlines..." He stuck his hands in his pockets. "Or they want you dead. Either way, they're out for blood."

"My bloodlines?" My voice sounded strained, even to my own ears.

Roland rolled his eyes. "You're a hark-Shifter, Layla. They are rare and considered valuable to Clans. You can hear the thoughts of animals. Can communicate with them while in human form. Hark-Shifters also have the ability to Turn into any animal they desire. It's a rare gift, Layla. One that hasn't been bestowed on Shifters for over two centuries."

"So they want...what?" My thoughts rattled around my head like an angry bee trapped in a jar.

Roland watched me carefully as I figured it out. It felt as though heavy stones were stacking within my chest, compressing my lungs and squeezing my heart. "My DNA," I murmured. My knees faltered, and I held my head with both hands, trying to steady myself.

Roland didn't move. "They want your lineage, your bloodlines. They anticipate your hark gene will pass to their descendants."

I lifted my head, my gaze resting on Roland. "And your Clan? Do they want the same thing?"

He scrubbed at his neck and looked at his shoes.

His silence was my answer. Anger flared within me, and instead of clawing his eyes out like I wanted to, I turned on my heel and marched back to my truck. I bit my lip, trying to keep my tears at bay.

"Layla, wait."

I heard his movement as he jogged behind me, but I quickly opened the truck door, holding on to it for support before I said, "You want to use me." My lip trembled.

"It's not like that," he said quietly. He touched his face, tracing the open cuts with his fingertips and it was then that I noticed we both had slashes on our left cheek. *His mark matches mine.* I drew my hand up to touch mine. I blinked, stifling a gasp. It stung, the wound still raw.

"You're special, Layla. My Clan wants to protect you," he said, his eyes piercing through me. I almost fell into their hypnotic trance, but I fought against it.

"In exchange for what? My cooperation? My *genes*?" I narrowed my eyes at him. "And let me ask you something. Are you just a lackey for the Clan, or do you have some significant position?" I threw the words at him like acid, and he stiffened. It was a subtle reaction, but it was enough.

"I'm a felis-Shifter," he started. "I can Turn into any cat species ever created." He straightened as he said this, pushing his shoulders back with pride. "Most Shifters have one true nature, but I can Shift into any cat species of my choosing."

With a sickening realization, I figured out how he fit into this messed up puzzle. *They want us to mate.* "You and I…" I struggled to put my thoughts into words. I swallowed back the dry lump that clung to my throat. "They want…you and I…"

His caramel eyes looked defeated.

My anger resurfaced, filling my veins with adrenaline. "You listen to me." I poked my finger hard into his chest. "I may be nothing more than a bitch in heat to you, but you can bet your ass, you will never get the pleasure of mating with me." I glared at him, scowling, then slid into the driver's seat, and slammed the door. Shutting out Roland, and his useless explanations.

With a shaky hand, I turned the key, careful not to look back at him. As I eased the truck back onto the road, I let my eyes finally lift to the rearview mirror. Roland was gone. I vowed to myself that I would fight against this part of me. The part of me that would *Turn* someday. The part of me that the Clans sought after- lusted after. *I will not be used as a breeder,* I thought. *There has to be a way to suppress the Shifter gene. I will gain control over myself again, or I will die trying.*

Chapter 10

Clocking in the next day, I was surprisingly chipper. I was looking forward to beginning my day. Although my job reminded me daily of what I truly was, it was still peaceful. Therapeutic even. I frequently had conversations with the animals I cared for, sharing with them snippets of my childhood or plans for the future. And they often shared theirs with me. As I mucked the coyote cage, I recalled last night's events with the crow. Learning his true identity and that I was being hunted by his Clan. My hands shook slightly, but I pushed past it, scrubbing harder and longer than I needed.

"What troubles you, Matriarch?"

I gasped. I should have been used to communicating with animals by now, but sometimes it still took me by surprise. I turned to face the female black bear in the cage across from me. She was lying atop a pile of fresh hay, her head elevated, watching me from her comfortable bed. I took a quick assessment of the Mammal Building around me. I was alone.

"Nothing," I answered.

"Come now. I sense your distress."

"You wouldn't understand," I said, turning to set back to work.

"I understand more than you think."

I stopped mid-scrub, focusing on the brush in my

hands before swallowing. "It's complicated," I muttered as I began furiously scrubbing a non-existent stain on the cement again.

"I imagine being a hark-Shifter is quite complicated."

I stilled.

"Being a bear is simple, so perhaps I don't understand all the responsibilities that come with your title. I know that when I awake each morning, I'll still be a bear. You on the other hand, you could awaken as any wild thing ever created by Mother Nature."

I swallowed and straightened. Her features were gentle, like those of a wise grandmother. I leaned my brush against the door and walked to her. Her tiny eyes observed me carefully, and her fuzzy ears shifted forward.

"What do you know of hark-Shifters?"

"It's the reason you can hear me. It's the blood that runs through you. In time, you will be able to take the form of any creature you desire."

I snorted. "Why am I the last to know everything?"

The bear's muzzle lifted in what I guessed was supposed to be a grin.

"This is common knowledge among the animal kingdom and those who can take our form. Humans are a fragile species, unable to comprehend the connection between Shifters and the animals they take the shape of."

"So why am I called the Matriarch?"

"Your gift is extraordinary, and rare. Almost as powerful as Mother Nature herself. Matriarch is the right title for a being so great. Take the elephant. Herds have always been overseen by females. Matriarchs

protect their species. One can only surmise that you were brought forth to ease the plight."

"What plight?"

"That I do not know. Being captive renders me ignorant of some of the issues stirring within the forest."

I admired her black coat as I thought about her words. It was thick and glossy and had never known the true harshness of nature's weather or domain. Well fed, medicated and cared for, she doesn't have the typical worries a wild bear would have. Without the need to forage, vie for territory, or evade danger, the bear has quite the comfortable life.

One could only hope that seeing her in person would help them appreciate animals and their role on Earth. It's Preston Park Zoo's hope that when people see the impressive animal in person, it will help them make a connection to the species. This connection encourages people to conserve resources, protect forests and save endangered wildlife. Zoos are vital in that way.

"Thanks," I said.

"I will always welcome your words, Matriarch. As long as you welcome mine."

I smiled at her and went back to work, lost in thought and lost in the physical labor of my tasks. After an exhausting nine hours, I was done for the day. I clocked out just as my phone rang. I pulled it out and checked the caller ID. Gwen. *Shit. I never called her.* I answered it.

"Hello?" I grabbed my messenger bag from my locker and headed out the building, scanning the trees that lined the parking lot as I moved. A car honked in the distance and I jumped, nearly tripping over my own feet. *Damn crow. I've been on edge ever since learning its name: Sid McCarty.* I shivered, nearly forgetting about the phone at my ear until I heard Gwen's voice.

"Are you there? Hello?"

"I'm here." I made my way across the parking lot, counting the steps until I was safely to my truck. *One, two, three, four, five, six...*

"You forget something?" Gwen asked. She was pissed, I could hear it in her voice. She hated to be stood up. By date or by phone.

I kept moving. "Yeah, I know. I'm sorry. I meant to call you, but—" *Seven, eight, nine, ten, eleven, twelve...*

"But?"

Thirteen, fourteen, fifteen. I heard a cawing in the distance, and for one terrified moment, I paused. Lifting my nose in the air, I caught a trace of cigar. Panic blossomed in my chest. My truck was only a few steps away. I slid my gaze to the left, and then to the right. No crow.

Gwen cleared her throat.

I sprinted the last several steps, my messenger bag banging against my leg as I moved. *Sixteen, seventeen, eighteen!* I unlocked my truck, checking over my shoulder just before diving inside. I slammed the locks down, then ran a shaky hand through my hair.

"What the hell, Layla?"

I closed my eyes and pinched the bridge of my nose. *Get it together.* I took a deep breath and opened my eyes. "Can I call you back?"

"No," she said simply. "Now tell me what is going on."

I sighed.

"Are you still pissed at me about Kurt?"

That rubbed me the wrong way. I scowled into the phone. *Hell yes,* I thought. It wasn't her fault that Kurt was a jerk, but she was the one who set me up with a complete stranger. "I'm not pissed at you, but no more blind dates," I replied sharply. "Deal?"

"Deal," she said. "Now, tell me about the new job. Do you like it?"

"I love it," I said smiling. The topic calmed me, and I nearly forgot about the crow. I started my truck and reversed out of the parking spot. "On my first day a guy got attacked by a lion." I pulled onto the highway, glimpsing in the rearview mirror a few more times than necessary.

"Get out of here!"

"He's fine," I assured her. "Just a few superficial wounds."

"Tis but a scratch," she said. Even through the phone, I could tell she was smiling. Gwen and I would quote the oddest things, at the most inappropriate times. Monty Python was one of our favorites.

"It's just a flesh wound," I added.

I heard muffled voices and static, so Gwen apparently covered the receiver with her hand. I strained to listen but couldn't tell who she was talking to. It was a deep voice, so I knew it was a man.

Gwen giggled, and her voice came through clear again. "Daddy says we need to stop quoting that stupid movie, and wants to know when he can get a tour of the zoo?"

I laughed. "Tell him when I'm allowed to bring guests, he'll be the first to know."

"Second," she corrected. "I'm always the first to know everything."

My heart squeezed. *I still haven't told her about me. I have to tell her,* I thought. *But how do I explain to her about Shifting? About being the Matriarch?* I bit at my lip, feeling guilty and suddenly lonely. I needed someone to talk to. Someone I could confide in, someone to hold me steady until I got a foothold on everything.

Then a memory surfaced of Roland, catching me in his arms when my body gave out after Kurt attacked me. *'I've got you,' he said. 'And I won't let go until you're ready. You say when.'* I pulled into my driveway and threw the truck into park. I sat for a moment, thinking about Roland and how I've been pushing away the only person who could help me through this.

Touched by regret, I shook the thought away and said, "Hey, I'm home now, so I'm going to let you go." I killed the engine, my eyes lifting to a crow circling in the sky. *Sid McCarty. He followed me.* I peered through the windshield at it. As if noticing me, it swooped and veered, disappearing in the trees.

"Call me later?" Gwen asked.

"Yeah," I said distractedly, closing the phone and fisting it. I swallowed hard before stepping out of the truck. My shoes crunched on the loose gravel, and I caught a whiff of a smoky cigar laced with the undeniable trace of a smoldering campfire. Just as I put my thoughts together, a strong hand covered my mouth, smothering my scream.

Chapter 11

I did the only thing I could do. I bit down hard and didn't let go until I tasted blood. A grunt at my ear fueled me to clamp tighter, until the hand snatched back. I whirled around and threw my very first punch. Ever. It was clumsy but effective as it connected. Pain shot up across my knuckles and spread to my wrist.

Roland cupped his jaw. "What the hell is wrong with you?" he shouted.

I shook my hand out, glaring at him. "With me? What is wrong with you?"

He stepped closer until he was looming over me, his lip curling as though he were suppressing a growl. My adrenaline rush must have been tapering off because I was suddenly frightened. I felt fragile and on the verge of shattering beneath his intense stare.

He slammed my truck door closed, causing me to wince, then his eyes darted past me, focusing on something in the woods. His pupils dilated, then constricted into pinpoints before I finally followed his gaze. My mouth parted upon seeing three figures in the distance, shadowed by the towering pine trees.

Roland let out a loud whistle and several wild boars emerged from the unruly thicket that grew around my property. Their putrid odor hit me, and I nearly wretched where I stood. The earthy cocktail of swamp water, mud, feces, and a fermenting compost pile forced me to breathe through my mouth.

"Run their asses out of here," he said to the group of reeking boars, his voice sharp with anger.

The boars *snorted* in response, then took off, kicking up dust as they tore through the trees.

Roland touched my shoulder, but I jerked away from him. I thought he was with Sid. I was sure of it when I caught his scent in the air, mingling with the man who hunted me. For a moment in time, I hated him for it.

The pain I felt when I thought he had betrayed me affected me far beyond the shallowness of hurt feelings or bruised egos. It was if he removed my very soul with a dull knife and left me hollow. Though brief, the emptiness scared me, and I knew I never wanted to experience that pain again. "I thought you were with Sid," I said quietly. "I smelled you both."

"Of course you did. I've been all over this area."

I turned, a look of question coloring my face.

"Patrolling," he continued. "Ensuring your safety." His eyes cast down to his open hand. My stomach sank when I saw my teeth marks marring his palm.

"Even after…"

His eyes lifted, holding firmly on mine as he spoke. "Yes. Even after you sent me away."

Why? Why would he do that? I glared at him, gauging his sincerity though I knew it wasn't necessary. He was loyal to his Clan and protecting me was his duty. His assignment.

"Unbelievable." He shook his head. "You just don't get it, do you?"

Annoyance flared within me. I balled my fist, my knuckles smarting, reminding me of the way my hand connected with Roland's chin.

"This isn't just about you," he said. "It's about our entire species." He turned on his heel and stalked toward the edge of the forest. "Sleep well tonight, Little Matriarch, knowing that there are those who wish to protect you, even after you've turned your back on them."

He stepped into the shadows, dissolving into the darkness without a sound. I looked at my shoes, allowing his words to echo through me until they settled on my heart. *I turned him away. But yet here he is, still trying to protect me.*

The sun sank in the distance, taking the warmth it offered. A cool breeze lifted my hair and carried the scent of blood. I shuddered, wondering who or what it belonged to. The boars? The menacing figures who lurked in the forest? Roland? My heart constricted at the thought and I suddenly felt compelled to search the shadows for him. I had to know if he was safe.

My footfalls were even as I easily wove my way around fallen limbs and logs. My sight was sharp, allowing me to move at a quick pace, but my search for Roland seemed futile. *He probably Turned into a tomcat and has slinked away somewhere,* I thought bitterly. An owl hooted somewhere above me, and I shivered. *Where is he?*

My stomach clenched; similar to hunger pains. I gripped my belly, trying to sooth the ache that gnawed at me. My skin soon prickled with scorching heat, running from my toes to the back of my skull. *What's wrong with me?* My vision went spotty around the edges, and I staggered, reaching out to a nearby tree for support. The bark scraped across my palms, but I clung tighter.

My head ached, and my eyes burned. I blinked, trying to bring some shred of relief. I fell to my knees, my fingers sinking into the dirt, trying desperately to steady myself. My blood raged like lava, surging through my veins and flushing my skin. Sweat dotted my temples and my skin began to itch uncomfortably. It didn't even feel like mine anymore. It felt tight and unfamiliar. I wanted to peel it off, and leave my flesh in a pile, right there in the woods.

I couldn't bear my weight a moment longer, the last ounce of strength I had evaporated, sending me face first into the dirt, my stomach flat against the ground. I sputtered, spitting out flakes of grass and leaf litter. As I lay there, the bones in my arms and legs felt as though they were being stretched, like candy on a taffy puller. I cried out, the pain unbearable as it surged through my spine.

"Layla?" Roland called from somewhere nearby.

I lifted my face just enough to scan the forest floor. My vision was blurry, barely able to make out the trees that surrounded me. Another round of pulsating pressure tore through me. Tears pricked at my eyes, and I didn't have the strength to hold them back. I sobbed openly, my tears mixing with the dirt on my face.

"Layla!" Roland cried again.

His heavy-soled boots came into view as a hazy shadow. I fought hard to focus on them, but my eyelids proved to be stronger. I felt his hand on the small of my back just as I surrendered, allowing my eyes to close and I didn't care if I ever opened them again.

****

I blinked, finding I was still in the forest. The

moon was casting a silvery mist through the trees, and the air was crisp. I gathered what little strength I had and pushed myself up, staggering as I tried to find my footing. I tottered clumsily before collapsing back into the dirt with a thud. Movement to my left caught my attention. I rotated my head and found Roland staring back at me. He swallowed and gave me a slight smile. Again I willed my arms and legs to cooperate, but something felt wrong. Different. I shifted, needing to evaluate my body. Take inventory of possible injuries. My head throbbed, but the pain in my limbs was gone.

"Layla, before you do anything crazy," Roland said. I looked at him, confused by his words. His arms were held up in surrender as though he were trying to coax me from jumping off a bridge. "I want you to know that I am here to help. I will guide you through this."

Help me with what? I pushed myself upright but was still unable to stand. My eyes drifted downward. My hands were gone! They were sharp black hooves. I tried to scream, but it came out as something primal, something unhuman. I flailed my arms and legs until I righted myself, my heart fluttering wildly, like the frenzied wings of a hummingbird. *I'm a goddamn deer!* My sanity was just as unstable as my wobbly knees. I wanted to run. Run away from it all, but Roland stepped in front of me.

"Layla. It will wear off," he said, his voice low and soothing. He knelt in front of me. "In time, you can control the Shifting, but for now you must allow it to run its course."

My eyes widened. *Wear off? Run its course? How long will that take?* I opened my mouth to ask, but the words fell silent. I grew frantic, my eyes darting everywhere until landing on Roland's. They held firmly to mine, as if trying to silently relay something important. My chest heaved, and my legs wavered, crumbling me to the grass. Roland sank to the ground beside me, lightly touching my neck, then my face. His eyes were soft, full of compassion and understanding. I leaned into his touch, as it was the only thing holding me together. As though without it, my humanity would fade into this other version of myself, never to return.

"It's all right, Layla," he said quietly as he strummed his thumb across my cheek. "I've got you," he said. "And I won't let go until you're ready." His caramel eyes searched mine. "You say when."

I lowered my head, inhaling the pleasant aroma of the grass. It was different to me now, no longer just an earthly scent, but now an inviting aroma. Comforting, like the tattered quilt my mother wrapped me in when I was sick. I breathed deeply, allowing Roland's touch and the blanket of warm grass beneath me to console me, heal my broken soul and come to terms with what I had become.

I'm not sure how much time had passed before the sensations came back—dim vision, mottled with black spots and spiked adrenaline. Fever that came in the form of fire coursing through my veins. Instead of pulled bones, this time they felt compressed, squeezed until they could no longer take the tension. Grinding my teeth, I endured the pain until finally, I had to shout out, fearing they'd snap from the pressure.

Roland held me as I thrashed and convulsed, my hooves splitting into fingers and my fur absorbing inward through my pores. Finally I was whole again.

Exhausted, I laid my head in Roland's lap, panting and trying to catch my breath. He drew his fingers across my forehead, pushing the damp hair from my face.

"You did good," he said softly.

I licked my dry lips. "Will it always feel like that?"

He shook his head, his lips curling into a slight smile. "It hurts like hell the first time, but eventually the pain dulls to nothing more than a slight discomfort."

I shivered, reliving the experience, the pain still raw and the ache in my head still present. "I don't think I can go through that again."

"It gets easier each time."

I examined my hand, spreading my fingers in front of my face. My nails were ragged, dried dirt was caked beneath them. "Why a deer?" I asked.

He cocked his head sideways, watching me with keen eyes. "As the Matriarch, your feelings manifested into the animal. My guess is…you're feeling vulnerable."

I nodded, chewing my lip as I thought about it. The few times I had seen deer in the wild, they were cautious creatures, always ready to flee at the snap of a twig. I recalled sitting in a tree stand with a then boyfriend as he set his scope sights on a massive male.

The buck was magnificent. His rack looked like carved ivory, sleek and beautiful. The memory still fresh as he pulled the trigger. As was the sigh of relief I let out when the bullet missed.

"Vulnerable. And hunted," I whispered.

A look of sadness flickered across Roland's features. "Come on, let's get you back home."

I let him guide me into a sitting position until I glimpsed my bare legs. My eyes grew wide as I became aware of my naked body. I folded inward, shielding myself as much as possible. "Why didn't you say something?"

"Because I knew you'd freak out," he said laughing.

I huffed at him, awkwardly adjusting my hands to cover the essential areas the best I could. "Where are my clothes?"

He motioned to the pile behind me. "I don't think any of it is salvable. They tore as you transitioned."

I groaned. "Great."

He smiled at my exasperation and rose up on his knees, lifting the hem of his shirt. "Here." With one quick motion, he striped himself of his dark green shirt, revealing a broad chest and deliciously chiseled abs. He tossed it at me, and I foolishly grabbed at it, removing a hand from its strategic place. My eyes lifted to his, and my cheeks warmed.

"Can you turn around?" I snapped.

The corners of his mouth curved into a devilish grin before he finally turned. "I told you before, nudity is common practice for Shifters," he said over his shoulder. "Better check your inhibitions at the door, Little Matriarch, because we'll be seeing a whole lot of each other's skin."

I was rendered speechless. My cheeks burned as I wriggled into his shirt. The soft material was saturated with his musk. It smelled of smoldering embers and candied apples. Much like Roland, the combination of rugged and sweet was contradicting, but utterly intriguing.

Taking a quick glimpse at my shredded work uniform, I sighed. He was right. Everything was beyond repair. Even my bra was snapped in two. Luckily, my hiking boots appeared to still be intact, so I pulled them on, without bothering to look down at myself. I could imagine what a sight I was, wearing an oversized men's shirt, the sleeves hanging over my fingertips, paired with clunky boots.

I collected my tattered clothes and looked over at Roland, my eyes lingering on his strapping back as silvery moonbeams shimmered across his tan skin. It was easy to be jealous of the moon, with it rays gently showering its warmth across his skin, touching him, caressing him wholly, the way I wished I could.

There were several ragged scars that ran along his spine. As I drew closer, I could tell they were old wounds that had long healed from the passing of time.

"Would you like me to take my pants off too?"

I halted, my skin flushing with embarrassment. "I…"

He turned and gave me a smug smile. "I could feel your eyes on me," he said, his voice low and husky.

I tucked my hair behind my ear, trying to pry my eyes from his, but failing. I licked my lips, not sure what to say or do.

"It's all right," he continued, strolling closer until he stood in front of me. With a hooded gaze, he said, "I liked it."

My cheeks flooded with warmth, but I held firm to his eyes, transfixed by their beauty. Even in the shadows, the amber color within them was undeniable. And this time, I was deeply drawn into them. My breath quickened at his proximity, the ill feelings I harbored for him receded like the waves of the ocean, replaced with the budding longing to kiss him. Slowly, I inclined my face to his, my eyes sweeping across his chin. My fingers itching to touch him, to run my nails along his stubble.

Roland lifted his nose, inhaling deeply before turning his head. I froze as he searched the air like a hound tracking a squirrel. Then, I caught the scent too. Boars. Before I could search for them, they materialized out the darkness. They were men now, dressed in worn jeans and tank tops. A man with a pony tail stepped forward.

"Carl," Roland greeted, stepping away from me.

"We ran 'em off," Carl began. "But they seemed hell bent on causing trouble for the Matriarch." He jerked his bearded chin in my direction.

Roland tensed, pressing his mouth into a firm line. His fist flexed and clenched repeatedly.

"Found this in your driveway," said a voice behind me. I turned to find a blond man holding up my cellphone. *I must have dropped it when Roland snuck up on me,* I thought. As he approached, I noticed his forearms were covered in tattoos. The strong scent of perspiration rolled off him as he handed the phone to me. His eyes briefly ran from my boots, across my bare legs and up to Roland's shirt. I shifted uncomfortably. *If I could Turn right now,* I thought. *I'd be an ostrich, so I can bury my head in a hole somewhere.* I knew all too well what this looked like. That Roland had sent them away to do his dirty work while he and I fucked in the woods. Inside, I wanted to die, but I looked at him directly, trying to override my embarrassment with false confidence.

"It was ringing," he said.

Like a clamp around my rib cage, my chest

squeezed. Late night phone calls only meant one thing. I swallowed hard as I checked the caller ID. Looking up, I said, "It's my father."

The men exchanged glances. With a trembling hand, I punched in my father's number, gnawing at my lip as it rang once. Twice.

"Layla." His normally confident voice was subdued, almost distraught.

"Hey. What's going on? Has something happened?" My tone was increasingly frantic, my heart pounding painfully in my chest.

"It's your mother. There's been an accident."

Chapter 12

My knees gave out. Thankfully, Roland caught me before I collapsed. My father's voice became distant as I forced myself to breathe, struggling to keep my mind focused.

"I'm on my way," I said, pushing Roland away before running blindly through the trees.

"Layla, wait," he called, easily catching up with me.

"It's my mom. Something's happened. I have to go." I ducked a branch, clutching my shredded clothes closer to my chest and pressing farther. Prickly vines and thorns scratched at my legs as I moved.

"Let me go with you."

I nodded woodenly without looking at him for fear that I'd burst into tears. The forest became suffocating, my breath burned in my chest as I pumped my legs harder. Finally the trees thinned out, and I could make out the silhouette of my house against the moon's light. When I finally broke free of the concealment of the woods, I felt free to breathe again. My boots crunched on the gravel as I ran across the driveway.

Half way across the front lawn, I paused, scanning the exterior of the house, my eyes zeroing in on all the pockets of black. My house was cloaked in darkness and for the first time, I was afraid to enter it alone. *Damn Victor Rizzo and damn Sid McCarty for taking away my sense of security. I may never feel safe again.*

Roland stepped up beside me. I gave him a side-way glance, admiring his strong profile in the moonlight. With him at my side, I no longer felt afraid. In fact, I felt stronger. I felt unstoppable.

Together we climbed the porch stairs. I dug through the pockets of my torn khaki's until I felt my keys. Willing my hands to cooperate, I unlocked the door and threw a nervous glance to Roland before opening it.

"The house is empty," he assured me.

"How do you know?"

"The only scent here is yours."

Our eyes touched before I hurried to my room. He stayed behind, waiting by the front door. I dropped my ruined clothes to the floor before ripping open my closet door. I snatched the first shirt I saw off a hanger. As I removed Roland's shirt, I inhaled one more time, savoring his delightful musk. A fleeting pang of disappointment unfurled in my stomach as I recalled our near kiss. *We were so close.*

Pushing the thought away, I shimmed into the snug cotton tee, pulling it over my stomach as I stepped out of my boots. Slipping into a clean pair of underwear and jeans, I quickly pulled my boots back on and darted down the hall, Roland's shirt in hand.

Roland was pacing a small circle. I tossed him his shirt, which he easily caught and slipped on.

"Let's go." I snagged a sweater from the coat rack and was out the door in a flash, with Roland on my heels. I rounded the hood of my truck, my adrenaline spiking further, making me feel jittery.

"You drive," I instructed, tossing the keys over the

hood. Roland caught them with ease and slid into the driver's seat. I climbed in beside him, stealing a peek as he revved the engine and backed out of the driveway.

"Where is she?"

"Greater Hope Hospital."

Roland looked comfortable behind the wheel, his eyes focused ahead, weaving around the stray cars that punctuated the otherwise deserted roads. His strong jaw clenched as he changed lanes and pulled onto the highway.

Shifting in my seat, I turned to look out the window. The night sky was completely black, not a star in it, reminding me of what my mother always said, '*A starless night means it's going to rain.*' Fissures formed in my heart at the thought of my mother lying in a hospital bed. I covered my chest, hoping to keep my heart intact until I saw her. *She's going to be all right.* I closed my eyes and pressed my forehead against the window, the cool glass soothing my aching head.

My stomach tightened when we pulled into the emergency parking lot. Roland jogged to keep up with me as I dashed across the pavement and through the sliding doors.

"Delia Carson," I said, skidding to a halt in front of the first nurse I saw. "Where is she?"

The woman blinked at me, probably taken aback by my wild-eyed expression. I wanted to shake her. *Speak, goddamn it!* She was small, and her blond hair was combed neatly behind her ears, giving her an elf-like appearance. I looked at her nametag. Paula.

"The nurse at the welcome station can give you that information." She stepped around me, making a bee line for the farthest point of the room. No doubt trying to escape me, and my craziness. I dropped my hands in defeat, turning in time to see Roland speaking to her.

"That's Layla Carson," he informed her. "Harvey will be pissed to know you blew her off like that."

He knows my father's name?

The woman seemed to be connecting my name to my father's, her expression changing as it registered. *Damn right, you know me. My father only runs this fucking hospital,* I wanted to scream.

"My apologies," she said, her tiny face blushing. "She's just been moved from ICU and is now on the second floor. Room two twelve."

I let out a relieved breath. *Moved from ICU, that sounds promising.*

"Thank you," Roland told her before we sprinted toward the elevators. One was just opening as we rounded the corner, so I threw myself inside, pressing my back against the wall as Roland followed me inside. The doors closed. My chest heaved, and I closed my eyes to ward off the vertigo that was stirring within me. The elevator soon dinged, and with it my eyes sprung open. I shot through the parting doors, my eyes searching for room numbers.

"This way," Roland instructed, veering to the right. The shiny floor reflected the bright fluorescent light bulbs, casting the empty hallway in a sickly yellow glow. We walked quickly, our footsteps echoing off the tile, as we scanned each door. *208. 210.*

The door was ajar, and I could hear the sound of machines beeping inside. I paused. *What will she look like? Is she awake?* I placed my hand on the door, pushing it wider. I swallowed back the lump of emotion that had collected in my throat and stepped inside. The room smelled like a mixture of disinfectant and iodine. The only light was emitted from a dim fluorescent bulb overhead.

Then, my gaze fell on my mother. She lay peacefully in the hospital bed, her eyes closed as though she were in a deep sleep. I couldn't take it a second longer. I rushed to her, choking back tears.

"Mama," I cried. I sought out her hand, ignoring her icy touch as I inspected her face. There were a few scrapes on her forehead and chin, but nothing serious. Careful placement of concealer would hide them easily. My eyes skimmed her body. The blanket was pulled only to her hips. Her abdomen was covered in thick bandages.

Her eyelids fluttered open, her lips straining to smile as she turned her head ever so slightly.

"Mom." I touched her forehead, running my hand through her dark hair. I smiled, though I know it was strained as I tried to put on my best brave face for her.

"Layla," her broken voice whispered. Her distant gaze drifted around my face before settling on my eyes. Her mouth parted as she stared into them, her brown eyes widening, as though she had seen a ghost. She licked her dry lips, then said, "Your father." She drew in a ragged breath. "Is he here?"

My eyes flicked to the room window. My father paced the hall, passing back and forth across the square of glass. His arms crossed as if to ward off any bad news, his features like stone. He occasionally paused to converse with a passing nurse. I pursed my lips before shaking my head. "No. He's outside."

"Get my purse and find my sunglasses," she

instructed.

Confusion spread across my face as I threw a worried look to Roland. He shrugged and looked equally perplexed. My heart clenched, wondering if she suffered a blow to the head or if it was the medication. "Mom, don't talk right now, just try to rest."

"Go." Her voice was stronger now, forceful and clear. "Now."

Startled by her vehemence, I released her hand. "Okay, calm down. I'm going." My eyes skirted the room until they landed on her purse. I walked toward it carefully, my boots scuffing the tile with each step. Voices drifted in from the hall.

"Hurry," she urged.

I reached into the oversized purse, rummaging through the contents until finally finding her tortoise shell sunglasses.

"Put them on, and do not remove them," she said, wincing and running a shaky hand across her bandages. "Do not ask questions."

I returned to her side, and slid them on, just as my father entered the room. Dr. Moore followed him, casting an insincere smile my way. I tensed at seeing him, taking my mother's hand into mine, seeking comfort, and restraint. Last time I saw Dr. Moore, was the night I walked away from my job, taking a rhesus macaque with me. My father slowly crossed the room, eyeing Roland briefly as he passed him.

"Did you wake her?" His tone was gruff, grating me to the bone.

"What happened?" I demanded, staring at our clasped hands.

"She let those damn mutts out to piss," my father

said, sounding frustrated. "I've told her repeatedly not to take them out late at night, but yet she does it anyway. Bet she'll think twice about it from now on."

I glowered at him. "Can you forget about your stupid need to be right all the time and just tell me what the hell happened?"

His frown deepened. "She was attacked." He stared at me, not offering any more.

"Attacked by what? Who?"

He exchanged a grim glance with Dr. Moore. "Komodo dragons." His face pinched, as though the words were acid on his tongue.

What? I studied him. *Was he serious?* "You're kidding, right?"

"This is neither the time nor place for amusement, and it chafes my ass that you'd think I'd be so insensitive."

My grip tightened around my mother's fingers. "I never said that."

"Then what are you saying?"

"I'm saying that it's impossible. Komodo dragons are indigenous to Indonesia."

"Well then, Miss Animal Expert, then you realize they are indeed far from home," he said, turning his attention back to Dr. Moore.

My cheeks burned, realizing I had been dismissed. Like a child. Like the countless times before when he turned his back to me upon uttering his 'final word', thus ending the discussion. Fuming, I said, "Look, I know what I'm talking about here. Komodo dragons do not live in South Carolina."

"That certainly is a fact, Layla," Dr. Moore countered. "But we have evidence to prove it."

"What kind of evidence?"

"For one, I saw the bastards," my father said, nearly shouting.

Dr. Moore touched his arm, quieting him, before saying, "Your mother has severe lacerations to her torso, caused by multiple serrated blades, or teeth. Her blood is already in the early stages of a bacterial infection. Komodo dragons carry up to fifty different bacteria strains in their salvia. Their venom can cause death in a victim in less than a week if not treated."

My chest tightened at the word *death*. My head felt heavy, as if it were filling with water, smothering my hearing and clouding my vision. I wavered.

Roland was behind me before I could even register his movement. He touched my shoulder gently, grounding me, comforting me. My father lifted a brow, his eyes probing as he observed us.

"Layla, who is this?" he asked, his tone sharp and cutting.

"Roland Stone," he answered.

Dr. Moore gave us a pensive look before turning to my father. "Harvey, I'm going review her current blood work. She may need different antibiotics, depending on the strains she carries."

My father nodded, "Of course." He followed Dr. Moore through the room, then asked, "You won't mind if I take a look myself?"

The door clicked shut before I could hear the doctor's answer. I sighed, sinking against Roland's strong body. I didn't trust my legs to support me without his help.

"I don't believe this," I said. "It's all too crazy. Nothing makes sense."

"They speak the truth," he assured me, his voice quiet as though he was trying not to scare me. "They were komodo-Shifters."

"How do you know?" My eyes drifted to my mother's bandages. They covered her entire torso. I didn't know what the wounds beneath them looked like, but from the number of bandages, I knew they had to be deep.

"Take a deep breath and tell me what you smell."

I turned slightly, looking at him over my shoulder. His face was serious, his eyes held firm to mine and he said, "Let your senses answer your questions."

I faced my mother again. She must have slipped back into a drug-induced sleep, her breathing was smooth and regular. I closed my eyes, inhaling deeply. I caught traces of blood, disinfectant, cheap detergent, iodine, burning embers, and something stagnant. Quickly identifying Roland's scent, and the smell of the hospital room, I homed in on the unfamiliar odor.

"What is that?"

"Infection," he answered.

Tears welled at my eyes. "Oh no."

Roland lowered his hands to my arms, stroking the length of them consolingly. "It's okay, Layla. She's going to be all right."

"How do you know?"

"Well, for one, she's being treated by top doctors." He stopped rubbing and leaned closer, whispering, "And two. She's got Shifter blood in her."

Chapter 13

I stood motionless as I absorbed this. *Shifter blood?* My throat closed, sealing my lungs from the scream that bubbled in my stomach, but also restricting my breathing. I needed air, space, and distance from Roland, the reminder that things were not normal. That *I* was not normal. I shook free of him, walked to the other side of my mother's bed. I gripped the sheets, steadying my swaying body and tilting vision. I closed my eyes, focusing on my breathing. *This can't be true,* I thought. I tried to imagine her Turning, wracking my brain for a memory that indicated that something was amiss. I came up empty. *She doesn't possess the Shifter gene.* She wouldn't keep that secret from me. *Would she?*

I opened my eyes, staring down at my mother. The gene was passed down through someone in my family tree, but it wasn't her. It couldn't be. She looked so normal, so fragile, so *human.* Then a nagging thought pushed its way to the front of my mind. *My eyes.* I ripped the sunglasses from my face, studying them, trying to fit the pieces together. *She knew my eyes meant that I had Turned, so she has to know about the gene.* She wanted to hide it from my father, but why? Was she ashamed?

I lifted my face to Roland. Our eyes met. The slight rise and fall of my mother's chest between us. Emotion starting to overtake me when I said, "I don't want any of this." My lip quivered. I bit down on it to keep my tears at bay. "Look what they did to her." My eyes flickered to my mother's face. It was relaxed, and she was every bit as pretty as she usually was, aside from her ashen skin and white lips. A tear slipped down my cheek as I stroked her hand. It felt frail and a bit too cold for my liking.

"With Victor Rizzo hunting you and your family, it seems to me that you don't have much of a choice." His tone irritated me. He acted as though I should take what fate had offered me with a smile.

Fuck fate.

"Why me?" I demanded, though I was pretty sure he wouldn't be able to answer me.

He stuck his hands in his pockets and looked at the floor. "I don't know."

"See?" My voice edged on hysteric. "No one can tell me why I'm so fucking important, so why would I believe any of this bullshit?"

His brows furrowed, and his eyes hardened, like flickering embers. "Isn't your mother lying in a hospital bed, half dead, an indication?"

I gasped at his callousness.

His eyes grew wide. He pulled his hands from his pockets and held them out, as though he were trying to tame a wild beast. "I'm sorry. I shouldn't have said that."

"You're damn right you shouldn't have said that." I was fuming, my ears and cheeks burned with anger as I glared at him.

"Look, Layla," he began.

"Just go," I ordered, shifting my eyes back to my

mother, her face still peaceful.

He frowned. "Fine." He lifted both hands in surrender. "Go on denying your destiny." He walked to the door and touched the handle. Looking over his shoulder, he said, "But it will only end up getting you, and your family, killed." He flung the door open and stalked away.

I closed my eyes, quelling the urge to scream, cry, or curse. I wasn't sure which, maybe all three. I breathed deeply, clenching and unclenching my fists. I stayed that way for a while, working through my anger until I trusted myself enough to know that I wasn't going to punch a hole through the wall.

Crossing the room, I slid a chair up beside my mother's bed. I sank into it, my body suddenly exhausted. Entwining my fingers with hers, I watched her, listening to the steady clicks and beeps of the hospital equipment. I studied her features. I imagined her nose growing, molding into a thick, pointed beak.

Then her skin lifting into scaly plates, as her legs fused into a fish's tail. I shook my head, ridding myself of the unsettling images. *Why didn't you tell me, Mom?* I squeezed my mother's hand, and then laid my head across my forearm, too tired to keep myself upright any longer. My body was just about to give into its exhaustion when I heard voices in the hall.

The door clicked open.

"Layla's still here?" My father's tone seemed surprised.

Remembering that I had removed the sunglasses, I kept my head down, pretending to still be asleep. I heard footsteps approaching, then movement around the bed. "Her vitals are strong," Dr. Moore said. My father stepped up beside me. I knew it was him by his scent. He always smelled of freshly oiled leather.

"Thank God." He sounded relieved, and for a moment I felt compelled to reach out and touch his hand.

"I'm certain she'll make a full recovery, but I'll be honest with you, Harvey. I don't foresee her going home anytime soon."

Silence.

I wondered what he was doing, what he was thinking. Was he scowling the way he always did when things didn't go his way? Was he getting emotional?

"She was lucky I was there."

I bit my inner cheek. *Of course. Mr. Perfect saved the day.* His footfalls seemed determined as he crossed the room, with Dr. Moore following close behind. They spoke quietly in the hall, their conversation all medical terms and jargon.

Their voices faded as they walked away. I lifted my head, sitting there in a stupor, my hands falling into my lap. *She has to stay here? For how long?* My eyes drifted across the bed and back to my mother's face. *I'm the reason she's here to begin with.* I watched her, trying to come up with a solution, a way out of this screwed up Shifter world, and back into the land of normal again. I came up empty. I stared at her so long I thought I was seeing things when her eyes fluttered open.

"Mom?"

She turned her head slightly. "Layla." She gave me a faint smile, a mere ghost of her usually bright grins.

"The doctor says you're going to be okay."

She gazed lazily at me, and I wasn't sure if she

even heard me, until she said, "Layla, I'm so sorry."

I searched her face. "For what?"

"For not preparing you. But you didn't bear a Mark."

Anger flickered deep within my gut like a sparked flint. *So it's true. She knows of Shifters, and she didn't tell me. She kept a secret, a terrible, yet vital, secret from me.* The realization hurt, but I refused to acknowledge it. I needed answers, and I needed them now. "A Mark?"

My stomach roiled with apprehension, but I was eager to hear her explanation. *Finally, some answers,* I thought.

She took a haggard breath, either framing her next words or fending off a wave of pain. Maybe both. "The gene has been in my family forever, passing from one generation to the next, manifesting in chosen descendants. The chosen ones are Marked, revealing their affinity."

"Affinity?" I mirrored.

"Some are born with a rough patch of skin, indicating their reptilian nature. Others have webbed toes, showing their kinship with the water. Canine Shifters have a fine line of hair down their back. Feline Shifters are usually born with a birthmark shaped like a paw print."

I thought about how that applied to me. Frowning, I realized I didn't have any of those.

"When you were born, I searched for the Mark, but found none. I was sure the gene had skipped over you..." she drifted into thought, her eyes washing over me with guilt. "I thought you had the chance to be normal."

"But I'm not normal. Am I?" I swallowed, staring at her, waiting for her to answer and confirm that I was indeed a Shifter, a freak of nature.

"I'm afraid not." She stared into my eyes, scrutinizing the details before saying, "Your eyes. They are a tell-tail sign. Shifters everywhere will know you possess the gene." She touched her ribs, it was obvious it was a struggle for her to move without wincing.

"Why are they cat-like, when…" I couldn't form the rest of the words. *When I Turned into a deer,* I thought.

"I don't know why they took the form of a feline. It's apparent you don't have an affinity for them."

"How do you know?" I asked, curious.

She gave a little laugh. "Well, for one, you despise cats." Her eyes flickered to mine, and for a moment they sparkled with familiarly. My old mom was in there. The one before she was brutally attacked by giant venomous reptiles.

"I don't despise all cats," I said, thinking about Roland and his warm, golden eyes. Then I remembered our last conversation, and added crossly, "Just housecats. They're annoying."

"Do you know what your true nature is, Layla? Has it revealed itself to you yet?"

I swallowed hard, moving my eyes to my fingers as I twiddled them anxiously.

"Layla?" She sought out my hand, latching on desperately. "What is it?"

I spoke to our mingled fingers. "I can hear things." My eyes lifted and fixed onto hers.

"What do you mean, you can hear things?" Her wide eyes implored me to elaborate.

"Animals," I whispered. "I can hear them."

Her soft brown eyes went round, as did her small mouth. "Hark-Shifter," she said softly. "You're bound to no animal."

"There's more." I licked my dry lips. "I've been told I'm the Matriarch."

"My God, Layla," she said, closing her eyes. "I had no idea."

"What does this all mean?"

Her eyes opened, every ounce of seriousness in her body shone in them. "It means that something is stirring in the Shifter world, and you've been chosen to resolve it."

I sat back, discouraged. "That doesn't answer anything."

"Your ability to Shift into any animal at will and communicate with them gives you the title as Matriarch. It's your destiny to right a terrible wrong, and you may need the help of the animals to do it. Your instincts will guide you."

I sighed, sweeping my gaze to my mother. "Are you…" My voice cracked a bit, forcing me to clear my throat. "Are you a Shifter?"

"No."

I felt a twinge of disappointment. I had hoped she could guide me through this confusing process, protect me from the unknown, teach me how to Shift. "Well then, who is? Anyone I know?"

"Your great-grandfather," she answered.

I frowned. He died when I was just a toddler, so I wouldn't be able to go to him with questions. "Anyone else?" I bit my lip as I waited for her to answer, holding desperately on to a thread of hope that there was someone out there I trusted, a family member to guide and comfort me through this process.

My mother's eyes welled with emotion, her voice wavering as she looked at me, her eyes washed with grief as she said, "Your sister."

Sister? I blinked at her and rubbed my ears as if to erase her words. Two simple words that threw my world into a total upheaval. "What did you just say?"

She looked away, sniffing before she whispered, "Shandy."

Shandy. Hearing her name made it even more real. *I can't believe this. Another fucking secret!* I jumped to my feet and loomed over my mother's bed. I couldn't breathe, I just stood there, clutching my chest in an attempt to keep my broken heart in place. "You never told me, why?"

My mother eyes were glossy with impending tears, but she ignored my tirade entirely. "She died a few hours after birth. She was Marked. You were not."

"Wait, what?" The pieces of information swirled around my head until they slammed into place, jarring me into comprehension. "Are you saying we were…" I paused, staring at her as she moved her head in a pitiful nod, her features twisted in a tight grimace as she said the word I couldn't.

"Twins."

Chapter 14

All I remembered after that was crashing through the door and hurling myself down the hallway. I jogged past patients on gurneys, blowing by nurses who watched me with wide eyes. I ran without looking back, not stopping until I burst through the door to the nearest restroom, locking it and pressing my back against the wall. My heart beat wildly within my chest. I slid down the wall until I was sitting on the cold tile. Leaning my head back, I closed my eyes, trying to make sense of everything. *I had a twin sister.*

I remembered how I used to wish for a sibling, especially on the nights my father proved to be extra cruel. A shoulder to cry on, a hand to hold when I was scared. Then, I thought about that for a moment. My father would've had another life to control, to mold with hurtful words and force to somehow surpass his exceedingly high expectations.

Perhaps it was best to endure that alone, I thought. *I wouldn't wish that on anyone.* I pressed my forehead to my knees. *This is all too much.* I wanted to rewind the last few weeks. Was it better to be ignorant? To remain normal? I thought about all the things I had learned recently. A world of Shifters, hidden in plain sight of humans. A world I had been sucked into against my will. The stuff of myth, stories, and fictional movies was now my reality. A surreal reality.

There was a knock at the door.

"Someone's in here," I called, not lifting my head.

Thankfully, footsteps faded down the hallway, and again I was alone. I stayed that way until my feet fell asleep, the tingling sensation annoying me enough to stand to shake them awake. *Why would she keep this from me?* I needed to know, so reluctantly, I pulled open the door and trudged back to my mother's room to get the answers I so desperately needed.

My father and Dr. Moore stood at the foot of her bed. Both men turned their gazes to me, their discussion tapering off until the room was silent. All that remained was the sound of my heartbeat in my ears, drowning out everything else.

"What's going on?" I asked, clenching my fist, instantly aware that I was without my mother's sunglasses. I stood at the doorway, frozen there by my uncertainty. Would my father notice my eyes, and what would he think about them?

"Just discussing your mother's condition," my father said, his tone clipped. "Why don't you go home and get some rest."

I looked at her as I weighed my options. She was fast asleep again, her face peaceful as she breathed evenly. I wanted to stay with her, to ask more questions, but perhaps they were right. No matter how badly I wanted to know, I knew I couldn't bear to hear the answers. *Not tonight anyway.*

Although I hated to, I nodded my head in agreement. My father gave me a smug smile, which tempted me to change my mind and stay just for spite, but my body objected. It needed rest.

"I'll be back tomorrow to check on her," I said

before turning away. My eyes washed over my mother one more time before I walked away.

***

When I pulled into my driveway, the morning sun was just beginning to rise over the trees. It was early, but I decided to call Rachael anyway and let her know what happened. She answered on the third ring.

"Hello?" she answered sleepily.

"Rach. I'm so sorry to call you so early."

"No worries," she yawned. "I have to feed the chickens anyway."

I felt relieved, having forgotten she had a small farm at home. Chickens, hogs, and even a goat.

"So, what's up?" she asked.

I told her about my mother's accident, careful to leave out the Komodo dragon part and replaced it with a dog attack instead.

"Damn Layla, that's horrible," she said. "I hope she gets better soon. Look, why don't you take some time off, spend time with your mom until she's doing better."

"Thanks, Rach. I appreciate that."

"Keep me informed."

"I will. And thanks again."

We exchanged goodbyes and hung up.

I stepped out of my truck and crossed my lawn.

I was dead on my feet, going through the motions as I unlocked the door, kicked off my shoes, and hung my bag on the coat rack. I padded my way down the hall, undressing along the way. Once I was in my room, I fell into bed. As soon as my face hit the pillow, I fell into a deep, dreamless sleep.

The sunlight streaming through the window didn't

wake me. It was the pounding at my door that did that. I groaned as I rolled over and peered at the clock through one parted eyelid. 1:06 pm.

The pounding continued. Suddenly worried it had something to do with my mother, I jumped up, adrenaline pumping through my tired body, awakening it with a jolt. I grabbed my robe, slipping it on as I dashed through the hallway, stopping at the door just long enough to peek through the peephole.

Gwen. She was standing close to the door, her face contorted like a mirror in a fun house. I touched the door knob, then caught a glimpse of her as she flinched. Curious, I watched a moment longer, uneasiness rolling through me like a morning fog. Something deep within me urged me to back away, shouting at me to not open the door, but I couldn't do that. Whatever it was that caused the hairs on my neck to stand erect, was out there with Gwen.

I licked my lips, and turned the door knob, steeling myself, from what, I wasn't sure. Just as the door pulled open, Gwen shouted, "Layla! Don't!" The man behind her brought the butt of his gun across the back of her head, knocking her unconscious. I reached out for her, but his grip held firm to her, her arms hung limply in front of her. My eyes shot to his, the fear giving away to anger as I glared at him. I recognized him by scent only. The smell of cigar wafted from him, and my stomach fisted with dread.

"What do you want?" I demanded.

"Isn't it obvious?" he asked, a disturbing smile pulling at his lips.

"Me," I answered. "I get that, but why?" I watched him, comparing his features to the crow that had haunted my dreams the past few weeks. His greasy black hair was combed back, slicked to perfection behind his ears. His dark eyes were beady, darting anxiously around my face.

"Victor has plans for you." His words sent a chill down my spine. His face was full of pockmarks, and I couldn't help but wonder if had been caused by sharp beaks.

I considered trying to fight him off, but considering he was taller than me, and he was still clinging to Gwen's unconscious body, I knew it would be useless.

His eyes drifted along my robe as it fluttered open in the breeze.

I cinched my robe tighter. "Fine," I said. "I'll go with you. But you have to promise to not hurt her." Gwen began to stir. Sid's dark eyes moved across her just before he shoved her into me. I caught her clumsily. She was dead weight, and I struggled to keep from dropping her to the ground. He sneered at me as he walked in my house, in *my* territory, as if I were insignificant, backing me up as he went. Anger flared within me, but I fought to contain it. For Gwen's sake.

"Might want to lose the robe," he said, slamming the door shut behind him. "Although I'm sure the boys wouldn't mind." He smirked at me. "Might encourage Victor to do things nature's way after all."

I swallowed. I knew exactly what he meant by that. They wanted me as a breeder, just as Roland's Clan did. Panic starting to well within me. How can I get away? With trembling hands and knees, I gathered Gwen into my arms, and hauled her down the hall and into my room, flinging her across my bed with a grunt.

"You've got five minutes," Sid called down the

hallway.

Flinching at his voice, I leaned across Gwen's body, shaking her shoulders.

"Gwen. Wake up," I whispered.

She groaned, her eyes fluttered open before she touched the back of her head. Wincing, she looked up at me, as it dawned her what had just happened. She sat upright. "Layla, what's going on?"

"Three minutes," Sid shouted.

Gwen gasped, her eyes widening with horror as I covered her mouth.

"Shh. I don't want him to know you're awake." I looked down the hall. Nothing. "I'm going with him."

She mumbled against my fingers, but I clamped harder and continued, "Get help. If you can, find Roland Stone and tell him that Sid McCarty has me." I tossed one more glance down the hallway. Still no sign of Sid. "Do you understand?"

Her blue eyes looked scared as she breathed heavily through her nose.

"Do you understand?" I repeated sternly.

She nodded and appeared on the verge of tears. I laid her back down, draping her hair across her face for good measure before I quickly dressed.

"Time's up," Sid said as he sauntered in, his eyes sweeping across Gwen before settling on me. "Victor's waiting." He motioned for me to follow. As I crossed the room, I gave a pleading look to Gwen who watched me, unmoving, just her misty eyes following me. Then, I turned and followed the man who had been hunting me for weeks.

****

Sid drove me to an isolated part of town, where the

paved roads turned to dirt and humans were outnumbered by livestock and stray dogs. I tried to look for a landmark, a street sign, anything that might be useful, but the only thing I saw was farmland and a few abandoned trailers. Sid lit up a cigar as we pulled onto a gravel road, taking me farther into the unknown. Panic crept its way through me like the slow progression of high tide. Lapping higher and higher until I thought I'd suffocate.

"Where are we?"

Sid looked over, drawing a deep drag on his cigar before saying, "The Lab." He blew out a puff of smoke. I watched as it swirled its way around his face then dissipated into the air, the smell overbearing in the small confines of his car.

"The Lab? What's that?"

"All in good time." He smiled a sick and twisted smile. "All in good time."

As we drove around a bend, I saw an expansive metal building up ahead. It didn't look threatening, in fact it looked like any other typical structure in town. All of the lights were on, and a few cars were parked outside. My heart pounded painfully in my chest as we pulled up to it.

Sid parked, and got out, calling to someone as he rounded the hood of the car. I told myself to stay strong, but still, I couldn't help but gasp when he snatched the door open, seized me by the hair and pulled me out of the car.

I winced, struggling to loosen his grip, but he only tightened it, pushing me forward, propelling me through the thick metal doors. The building smelled sterile, like a hospital, but I caught traces of animal dander and musk.

Sid led me through the halls, turning and rounding corners until I lost track of where I was. The sound of footsteps fell into step behind us.

"Yes boys, here she is in the flesh. I did, what you couldn't," Sid said mockingly, cinching his grip so tight, I thought he'd rip my hair out of my head. Tears pricked at my eyes, but I blinked them back. *I'll be damn if I let them see me cry.*

Two men flanked us, but I couldn't see their faces, only catching glimpses of their sleeves or boots as they moved. Sid pushed me through a final set of doors, into what appeared to be an office. A sturdy desk was centered in the room, a leather chair behind it and several large potted plants. A map of South Carolina was framed on the wall, gold lines were drawn over it, like a grid, marking territories that I didn't recognize.

The door behind us clicked open, and I heard heavy footfalls coming up from behind, then a man stepped in front of me.

He was stocky, and his sideburns flared out across his cheeks, nearly touching the corners of his mouth.

Sid took another hit from his cigar, blowing smoke in my face as he thrust me forward, causing me to stumble. The man cocked his head, his gray eyes studying me intensely.

"So this is our Matriarch?" he said, a smug smile pulling at his lips. He leaned closer, inspecting my eyes. "You've already earned your mammal Mark, I see."

I couldn't hide my surprise. I stared at him, waiting for him to explain.

He lifted an eyebrow at me. "Have you earned any others?"

I licked my lips. "I don't know what you're talking about."

He chuckled. "Such a big title for someone who knows so little." He walked around the desk and took a seat behind it, then motioned for me to do the same.

As I sat down, I noticed the two men who had been lurking around me and Sid since we walked in. Identical twins. Their matching dark skin looked like old leather, their small eyes watched me as though I had crosshairs set over my heart.

I didn't recognize them, but there was something about the way their short arms bowed, that made me look twice. I inhaled deeply, trying to place them. The scent of infection filtered through my nose, and my lips parted as I panted, the urge to growl clawing its way up my throat.

Komodo-Shifters. Adrenaline flared within me, and my fingertips ached, feeling as though blades were being pushed beneath my fingernails. I gripped the armrests, digging my fingers deeper into them, trying to keep myself grounded, to keep from hurling myself at the men who attacked my mother.

Something ripped.

I looked down at my hands. Instead of my fingers, long claws gripped the armrests, wrapped so tightly they tore into the leather. Shocked, I withdrew my hands, turning them over before me several times, inspecting the sharp claws that now replaced my fingers. I watched, in disgust and awe as they morphed slowly back to normal.

"What got your inner beast raging?" The man asked, the corner of his mouth inched upward arrogantly.

"They attacked my mother," I hissed, narrowing my eyes at him. "It's just a matter of time before I make them pay for it." My eyes darted to the men, who rumbled like caged animals, ready to break loose.

The man laughed. "A little spitfire," he said. "I like that. It makes things interesting."

I glared at him.

He shifted his gaze to the men. "Jamal. Antwon. You may go," he ordered, the leather chair squeaking as he sat back.

The men protested but were cut off by Sid. "You've been dismissed," he snarled.

The komodo-Shifters grumbled as they filed out of the door, taking their rancid stench with them.

"Now. Let's get down to the quick of things," the man said, pressing his fingertips together. "You're a desirable piece of skin, Miss Carson. If it wasn't my Clan that claimed you, in due time it would have been another."

I thought about Roland, and how his Clan wanted me to be his Mate. My cheeks flushed thinking about it, and right then, I cursed myself for not accepting.

"And you are?" I already knew the answer, but I wanted to hear it from him.

He smiled at me. "Victor Rizzo. Head of the Croix Clan." He stood, gesturing to Sid. I felt a hand clamp down on my arm, yanking me to my feet.

"Let's go on a little tour, shall we?" Victor said, leading the way out of his office. He walked ahead of us, not bothering to look back when he said, "This building is the Croix headquarters. Shifters who have pledged themselves to this Clan assemble here much like mortals convene at a Town Hall."

He kept a steady pace, winding us through the halls until we came to a set of glass doors. He pushed a button on a wall and the doors flung open. Cold air gushed outward, cutting through my clothes. As we entered, the odd hospital smell strengthened. Tile floors reflected the fluorescent lights overhead. Several workers in white lab coats eyed me curiously as we walked by.

We passed doors that were labeled: Biohazard, Toxic Chemicals, and High Radiation Area.

"This area is known as The Lab," Victor explained, still keeping his pace as we turned down an isolated wing. "I am fascinated with evolution, Miss Carson. To learn how we came to be the dominant beings we are today is important to me, as well as my Clan. Which is where you come in." He finally stopped and turned around, his back to a glass door that read: Genetics. My eyes drifted past him, trying to see inside, but could only make out a steel table.

Victor stepped forward, invading my personal space and bringing with him, the smell of wet dog.

"Immersed within your blood, lies the ingredient for a superior Shifter race. And in time, I will harvest it, and create a breed of Shifter strong enough to eradicate the useless mortals of this world."

He pulled the door, holding it open so Sid could shove me inside. I stumbled forward. With fear slinking its way through me, I looked around. There was a workstation much like the one in Greater Hope's laboratory, and metal cabinets lining the wall. Dozens of microscopes, glass beakers, and other equipment filled a lab table.

"So after you take my DNA, then what? Will you

let me go?" I asked, turning to Victor.

His smile turned sinister. "Dear, dear, Matriarch. I'm afraid you're here to stay. I can't just let you go, and chance you'll lose your good senses and attempt to do what you were brought on this Earth to do."

"Which is what?"

His gray eyes flashed something feral, and dangerous. "Stop me from taking over the world."

Chapter 15

My mouth parted, and I searched his face for some hint of sanity, humanity, something to give me a thread of hope that I'd get out of there alive. He sneered at me, before motioning Sid forward with a jerk of his chin. Sid pushed me, forcing me to follow Victor through the room to an examination table.

"Lie down," Sid ordered, shoving me hard into the table, my knees connecting with it, sending a throbbing ache through my legs. *Stall. Stall. Stall.* I whirled around, my back against the table as I asked, "Are you going to kill me when you're through?"

Sid and Victor exchanged looks. Panic welled through me as I watched them. I grew antsy, wanting desperately to flee, but I knew I wouldn't get far. Besides, I had no idea how to get out, and the building was crawling with Croix Shifters. I thought about Turning.

Could I Turn into something strong enough to take them both out? What about the rest of the Croix Clan? Would I even be able to Shift? I hadn't learned how to hone it yet. Too many factors led to a suicide mission, so instead I was forced to wait. Wait for someone to come and rescue me from these mad men. Deep inside, I prayed it would be Roland. Silently, I spoke directly to him. *Please come for me.*

"Your blood is more valuable to me alive," Victor

finally answered. He turned to Sid and said, "Go find the doctor."

Sid nodded and hurried out of the room.

"You're about to be part of something monumental," Victor said seriously.

"Against my will," I countered.

His lips lifted in smile. "In time, perhaps you'll be more willing to donate your genes to the cause." His eyes trailed down the length of me, making me feel uncomfortable. Violated. "Course, we *could* do it the traditional way," he said. His voice husky as he stepped closer, the nauseating smell of mange drifting around me. "Like Adam and Eve, we could conceive a population of powerful Shifters. From our blood, we'll spawn an entire new breed, one that will bring our kind to the top of the food chain. Where we belong." He reached out to touch my hair.

"You mean, with *my* blood." I looked directly at him, packing all of my bitterness and hatred into my next words. "Cause by the smell of you, you're just a filthy mutt."

His gray eyes darkened, and he backhanded me. The force knocked me back a few steps. Pain shot through my cheek and cut right down to my teeth. I brought my hand to my face, tracing the welt with my fingertips. Tears sprang at my eyes, but I refused to cry. I glared at him, breathing heavily as I considered launching myself at him.

He examined the back of his hand, before settling his eyes back on me. His lips quivered into a snarl. I swallowed and squared my shoulders. I am dominant. I am Alpha. I am the Matriarch. We stared at one another for what seemed like eternity, sizing each other up, willing the other to bow down. Neither of us did.

The door behind me opened with a loud clang. Jamal skidded to a stop, his eyes wide when he said, "There's been a breach."

My heart skipped. *A breach? Is it Roland?*

"What kind of breach? Do you know where?" Victor stalked toward Jamal, his hands tightening into fists.

"We're not sure, but rest assured, boss, we're on it."

"Then get your ass back out there and find the scum who's foolish enough to invade my compound!" He slammed his fist onto the steel table, rattling the glass beakers.

An alarm blared through the speakers in the corner of the room. I shrank back, covering my ears. I took a quick glance at Victor. He looked disoriented, unsure what problem to focus on first. Me or the intruders. *Now's my chance,* I thought. I called upon my true nature, to Turn me into something fierce. Something powerful.

Adrenaline spiked within me, and my bones started to pull and stretch violently. I felt the prick of sharp incisors sinking into my bottom lip. I ran my tongue over them, feeling the pointed fangs that now filled my mouth. A growl rumbled in my throat.

Victor's gaze fixated on me, his eyes narrowing just before he rushed me, slamming his shoulder into my gut. The air was knocked out of my lungs. I wheezed, shaking my head to clear it. His fingers dug into my skin as he grabbed me, shaking me almost incoherent. I snapped at him, trying to sink my teeth into his flesh.

Again, he backhanded me.

I felt the bruise on my cheek flare angrily. I touched it, realizing my fingers were normal. I hadn't finished Shifting. Victor grabbed me by the neck, steering me backward to the examination table. I resisted, fighting against him with every fiber in my muscle, but he cinched tighter, restricting my airway until I thought I'd pass out. When he finally released me, I sputtered, wheezing as I struggled to fill my lungs with air. Before I could, he tossed me on the table, the paper crinkling beneath me, as I lay sprawled upon it. I thrashed beneath him until he swung his fist, punching me squarely on the temple. My vision spotted, and my head ached with a pain so overwhelming, I thought he had crushed my skull.

He snatched open a drawer, nearly ripping it out completely. He reached inside and withdrew a syringe. "You will give me what I want, Matriarch. One way or the other, I will rip that DNA from your blood." He tossed the syringe onto the metal medical cart beside the table.

I straddled the line of consciousness, fighting to stay awake when someone burst into the room. The alarm finally stopped blaring, but the ringing in my ears didn't. Victor looked up, his face pinching as he scanned the laboratory door. Through blurry eyes, I strained to make out the figure standing at it.

"We located the breach," Jamal said, his voice confidant until he continued. "But we haven't been able to track the intruders,"

"Intruders?" Victor hissed. "You mean there is more than one?"

"It's the Wanderlust Clan," Jamal said swallowing.

"The entire, *fucking* Clan?"

"No," he answered. "Just a few high rankers."

Victor loomed over me as I lay there helpless on the examination table. "Well, find them," he ordered.

I wanted desperately to feel relief knowing that Roland's Clan was infiltrating the Croix's compound, but with Victor so close, I could not feel anything but fear.

"What do you want us to do with them?"

Victor looked down at me, his lip curling into a sneer. "Kill them."

I panicked. *Roland!* I struggled to sit up, but Victor retrained me, tossing one more look at Jamal. "Get the hell out of here!" he barked.

Jamal disappeared, and my chest tightened. He was on his way to find Roland, and if he did, he was given orders to kill him. I had to do something.

Victor bent closer, his breath on me as he brushed the hair from my forehead.

"Dear, sweet Layla. Why do you have to put up such a fight?" He scowled, tracing a finger down my swollen cheek. "Forcing me to spoil such beauty." His gaze drifted along my face, a smile replacing his frown. "No matter. I still want you to carry my young."

I spat in his face.

He flinched, looking amused as he wiped himself clean. "In the meantime, I'll get your DNA through an alternate method." He lifted a syringe, topped with a shiny, pointed needle. He straightened my arm, smoothing the delicate flesh in the crook until the veins popped out. I cringed, swallowing back a scream as the fluorescent laboratory lights sparked off the needle.

The lab door suddenly clicked open, and Victor

turned his attention to whoever entered. His body blocked me from seeing who it was, but I could tell from his body language, it wasn't someone from the Wanderlust Clan. He visibly relaxed at the sight of them.

"There you are," Victor said sharply. "I almost did it myself."

"I'm sorry, Victor. I came as soon as I could." The voice was familiar, but through the haze of panic, I couldn't quite place it.

"Just get over here and do what you're getting paid for."

Victor stepped away, still holding the syringe high in the air as he moved. My stomach fisted when my eyes fell on the man in the white lab coat.

"Layla," Victor said condescendingly, with a smirk of his lips. "You already know Dr. Moore, don't you?"

Chapter 16

I stared at him with wide eyes.

"Why?" It was one simple word, but it was packed with so many inner questions. *Why are you involved with Shifters? Why are you working for Victor Rizzo? Why are you doing this to me?*

Dr. Moore has been a friend and colleague of my father's for the past twenty years. I met him when I was six years old. I watched him and my father exchange golfing tips over dinner. I knew him well, even before I started working with him at Greater Hope Hospital.

"Layla, do not think of me as cruel. I am simply researching. Trying to learn more about this fascinating genetic abnormality within the human race." I noticed Victor tense beside him. "And you're an absolute anomaly," he continued, smiling. "Imagine the progression science, and humanity can achieve if we could isolate your gene." He stepped closer, taking the syringe from Victor, practically salivating at the thought.

Victor fastened my legs down with thick straps. I was bound to the examination table. Panic gnawed within my gut. I fought against the restraints, but Victor pinned my arms down. I screamed as the needle took aim for a pulsating vein.

The laboratory door broke loose from its hinges with a loud bang. All of our eyes darted to the sound.

Dr. Moore stumbled backward, still clutching the needle, while Victor growled, his gray eyes narrowing at the cheetah that was coming toward us, its teeth bared as it approached.

Victor's skin rippled oddly, his mouth and eyes twitching like mad and I knew he was Shifting. Fear gripped me like a corset, cinching my chest and limiting my air.

The cheetah stopped short, crouching on its lean legs, as it studied the two men. Its long tail swished back and forth like a lure, before it leapt on Victor, ripping at his face and chest with its pointed claws. Victor finished transitioning, his human form now replaced with the body of a coyote. His gray fur stood on end, his muzzle bleeding from the gash the cheetah inflicted.

Dr. Moore didn't waste the open opportunity. He turned toward me, repositioning the syringe in his fingers. With snarls and growls around me, the commotion proved to be too much for my true nature. Feeding off the frenzy, I smiled as adrenaline flared and coursed through me. I gritted through the pain of stretched muscles and contorting bones, my body convulsing until it snapped the leg restraints in two.

Coarse fur replaced my skin, and my sense of smell heightened. Letting out a ferocious roar, I shambled off the examination table. Dr. Moore scrambled backward, his eyes darting wildly around the room, looking for a way out. The only one was behind me.

Moving on four legs rather than two was still a difficult task. I took clumsy steps toward him, until I had him cornered. I knocked the syringe to the floor. Dr. Moore hollered. Blood dripped down his fingers. A huge gash ran from his forearm to his palm. I felt a twinge of shock, and remorse, seeing what my claws could do so easily. I clambered back, staring at my paw. My eyes swung to the blood pooling on the floor, the coopery scent overwhelming my senses.

A yelp rang through the air. I turned, noticing the cheetah had Victor by the throat. The two thrashed around, becoming a blur of just fur and teeth until two more figures crashed into the room. I smelled them before I saw them. *Komodo-Shifters.* The lizards slithered into the room, lumbering toward me on short, bowed legs. Their tongues flicking outward, tasting the air, sensing the blood.

One of the lizards swung its powerful tail, whipping the cheetah across the shoulder, an ugly red gash left behind in its wake. The cat flinched but did not release its grip on Victor. The other Komodo hurled itself toward me, its mouth snapping dangerously close to my fur. I raised my paw and smacked the lizard with a force that sent it flying through the air. Its scaled body slammed into the table, the sound rung off the steel like a church bell.

Rolling onto its feet as if nothing happened, the great lizard scurried back toward me, its feet slipping on the smooth tiles as it ran. It was clear it wanted me dead.

I let out a warning growl, but the Komodo didn't slow its pace. Terrified of its infectious bite, I stood on two legs, bringing myself to a towering height. The lizard snapped its lethal teeth, and nipped at my fur, pulling it from its root.

"You put up more of a fight than your mother," the creature said into my mind.

My eyes widened at the vicious words. Anger flickered within me. Not the usual anger. This anger was savage, and untamable.

"I don't want to kill you", I thought back. *"But I will."*

"I tasted her blood, and now, I will taste yours!" He practically shouted the words in my head as he charged, his jaws snapping wildly. Unable to stop him any other way, I brought my foot down, stomping on his back until I felt his spine snap under my weight.

The Komodo's body jerked once, its tail curling and whipping madly before stilling beneath my paw. I stepped away from the unmoving body, relieved the Komodo was dead, but also sickened by what I had just done.

Needing to look away, I glanced over my shoulder—Dr. Moore was gone. He must have gotten away during the commotion. My eyes jumped to blur of movement across the room. The cheetah, overpowered by Victor, and being held at bay by the other komodo, had slash wounds to his abdomen. They were clean wounds, which meant they were likely from the komodo's powerful tail—not his teeth.

"Go!" the cheetah suddenly urged me. I snapped to a clear focus—I knew that cheetah. My gaze held firm to the cat, recognizing Roland's voice as easily as I'd recognize my own.

"I won't leave you", I said, refusing to budge.

The komodo's eyes slunk its way around the room before falling on the unmoving body of his brother. Its tongue shot out, tasting the air.

It let out a horrible, pained scream.

My body quivered with adrenaline. I had to be

ready for another round of brutal fighting. Could I do it? Could I kill again?

The komodo turned its long slinky body toward me. Roland reached out, and swiped a paw down the lizard's back, shredding its thick skin into shreds. This only slowed the enraged reptile.

"Layla, go!" Roland shouted.

For one moment, our gaze touched. Roland's eyes were pleading.

"Please. Lives, not just mine or yours, depend on you."

The komodo-Shifter opened its large mouth, its pointed teeth resembling switchblades.

"I will come back for you", I said, my tone strong and determined as I lumbered away, moving my big bear body as fast as it would move. I rounded the threshold and ran down the hallway. A few men dashed about, but I barreled through them, knocking them into walls.

I followed the twists and turns of the building, not slowing my pace when I came to a double set of glass doors. I ran straight through them, shards of glass splinting and shattering around me, but I kept moving.

I made it. I was outside. It was twilight, and a light rain floated through the air like a mist. I ran toward the same gravel road that had brought me. A pair of headlights flicked on in the distance. I winced from the brightness but kept moving. *I have to get help! I have to save Roland!*

My legs suddenly ached with the familiar restricting sensation of shrinking bones and distorting muscles. *Oh no! I'm Shifting back!* With a pained grunt, the hair sucked back into my pores, my claws retracted.

I fell to my knees, shrinking back into my human form in the wet gravel. The rain came down harder now. Ice cold on my bare skin.

"Layla?"

I lifted my head, peering through the rain. "Gwen?" My voice was strained, almost hollow.

Her eyes were round, her movements tentative as if unsure she should get too close.

I ground out a curse, pained to see my best friend scared of me. "Gwen, please…" I broke off, unable to finish. The wake of the transitioning was still raw, like being doused with water after being ablaze with fire. I slumped back into the earth, the ground sodden and muddy beneath me.

"Oh my God, Layla." She ran up to me, her eyes wide as she stared down at me, her wet hair sticking to her face. I could sense her hesitation before she sank to her knees beside me. "Layla, what the hell is going on?"

With great effort, I lifted myself onto my forearms. The hard rocks dug into my skin, but I ignored it, fighting hard just to look up into her face. Her look of fear now replaced with a wounded look of betrayal.

"Answer me," she demanded. "Why the fuck are you out here, naked, and running as though your life depends on it?"

"What…" I cough, testing my voice. I swallowed down a dry lump before I try again. "What are you doing here?"

"Roland told me stay here and wait for you."

I wiped the rain from my eyes. "How did you find him?"

"I didn't have to," she explained. "He found me.

As I was leaving your house, he just appeared out of nowhere. Then we drove out here, to the middle of nowhere, and he told me sit here and wait. So I did." She looked me over, concern etching her face. "What is going on?"

I drew myself onto my knees and wrapped my arms around myself in a vain attempt to warm myself. "Why don't you just ask the real question?" I narrowed my eyes at her. I knew she saw me transform. "Ask me how I turned into a bear." My lips trembled. I was freezing, the cold rain felt like falling ice.

Her face grew ashen. "So I wasn't seeing things." She touched her temple, sinking to her knees. "I feel a little dizzy."

"Gwen." I clutched her shoulder, trying to steady her and myself at the same time. "Gwen. Are you all right?"

She took my hand from her shoulder, squeezing it tight. "My God, Layla. What is happening?"

The siren started blaring once again from the Lab.

Gwen jumped at the sound. "Come on. Let's get out of here," I said, attempting to stagger to my feet.

With Gwen's help, we dashed to her car, the rain now coming in heavy sheets. As I slipped inside, Gwen started the ignition, and turned up the heat, trying to knock the chill from the air. I shivered. She reached into the back seat and handed me a hoodie.

"It's all I've got, sorry."

I pulled it on, flipping the hood over my head and cinching it tight. "Thanks." I rubbed my hands together, trying to warm my frozen fingers.

I could feel Gwen's eyes on me.

"Why did you hide all of this from me?"

I looked over at her, my heart squeezed at the sadness that was so plainly written across her face. "We're best friends Layla, why did you keep..." She waves her hand along the length of me. "whatever *this* is from me?"

"I didn't plan to. I just wasn't sure how you'd react...hell, I'm still trying to figure it all out myself. Trust me. It's a whole lot more complicated than you could ever imagine." I began to fiddle with the hoodie's drawstrings, not knowing what more to say. I knew she was hurt, but there wasn't much more I could offer her, except an apology. "I'm sorry, Gwen."

She breathed in deep but didn't say anything else. The pit of my stomach twisted. I couldn't tell her about Victor Rizzo and Dr. Moore. It was too dangerous. Withholding anything from Gwen felt wrong. Unnatural. But I simply couldn't tell her anything else. The more she knew of my new world, the more danger she was in. It was best she stayed in the dark.

Changing the subject, I said, "We need to go. Now." My eyes shifted to the building. The Lab. Roland was still in there, and I was leaving him behind. My heart ached, but I couldn't take on the entire Croix Clan. Not now anyway. I needed help.

"What about Roland?" She followed my gaze. "Are we leaving him here?"

My stomach churned. "Yes," I whispered.

There was a knock on my window. Gwen and I jumped. I clutched at my chest, while Gwen screamed in surprise. It was Carl, the boar-Shifter. His hair hung over his ears in wet clumps.

"Unlock the door," I told her.

"What?" Gwen stared at me, confusion spread

160

across her face.

"It's all right. I know him."

With a shaky hand, she hit the button on the door panel, and the locks clicked open.

Carl slid in the back seat, the smell of mud and grime following him like a shadow. "Matriarch," he began. "Our men are out. Roland is all that remains."

"I'm going back for him," I declared.

Carl shook his head. "Now is too risky. They are on high alert, and it would be a death mission to walk through those walls right now."

"I meant after I recruit help," I explained. "I'm not going to just let Victor have him." My hands curled around the hem of the hoodie, into tight fists. "Who knows what they'll do to him."

"Our Clan will back you," Carl said. "But right now, they are like ants, scattering to protect their home. Let them settle." He moved to exit the car, then stopped. "They won't kill him, you know."

I looked at him, trying to read his face.

"Victor knows you will return for him. So the Clan will keep him alive until you do." He opened the door and stepped out. "Be careful, Matriarch. We will be waiting for your call." He pressed his fingertip against the glass and wrote out a phone number in the fog before shutting the door behind him.

"Take down that number," I instructed. "Hurry. I'm going to need it."

Gwen punched it into her phone, then lifted her face. "Okay, Layla. Spill it. Who are all these strange men, and why did he call you…Matriarch?" ·

As I stared at her, I tried to frame the right words. They were all right there in my head. The words that would explain that I possessed a flawed gene that enabled me not only to Change into an animal, but also communicate with them.

The words that said, *'I've been chosen to stop Victor Rizzo from eliminating the human race and replacing it with a world of Shifters.'* But how do you say those words out loud without sounding insane? I bit my cheek, pondering all of it, when Gwen broke my thoughts by grabbing my hands.

"You can tell me."

"No matter how crazy?" I asked, lifting my gaze to hers. Her face was kind and trusting. The same face that loved me unconditionally, like a sister. The same face that watched me confess that I tore her favorite poster in middle school but didn't let the anger show. She touched me with the same hands that held me as I cried my way through my first breakup. My gut told me, I could tell Gwen anything.

She gripped me tighter. "Layla, it's me you're talking to. I'm the definition of crazy."

I gave a slight laugh. "I think our definitions of crazy are quite different."

"Well, try me." She let go of my hands and put the car into drive. She did a U-turn on the gravel road, pointing us back home, and away from the Lab. Away from Roland. My stomach sank with unease. I hated leaving Roland there. What were they doing to him? Was he hurt?

As I watched the building grow smaller and smaller behind us, my heart clenched like a knot on a noose, knowing that I was leaving him behind. Carl's words offered little consolation. *'They know you will return for him. So they will keep him alive until you do.'*

"So are you going to explain how a furry bear ass, turned into *your bare* ass?" She lifted a brow at me.

Her humor helped ease my apprehension, so I pulled the sleeves back over my fingertips and began my explanation. I didn't leave out anything, the words just kept flowing, barely allowing me to slow for a breath, until I was done. I watched her carefully, shifting in my seat as I waited for her to break the silence.

She continued to drive, both hands tightly gripping the wheel, until finally, I couldn't take it anymore.

"Gwen?" I hedged. "Damn it, would you say something?"

She was quiet for another long moment, then she said, "Are we talking about *Teen Wolf* kind of shit here?"

"Well, no, not really." I crossed my arms. "I'm not a fucking werewolf." I slid my gaze back to her, and tried to lighten the mood by adding, "I don't chase cars and bite the mailman."

Still looking straight ahead, she grinned, then slowly turned to face me. "You don't scare me, freak." She winked.

And with our silly quotes from *Teen Wolf*, the awkwardness evaporated into thin air. We were back to just being Gwen and Layla again. Best friends who just happened to be a Shifter and a human.

Chapter 17

The rain let up just as Gwen pulled into my driveway. After I changed into some dry clothes, I told her my plan. It was a flawed plan, but it was the only plan I had.

"I'm going with you," she declared.

"No, you're not," I said sternly. "You could get hurt."

"And so could you," she countered. "I won't let you go alone."

I crossed the floor and stood by the front door. "With any luck, I won't be." I pushed the door open, looking out into the darkness. "Keep the doors locked and whatever you do, don't go outside."

"But—"

I looked over my shoulder, pleading with her now. "Gwen, this is serious. Please. For me."

She only responded with a small, child-like nod.

I stepped out into the night. The cool air nipped at my cheeks as I wove myself through the depths of the woods. My animal senses were on high alert. My ears caught every rustle and every scamper. My nose filtered through each scent, filing them away neatly in my head. Owl, oak, fox, bat, moss, lichen and more.

It wasn't just my senses that worked flawlessly. My gait had become loose, and nimble. My footsteps fell soundlessly on the forest floor. Going by gut alone,

I finally stopped. I stood in a small pocket of moonlight, tall oak trees surrounding me, the crisp night air cutting through my sweater.

"I ask for your help," I said firmly into the darkness. "Someone important to me is being held captive by a coyote-Shifter named Victor Rizzo," I continued, fully aware that to the human eye, I appeared to be talking to empty air. But I knew better. I knew many ears were listening. "I need your help."

I waited, the sound of my own breathing was all I heard for a very long time, until finally there was a rustle in the bushes. A large wolf emerged from the underbrush. Its beautiful gray coat matched the silvery moon beams that filtered through the trees.

"We will assist you, Matriarch."

"Thank you," I said, pushing my shoulders back to show dignity and strength, though inside I was a wreck. My mind was completely consumed by Roland. I not only worried for his safety, but a dawning of feelings hit me like a freight train. I loved him. I couldn't explain how it happened. But just like everything else in my life now, I ran off pure instinct. My instinct told me that Roland was mine. And I was his.

"Where do you need us?"

"Croix compound. Do you know it?"

"My pack knows of the Clan. We have crossed paths many times with the leader. He is a calculating man and a vicious coyote. That makes for a dangerous being."

"That is exactly why I must stop him."

"I will alert the pack, as well as some other allies."

"I'm in debt to you."

"Your duty here on Earth is enough."

I stared at him, not sure I understood what he meant.

Its dark eyes, like lumps of coal, were alert and sharp.

"My pack knows the Croix Clan compound. We will meet you there at the next moonrise. We will help you get your Mate."

My Mate? I was shocked by the term but was unable to dispute it. Something in my soul told me Roland was important to me. And more than just simply attraction. It was something essential, something vital—like breathing.

The wolf turned to leave. *"We will be at your side, Matriarch."* He trotted away, melting into the darkness from which he appeared.

I easily picked my way back through the dense forest thanks to my newly keen eyesight. I hurried across my lawn and took the porch steps two at a time. Gwen met me at the door.

"I told you to keep the doors locked," I snapped.

"Sorry. I was getting antsy waiting on you."

I pushed past her, pulling her inside. I shut the door and flipped the lock.

"We're going back," I told her. "Tomorrow night."

"We?" A slow grin broke across her face.

"Yes, *we*." I sighed. "But you're not going inside the Lab," I explained. "I want you to wait on the road again, in case Roland is hurt and can't run."

"So I'm the getaway car?" She clapped her hands eagerly.

"As much as I hate to say this, but yes…you're the getaway car. Do you have a problem with that?"

"Hell no," she said smiling. "This is going to be fun."

****

I don't know how I did it, but I survived the wait of the passing hours by either pacing or calling to check on my mom. There wasn't much change. She was still responding to the medication and spent most of the time drifting in and out of consciousness. Gwen went home for a few hours to change and raid her father's closet. We figured it would be a good idea to bring extra clothes, in case Roland and I Shifted.

"Let's do this!" Gwen said as the sun winked out of sight.

I rolled my eyes as I followed her out the door and to her car. "Turn it down a notch there, eager beaver. You're entirely too excited about this," I said sinking into the passenger seat.

"Sorry. I can't help but feel like we're Charlie's Angel's or something."

"Gwen, this is serious. We're not private investigators, and I'm sure as hell not Farrah Fawcett."

"Well, actually," she said starting the engine and backing into the road. "I thought you'd be Kate Jackson and I'd be Farrah—"

"Gwen!" I slammed my palm against the dashboard. "Damnit. You're going to get yourself killed if you keep living in la la land over there. You better wake up and face reality. You're driving me into a hornets' nest, and there's a good chance I won't make it out."

She tossed me a worried look. "Stop it. You're scaring me."

"Good," I snapped. "I want you to be scared cause

I'm scared shitless. I'm in deep here, Gwen. This is real life or death shit we're dealing with."

She grew quiet. By the way her hands shook on the steering wheel, I knew she was nervous. I refused to give her a pep talk. She needed to understand the seriousness of the matter. Roland could be in bad shape. I could even die trying to rescue him.

I swallowed at my dark thoughts.

As we drove farther away from town, and closer to the Lab, Gwen asked, "So, how are you getting in?"

I looked out the window, searching for traces of my allies, but found none. I put trust in that wolf. Hopefully he would come through.

"I asked the animals for help." I kept my voice steady, hoping it didn't sound as ridiculous out loud as it did in my head.

She took a sideways glance at me before turning on the gravel road. The tires of the car shook and crunched over the loose rock, bringing me closer and closer to the Lab. My stomach grew tighter and tighter. Just before the bend, I instructed Gwen to stop the car.

"This is far enough. I don't want them to know you're here," I said. "If anyone, and I mean anyone you don't know comes, you just get the hell out of here. You understand?"

"I won't leave—"

I cut her off. "You have to. Tell my father that Doctor Neal Moore has been researching DNA without consent."

"How will that help?"

"Hopefully it will put a stop to the mayhem that's brewing inside that building. Now promise me you'll do it."

She licked her lips and nodded woodenly. "I promise."

I gave her a firm nod in return, then climbed out of the car. Shutting the door, I made my way along the edge of the compound. It was disturbingly quiet, and I wondered if it was a signal of what was to come. Would I face this alone? I chewed my lip, waiting, listening for an indication that my help had arrived, but the darkness remained still.

How am I going to get Roland out of there? I felt panicky, unsure on how I'd pull this off by myself. The truth was, I wouldn't. I *needed* help.

I crouched near a fallen log, surveying the Lab, trying my best to formulate a plan when the lights flickered on and off in the building. A security light in the parking lot blinked, and I thought I caught a glimpse of something stirring in the stream of light.

I squinted, attempting to make out the figures in the distance. They moved in unison, like rippling water across the ground.

Rodents.

What were they doing?

I sensed a presence behind me. The tiny hairs along my neck stood up. I whipped around, muffling a startled *yelp* with my hand as I faced the great wolf I met last night.

"I'm sorry, Matriarch. I didn't mean to frighten you."

"What are they doing?" I asked, turning back around. "The rodents?"

The wave of tiny furred bodies glided around the back of the building. The lights in the front of the Lab went off, shrouding it in complete darkness.

"Causing havoc."

I looked at him over my shoulder. His eyes were set on the Lab.

"They will cause confusion by eliminating the lights. You will need to rely on your senses to locate your Mate."

My senses? I acknowledged that my senses had indeed improved since discovering my abilities, but they were no way near precise. "Forgive me, but my senses aren't quite like yours. I'm not certain I trust them enough to rely on them without sight."

All final traces of light suddenly extinguished. The rodents must have chewed through the final set of electrical wires. I imagined the chaos going on inside. People running around, flipping switches, some even Shifting, in order to see better.

"You have no other choice. We must act now."

He took off in a sprint, his paws quietly kicking up dirt. I ran to keep up, debating on whether or not to Shift. I could move quietly and see perfectly in human form, but once I entered the building, I would be an easy target. I decided to Shift.

Once I got closer to the Lab, I willed my body to change, using my anger toward Dr. Moore and my hatred of Victor Rizzo as my fuel. My adrenaline spiked, and a fever broke loose through my veins. My bones felt as though they had boiled into a soupy mass, before congealing into thick skinned body of a lizard.

I lay flat on the ground, collecting myself. The view from the ground was startling, but I quickly adapted, leaping on the side of the metal building, clinging to it with the velvety pads of my feet.

"Use your senses to search the building."

I looked down at the wolf, my tongue slipping out involuntarily. The scents in the air exploded in my mouth, the sensation was odd, but fascinating. I skittered across the wall and slipped through an opened window. I moved quickly through the halls as Shifters darted to and fro, some carrying flashlights while others with keener eyesight maneuvered easily in the darkness.

"The breaker hasn't been tripped," said a voice.

"Check the transformer," instructed another.

I hovered just below the ceiling, keeping close watch of the activity beneath me. I quietly rounded corners, only stopping every now and then to taste the air, searching for Roland's woodsy scent. A fox and a badger scurried through the halls. Being nocturnal, the blackout didn't hinder their sight.

The commotion below persisted, but I pressed on, the darkness not bothering me at all until the sound of flapping wings froze me into place. The familiar smell of cigar wafted through the air. *Sid.* I remained motionless, my mind a frantic mess of possibilities. *What if he recognizes me? What if he doesn't, but eats me anyway? Birds eat lizards. Dear God, what do I do?*

I stayed still as a statue, fearing that if I even blinked, he'd see me. *Should I Shift?* Sid squawked once before fluttering down the hall. Thank God, he didn't notice me. I waited until his scent disappeared completely before I moved again.

The emergency light boxes flickered on, casting a dim glow across the hallway. I hesitated, unsure if anyone would question a gecko on the wall. I decided I didn't have time to worry about that—I had to move, and fast. I scampered across walls, tasting the air, until finally I found a trace of smoldering campfire.

I honed in on it, locating Roland in the next room. Surprisingly, it wasn't guarded. I looked down the length of the hall. It was relatively quiet, only a few Shifters still in human form wandered around the now partially lit hallway.

I moved easily down the wall, slipping through the opened door across from where Roland was being held prisoner. It was a deserted storage room. Rows of neatly arranged medical supplies, from rubbing alcohol to paper gowns lined nearly every inch of the room.

Dropping to the floor, I quickly zeroed in on the chemistry of my body, willing it Turn and expand into its grizzly bear form. It was agonizing to shift from such a small form, to a four-hundred-pound animal, but I needed something strong enough to take down the door, and I had grown accustomed to the function of the bear's stalky limbs and wide girth. Barely fitting inside in the storage room in my new body, I was forced out of it. Filling up the hallway, the Shifters quickly recognized me in this form from the previous night. Their voices rose with alarm as they shouted to one another.

With the weight of my body behind me, I slammed myself into Roland's door, crashing in on it and easily ripping it off its hinges. I took in the room quickly, my eyes falling on Roland, naked, in human form, pressed against the far corner of the room. He had a purple bruise across his chin, and appeared exhausted, but otherwise he seemed unharmed.

"Layla?" he questioned, his golden eyes searching mine.

A few men hollered something behind me, but as they closed in, I whirled around, wielding my paw like a dangerous weapon, swiping blindly at the bodies. The feel of torn flesh beneath my claws didn't slow me down. In fact, I charged them with teeth blazing, snapping and growling.

A low snarl to my right caught me off guard. Turning to it, I saw Roland, now back in cheetah form clawing right along beside me. He easily shredded a Shifter's arm, rendering it useless. I backhanded another, sending him into a wall. His body slid down limply, falling into a heap on the floor.

A large ram rushed at me, his thick, curly horns crashed into my side, knocking the wind out of me. I shook my head, trying to clear my clouding vision, blinking repeatedly as he collected speed to do it again. This time I bent, jamming my shoulder squarely into his throat. The ram's body stilled upon impact and flopped to the tile.

"Run!" Roland's voice urged me as he leaped gracefully over the bodies.

I tore after him as he bounded around corners, hissing at startled Shifters, and even swiping his claws at some who tried to reach out to stop him. I barreled through, not slowing for anyone or anything, keeping Roland in sight as I crashed through the halls. Up ahead there was a set of metal double doors, and Roland slowed, as if knowing he wouldn't be able to get past them. Without losing momentum, I hurled myself at them, colliding with the steel.

Pain shot through my body, but I refused to acknowledge it. I was going to get us out. No matter what. I reared back again, plowing into it with all of my strength. The hinges buckled. *One more good shove,* I thought.

A throaty bark behind me made my blood turn to ice. Taking a quick look over my shoulder, I saw him. Victor. He was snarling, slowly closing the space between us. *Stalking his prey,* I thought with a shiver.

Roland hissed, lunging at him without hesitation. As the two rolled furiously on the ground, I slammed the metal doors again with my shoulder. A sliver of moonlight filtered through the gap, and the smell of the outdoors renewed my strength. Crashing through the unforgiving metal one last time, it gave and out I stumbled into the darkness.

For a fleeting moment, I felt victory. Then, low growls permeated the air around me, making my fur stand on end. A dozen or more wolves surrounded me, some snarling, their lips drawn over their razor-sharp teeth, others preparing to pounce.

Slowly, I backed up. *"Roland,"* I eked out, chancing a quick look over my shoulder.

He was still tussling with Victor, his claws embedded within Victor's skin. But sadly, Roland did not have the upper hand. Victor's teeth were sunk deep into his flank. Each of their fur bodies were now matted with salvia and blood.

I had to help Roland. Forgetting about the wolves, I lumbered toward him. *"Roland,"* I called. *"I'm coming!"*

Victor tightened his grip. I saw the pain flicker in Roland's beautiful, golden eyes. Red hot anger singed the edges of my vision. I roared, then charged full speed. Victor's eyes bulged, watching and waiting for me to hit my mark.

"Release him!" I shouted, just before snatching Victor up by the nape of the neck. For one scary

moment, I thought he'd shake his head, surely ripping off a chunk of Roland's flesh.

He didn't have time to react. I didn't give him the chance. He lost his grip on Roland and I took full advantage of the moment. With all of my might, I swung him around, feeling his bones snap beneath my teeth. He yelped, and I suddenly felt sick to my stomach, the taste of him vile on my tongue. I flung his limp body toward the wolf pack, praying they were my allies, not Shifters.

When Victor's body hit the ground, the wolves descended. Their furred bodies closed in, blocking him entirely. But I didn't need to see him to know his fate. His cries, first animal-like, then clearly human were eventually drowned out by the sounds of ripping and shredding and snapping bones. My stomach roiled, bile stinging my throat as I watched the collective bodies of the pack work together as a unit, disemboweling Victor.

"Layla", Roland urged. *"We need to go."*

I stumbled along, forcing my legs to follow Roland as he sprinted away. I watched his tail swish back and forth, trying my best to ignore what was going on behind me. *I will not look back. I will not look back.*

We ran until we reached the forest edge. I was relieved when Roland finally slowed, my legs burned with exhaustion.

"Gwen is waiting on the road," I told him.

Roland turned to look at me, his pink tongue hanging low as he panted heavily.

"On the gravel road. We're not far", I continued.

A wolf howled in the distance, triggering us to take flight again. Branches whipped by my face, snagging on my fur as I ran, but I refused to stop until we reached

Gwen. I had to know she was safe, and I had to know we were too.

I finally saw Gwen's Honda. As we drew near, the car lights switched on. Roland slowed his pace, Turning as he moved. Somehow he made it look so easy, so graceful. He never missed a beat, still running on two legs as the last of his tail disappeared, his firm buttocks taking its place. I had to stop, my paws skidding in the gravel as I urged my human form to emerge from within my inner beast. I cried out, the pain excruciating now since my muscles were so sore from fighting.

Roland stopped, doubling back quickly, kneeling beside me as my fur sucked inward and my nails retracted. He held me as my limbs reformed, perspiration spotting along my back and forehead.

Finally, I had Turned.

"Are you all right?" he asked as he lifted me from the ground. I could only nod. My legs felt like rubber, and my arms were heavy. He carried me with ease. I tried my best to ignore our bare skin touching, and the proximity of our exposed parts. Gwen on the other hand—couldn't.

She peered around the front seat as we got in the backseat. "Damn. I haven't seen this much ass in one day since I agreed to help Aunt Rainey buy a thong." She shuddered. "And let me tell you that was not fun. She's sixty-eight."

I reached for the spare T-shirt and pants I brought, pulling them on as discreetly as possible.

"Gwen brought you some of her dad's clothes," I said to Roland, feeling the heat fill my cheeks as I tried to keep my eyes trained on his. "They should fit."

Gwen handed Roland a wad of clothes. "They may

be a little tight, but at least they'll cover your junk."

He smiled, and started to dress, though it was awkward with us both in the back seat. He knocked me a few times with his knees and elbows, so I scooted away, trying to give his large frame ample room. When he was done, I assessed his outfit.

His white T-shirt was a bit small, stretching tightly across his chest and shoulders. The short sleeves cut across his biceps, enhancing his lean muscles. His jeans were snug, but at least we were both finally covered. I wasn't sure how long I could hide the fact that my body was reacting to his nakedness.

"So what the hell happened back there?" Gwen asked, thankfully pulling my thoughts away from Roland and his perfect body. She turned the car around and punched the gas.

"It's over," I said, my voice small since I really couldn't believe it myself. Victor Rizzo was dead. I hugged myself, recalling the wolves and the awful sound of ripping flesh. Then, a terrible thought surfaced. Sid McCarty. He was still alive. Did that matter? Would he pursue the sick idea of eradicating humans and replacing them with a genetically engineered breed of Shifters? I swallowed hard, my hands starting to tremble at the idea.

"Or is it?" I questioned, looking up at Roland. "Will the Croix try to finish what Victor started?" I searched his face, trying to read it.

"Clans govern themselves a whole lot harsher than humans. The surrounding Clans will vote on what happens to the remaining members. Some may pledge loyalty to other Clans. Some may try to go rogue. Some, like Sid McCarty, will be captured, tried and more than likely, imprisoned or executed for their involvement."

"What about Dr. Moore?" I asked. "He's human."

"Humans who run with Shifters, will be accounted for as Shifters," he said grimly, his eyes moving to Gwen's in the rearview mirror. "Lucky for you, you chose the right side." The corner of his mouth lifted into a mischievous smile.

"Damn straight I did. My girl can go from bumble bee to bear in two point three seconds."

I laughed. "I've never been a bumble bee."

"But you've been a bear. I've seen your bear ass twice, in both sense of the words. And frankly, Layla, that's two times too many. I love ya, honey, but not enough to keep seeing your skinny ass naked all the time."

"You do seem comfortable as a bear," Roland pointed out. "Must be your mama bear instincts coming through."

I stopped smiling. "What are you talking about?"

His gaze lifted to Gwen for a second before moving back to me. He seemed a bit uncomfortable, shifting in his seat before saying in a low voice, "Remember what I said before?" His eyebrows lifted in question. When I only replied with a blank stare, he whispered, "Your fertility is peaking." He rubbed his palms on his knees. "Plus, I'm guessing with me being held captive…your possessiveness took over and—"

I lifted a hand to cut him off. "My…*possessiveness?*" I snorted and gaped at him, dumbfounded. I cared deeply about Roland, but I hadn't told him as much. I wasn't even sure he returned my feelings. Suddenly insecure, I got defensive. "Let's get this straight," I said. "I rescued you, only because you rescued me first."

His mouth hung open for a beat, then a goofy grin spread across his features. "You're kidding, right?"

I scowled at him, crossing my arms over my chest.

"Are you really saying that the only reason you risked your life in there, was because you owed me?"

I glowered at him, allowing the seconds to stretch into minutes, until finally Gwen pulled into my driveway. The three of us sat quietly until she said, "Okay, the sexual tension in here is so thick it's fogging up my windshield and possibly impregnating me at this very moment, so I'm getting out of here. Get the hell out of my car. The both of you."

I frowned at her too.

"Out," she repeated, hitting the unlock button on her door panel.

I climbed out of the car without saying a word. Roland was right behind me.

"You're welcome," she called out the window.

I tossed her a glance, squelching the childish urge to stick my tongue out at her.

She smiled and beckoned me closer with her index finger. Reluctantly, I stepped up to her window.

"I'll be your getaway driver anytime, Layla, but I refuse to be a third wheel. That man wants you and I think the feelings are mutual." She smirked at me. "I'll call you tomorrow to get all the dirty details." She winked and pulled away before I could say anything.

I turned to find Roland waiting on my porch steps. I watched him carefully as I slowly crossed the lawn. He held firm to each handrail, blocking my way.

"Are you still holding on to that weak theory?"

"Theory?" I mirrored sweetly, cutting my eyes as I tried to pass him.

He didn't budge. "Yes. That load of bull you tried to feed me back there. How you only saved me because I saved you first."

I stuck my chin out. "That's right. We're even now."

He laughed mockingly. "So, let me get this straight. Whatever I do first, you'll counter it until we're even?"

I nodded, watching him, trying to figure out where this conversation was headed.

"What if I kissed you?" he asked, his face inching closer to mine. His golden eyes glimmered, ensnaring me into place. "Would you kiss me back?"

My insides quivered, heat pushing through my veins with need. No matter how infuriating this man was, I wanted him. Wanted to taste his mouth, wanted to feel the touch of his hands against my skin. With our eyes never straying from each other, I whispered a weak, "Yes."

The corner of his lip curled, and his eyes became feral, and hungry. His scent became bold, the woodsy musk of him tempting me, seducing me. When I felt his hot breath against my face, my own breath caught in my throat. He wet his lips just before pressing them tenderly against mine.

It was an innocent display of affection. As if we were testing the waters, unsure if we were ready to take the leap into deeper, more turbulent waves. But then, just as our mouths separated, they sought each other out again, this time more eagerly.

My hands slid up his shoulders and wound around

the back of his neck. His arms encircled my waist, lifting me up, and holding me close, chest to chest. In that moment, we breathed in one another, as if that was all we needed to survive.

When our mouths parted, we stayed wrapped up in each other, panting, our foreheads touching.

"I've been dreaming about that," he said quietly as his eyes closed.

My heart fluttered. My pull to be close to him wasn't one sided. He felt it too.

He opened his eyes. The usual fierceness was gone, now replaced with exhilaration. He gently lowered me until my feet were back safely on the wooden step. I stood looking up at him, wondering how we made it to this point. How this ruggedly handsome stranger slowly became a protector, an ally, and now he was so much more.

"You should get some rest," he said. "With all of the Shifting you did, your body is going to hate you tomorrow."

I frowned at the thought of being apart.

Roland smoothed the crease in my forehead and gave me a little smile. "I'll see you tomorrow." He kissed my cheek, his scruffy chin tickling my skin. I watched him leave, lightly treading down the porch steps, then across the front lawn. His movements were slinky, his feline nature evident in the seductive way his limbs worked effortlessly in time with one another. I admired his toned muscles and the graceful swagger in his step.

He stopped at the edge of the forest and gave me sweet smile before dissolving into the thick of the trees.

I stood there, unmoving, my heart overflowing

with too many emotions to name. The taste of his kiss still on my lips. There was no doubt about it. Roland Stone was mine. My heart. My soul. My mate.

Chapter 18

I awoke the next morning thinking of Roland. I touched my fingertips to my lips, still feeling the warmth of his mouth. When I sat up, I realized how badly my body ached, just like Roland said it would. I stretched, trying to loosen all the knots of tight muscles. I took some pain reliever and sipped at coffee as the medicine worked its numbing effect on my sore muscles.

I sat my mug on the table, thinking about Roland and his alluring golden eyes. Lost in cloud nine, I dressed and combed my hair in a silly, love-fool daze, then grabbed my keys and headed out the door to visit my mother.

As I drove, my cell phone rang.

I answered, though I didn't recognize the number.

"Hello?" I said, turning into the entrance of Greater Hope Hospital.

"Hi," the husky voice said.

My heart shattered into hundreds of excited butterflies.

"Roland," I breathed.

"I want to see you," he continued.

I smiled. "I want to see you too."

"My gut is telling me to run to you right now. Where are you?"

I glanced at the entrance sign to the outpatient

building. "At the hospital," I answered as I pulled into a parking slot. "I'm checking on my mother," I added, killing the engine to the truck.

He was quiet.

I got out, making my way through the parked cars and up to the entrance doors.

"Roland?"

"I'll be there soon."

Before I could say anything, he hung up.

I looked at the phone, puzzled, then tucked it into my pocket. Before I entered, I peeked inside my purse, making sure my sunglasses were there—just in case. Mom was persistent—almost demanding—that I shield my eyes from my father. Not understanding the reason why, I chose to do as I was told. Other than Roland, my mother was the only person linked to the Shifter world who I trusted. If she said to wear the sunglasses, then damnit, I was going to wear the sunglasses.

I rode the elevator up to my mother's floor, oblivious of the people entering and leaving. Leaning against the back wall, I wondered how I got there. How everything had changed so dramatically—so quickly.

The elevator dinged, and the doors parted. I stepped out, shaking away my reverie, anxious to see my mother. I hoped she had progressed since I last saw her.

I moved through the hallway, smelling the sterile air, ignoring the niggle of thought that wouldn't go away. *Why was Roland so insistent on seeing me now? Why here? Why at the hospital?* I should have felt flattered, but instead, I was troubled. *What did it mean? Did he sense something? Something dangerous?*

The door to my mother's room was wide open. I

walked inside, finding her awake, watching her favorite soap opera on the television. She turned, a smile lighting her face when she saw me.

"Layla." Her voice was stronger, and her color had returned.

"You're looking good, Mom," I said. "How are you feeling?" I took a seat beside her bed and reached for her hand. It was warm again, and not as frail as before. I squeezed her, happy to feel her strength again.

"Much better. Your Daddy says I can go home soon," she said with a smile.

"That's wonderful," I replied. "Where is he anyway?"

"In surgery. They needed him, and who am I to keep him from saving someone's life?" She turned, her hair falling around her pillow as she faced the TV again.

I watched her, biting my lip, wondering if I should tell her about Victor Rizzo.

"So how are you faring, Layla," she asked, not looking at me. I followed her gaze, noticing the actress on the screen crying theatrically in the shower. I rolled my eyes. *How can she watch this?*

"You'll have to be more specific, Mom," I said. "Faring well with what? That you were attacked by komodo-Shifters? That *I'm* a Shifter? That I had a twin sister, who I never knew existed?" I didn't mean to sound so hateful, but the weight of everything was becoming too much to bear.

Her eyes lowered, but she still did not look at me. Taking a deep breath, she said, "I'm sorry, Layla."

"Again, which are you sorry for?" I spat. "Sorry for all of those things happening? Or sorry I found out?"

She turned, her eyes wide and rimming with tears. "I thought I was protecting you."

"By keeping me in the dark?"

I heard footsteps approaching, and she must have heard them too because she didn't answer me, though she pressed her lips together tightly. I inhaled, trying to catch his scent. I frowned when I recognized my father's leathery odor, not Roland's woodsy smell. I quickly grabbed my sunglasses out of my purse and slid them on.

His shoes clicked on the tile as he crossed the room. "Layla." He said it so tersely, he may as well be addressing a fellow colleague.

"Father," I said, resisting the urge to salute him. He was in his crisp white lab coat, a stethoscope around his neck.

"Your mother is doing well. I'm confident that she will be released soon."

I shifted my eyes back to my mom. She gave my father a strained smile, then looked back at me.

"That's good news," I said.

"Yes, it is," he agreed as he checked her chart. I watched him as he slid the clipboard back into its slot and rounded the bed to my mother's side. "I'll be back to check on you," he said just before pressing a chaste kiss to her forehead. His eyes focused on me. "Don't exhaust her."

I opened my mouth to say something, but a gentle knock at the door interrupted me. I turned, catching a glimpse of Roland's tanned skin. He smiled at me, which only enhanced his handsome features.

"May I help you?" my father asked, his face pinched in annoyance.

"He's with me," I said, my tone cutting.

My father arched an eyebrow as he scrutinized every inch of Roland. "Is this a new boyfriend of yours?"

Boyfriend? Roland and I had never discussed our relationship, but the term *boyfriend* seemed inadequate. We were much more than that. Something more significant, more solid, and more permanent.

"He's…well, we're…" I stumbled over my words, not sure how to answer. Roland saw me floundering but offered no help.

My father looked from Roland to me, his brows furrowing deeper and deeper by the second. He raised his hand, signaling me to be quiet. "Never mind," he said, walking out the door.

Roland and I looked at one another for a long moment, then my mom spoke.

"Are you a Shifter?" she asked, her voice quiet.

Roland's gaze moved from me to her, before he answered with a straightforward, "Yes."

"What Clan?"

I looked at her. Her knowledge of Shifters still stunned me and hearing her speak of it was strange.

"Wanderlust," he replied.

She gave a knowing nod. "Admirable Clan."

My eyebrows shot up. "You know of them?"

Her coffee colored eyes scanned Roland, then rested on me. "Yes I do. Your great grandfather belonged to the Harvest Moon Clan."

"Close allies of the Wanderlust Clan," Roland said, stepping up beside me. "They are a group of farmers," he explained. "They have provided well for my Clan in the past."

"Yes, that seems to be what they do best. My grandfather was either tending to the crops, or forcing you to eat them," she said with a laugh.

"What was his true nature?" I asked, astounded to learn more about him.

"A hare." She snickered. "Which was ironic, being that he was a farmer. Turning into one of the biggest pests of the farmland was a running joke with the Clan."

Roland smiled, and I found myself grinning as well. I pictured the man in the old black and white photograph in my mother's album, imagining him Turning into a floppy-eared jackrabbit.

"And you?" my mother asked Roland. "What is your affinity?"

"Felis-Shifter," he answered.

"Ah." Her features softened, and her eyes shone with a newfound fondness of Roland. His genes and dynamics must be impressive among the Shifting community. *Which is why his Clan wants to pair us. Parents with strong genes will result in strong offspring.* Slightly irritated, I pushed the thought away.

A nurse entered the room. "How are we feeling Mrs. Carson?" she asked in a pleasant voice.

"Well, thank you," my mother answered.

"Just checking your vitals and changing your bandages." She buzzed around my mother's bed, checking the machines, punching buttons and securing plugs.

"I'm going to give her some privacy," Roland said, touching my shoulder. "Want some coffee?"

"Yes please."

He gave me a little squeeze and smiled. "I'll be

back before you have a chance to miss me." He touched my cheek, then stepped out of the room.

The nurse removed my mother's bandages carefully, taking her time and being as gentle as possible. I couldn't help but stare as she slowly unwound them. Watching her fingers work with precision, I braced myself for the hideous wound. When the final slip of gauze was gone, I was surprised to find only clean, sutured flesh in place of the once bloody, angry, torn skin that had once been there. The nurse dabbed on a bit of betadine, then dressed the wound in fresh bandages.

"There you go, Mrs. Carson. Everything is healing wonderfully," she said, tossing the soiled bandages in the trash. "And quickly," she added. "Must be your husband's golden touch." She smiled and let herself out of the room quietly.

The mention of my father had me on edge. I stood and walked to the doorway. Hospital staff moved about the hall briskly, going in and out of patients' rooms and elevators. Roland was at the far end, strolling toward me, carrying two cups of coffee. I smiled at him, and he returned it, making my heart melt. His chiseled features were so rugged, he could have been carved out of sandstone.

The elevator dinged to my left, and out stepped Dr. Moore. My chest tightened, and I felt nauseous at the sight of him. He was poring over a chart, his hand bandaged from his wrist to his fingertips.

I did that, I thought, recalling the sensation of his skin ripping beneath my claws. As if sensing my stare, he lifted his head and our eyes met. He instantly paled, swallowing hard as he slowed his pace to an abrupt halt, not daring to come too close.

He floundered for a moment, his eyes darting wildly around him, as though searching for a way out. I glared at him, striding out into the hallway, and squaring my shoulders. I wasn't backing away or down.

Roland came up beside me, a low growl rumbling in his throat.

"Why's he here?" I asked, not taking my eyes off the doctor.

"Clan must not have caught up with him yet," Roland answered through gritted teeth. "Or…"

"Or?" I repeated, looking at Roland. His eyes were narrowed at Dr. Moore. They flickered menacingly, as though he was using every bit of willpower to restrain himself.

"Or, they don't know of his involvement." He finally tore his gaze from the doctor and looked at me. "We'll meet with the Clan's leaders and find out." His lip curled into a snarl. "He will be dealt with. One way or another."

My throat went dry. *Clan leaders?* The same Clan leaders that wanted me to mate with Roland just because of my genes? My breed, my pedigree, my stock? All of it sounded like I belonged in a dog show somewhere, and it made me sick.

Dr. Moore looked baffled, standing there in the hallway, trying to look normal to his fellow staff, but he was too much of a coward to get too close to Roland or me.

"The Clan leaders had no idea that Victor wanted to genetically produce a new breed. They just thought he wanted to use you as a breeder," Roland explained.

I flinched at the word, *breeder*, but I let him

continue.

"They need to be told, Layla, by *you*, so they can handle the Croix's accordingly."

I nodded stiffly.

Together, Roland and I went back inside my mother's room, allowing Dr. Moore to escape. There wasn't much we could do in a crowded hospital, and as sure as the sun rises each day, the Clan would soon catch up with him.

"That must be what I sensed this morning," Roland said in a low voice. I recalled the urgency in his voice when he said, '*My gut is telling me to run to you right now*'. "Something told me you would need me"

"I'm glad you listened…"

"As a Shifter, you should *always* listen to your instincts. Remember that, Layla."

It was difficult, but I pulled my gaze from Roland, and focused on my mother. She looked surprisingly lovely laying there, a healthy pink tinge returning to her cheeks and her lips no longer pasty and dry. "Mom, we have to go, but I will call and check on you soon." I bent and kissed her cheek. "I love you."

"I love you more," she replied, smiling at me as I closed the door to her room.

Chapter 19

Roland's SUV bounced along the unfamiliar back roads. I gripped the dashboard so tightly, my knuckles were white. Finally, we pulled up to an expansive log cabin. It had a massive porch that wrapped around the side of the building and a brick fire pit in the front yard. Wanderlust headquarters were much homier than the Croix's. I tried not to think of the stale air, and the barren, almost clinical atmosphere of the Lab.

As I stepped down from the SUV, I could smell the other Shifters. I tensed, realizing there were many different scents in the air. Bird dander, musk, wet fur, and something putrid, like rotting meat. Other than Roland, I knew no one there.

Pushing back my shoulders, I reminded myself, *I am the Matriarch. There is no reason to be afraid of this Clan. They are the good guys*.

Roland touched the small of my back and led me up the stairs.

"Don't be nervous," he said, pushing open the front door.

I took a deep breath as the room opened up before me. Rustic furniture arranged in a cozy nook across from a stone hearth were occupied by a few men. They were in deep discussion, until we walked in, that is. They went completely silent. Their eyes probing me, the subtle flare of their nostrils telling me they were identifying me.

Roland greeted them with a curt nod and steered me down a wood-paneled hallway.

"Our leader is Wade Walker," he said. "You can trust him."

I slid my gaze to him. "Do you?"

"With my life." He rapped the door with his knuckles. That was enough for me. If Roland trusted him, then so did I.

I pursed my lips, trying my best to combat the nerves that was threatening to overtake me. I ran my sweaty palms over my jeans, shooting Roland a look of apprehension.

"It's okay," he mouthed, his eyes kind, and understanding.

"Come in," called a gravelly voice.

Roland opened the door and pushed it aside. Behind a desk sat a barrel chested beast of a man with pure white hair, combed into a slick pompadour. He smiled pleasantly, as if expecting our company.

The room smelled of pine and leather, like an old weathered barn. I entered hesitantly, with Roland at my side. Unsure what to say or do, I stood awkwardly, my arms at my sides. Roland's fingers fleetingly brushed mine, and for a moment I thought about taking his hand for support.

"Wade," Roland began, stepping up to the solid oak desk. "This is Layla Carson."

"I know," Wade said, standing from his chair. He stood as tall as Roland, but twice as round. "It's an honor to be in your presence." He took my hand and bent slightly in a small bow. His knuckles were covered in unruly white hair. I wondered what his true nature was. Taking a peek at his bushy eyebrows, I knew it had to be something hairy.

He had a thick beard that was braided into two strands and the kindest eyes I have ever seen. They were gun-metal blue, which sparkled with warmth, and his smile seemed genuine.

He gestured for us to sit, before fitting himself into his oversized office chair. I sank into the leather seat, taking in the rest of the room. There were pictures of what I assumed were Wade's grandchildren on his desk. Two small boys and a teenage girl smiled behind a wooden frame. A wagon wheel and a dream catcher hung from the wall. He had a perfectly normal desk, equipped with the usual items. A coffee cup, pens, folders and a phone. Again, I tried to figure out what he Turned into.

Wade leaned forward, elbows on the desk as he waited for me to speak. He gave me a reassuring smile.

I began to relax, sensing his sincerity. I cleared my throat and began to tell him everything that had occurred within the horrible walls of the Croix compound. When I was through, he knitted his bushy brows and frowned slightly.

"Somehow Victor was able to keep the doctor's involvement concealed." His frowned deepened, and his eyes shifted to Roland. "His actions…will have consequences. I'll get some men together to track him. We'll have him by morning."

"I'd like to go," I said, feeling Roland tense beside me.

"The Clan is capable of bringing him in," Roland replied. "There is no reason for you to go." His jaw ticked as he ground his teeth together, his hands rigid around the armrests.

"I want to," I said. "I've known the man for over half my life, and in a matter of minutes, he was able to shatter what trust I had in him. He stamped out the trace of humanity he had left when he tried to rip my DNA from my blood by force. I will never forgive him for that nor will I ever forget it."

I recalled the rhesus macaque, and the fear in his eyes. This wasn't just about me. *Dr. Moore tests on animals, and now Shifters. He has to be stopped.* And I was going to make sure of it. With a steady voice, I said, "The man deserves whatever the Clan has in store him."

The corner of Wade's mouth inched upward, and his eyes shone with, admiration? Amusement? I wasn't sure which one, but I continued anyway. "I'm going *with* the Clan, or I'm going *without* them."

Roland pursed his lips together, scowling.

"Very well," Wade said. "I'll send a few trackers to accompany you."

"What?" Roland slammed his fist to the armrest. "You're allowing this?"

"He's just a man Roland, what could he possibly do?" Wade lifted a questioning brow.

"A man who she's grown up with," he countered. "What if he pleads for mercy? What if she can't bring herself to take him in?"

A seed of anger grew within me. Roland was talking about me as if I wasn't even there. Worse yet, he acted as though I was weak.

"I feel she will do what's right," Wade replied, interlacing his fingers in front of him. "Besides, she doesn't have to be the one to seize him. I'll send capable men with her. She can just lead the way. Let her do this, Roland. It's her right."

I glared at the two men, my irritation level rising by the second. *I am right here, damn it!*

"What if she gets hurt?"

"She could have gotten hurt when she went back for you," Wade shot. "I don't see you arguing against that."

"I had no control over that," Roland said through gritted teeth.

"Will the both of you just stop it?" I shouted, jerking myself into a standing position. Wade leaned back in his chair, taken aback by my outburst. "Neither of you have control over what I do." I narrowed my eyes at Roland. "I'm going to get Moore. You can either come with me, or stay behind, but you will not stop me."

"I just want you to be safe, Layla," Roland answered. "I don't want you to risk anything just to prove a point to a useless human."

It felt as though my breath was snatched away from me. "Useless human?" I touched my chest. "Until about a month ago, I was a useless human."

"I didn't mean it like that," Roland said, paling a little. "I just meant that he's not worth it. The Clan can handle it. You always seem to forget how important you are, and it would be a waste to risk your life for someone so insignificant."

My ears felt hot, so I knew I was about to boil over. "What part of me is so important, Roland?" I moved my gaze to Wade. His friendly face was now replaced with a look of worry. "Or maybe you can answer that, *Wade Walker*." I balled my fists at my

196

sides so tightly I could feel my fingernails digging into my palms. "What part of me is so *fucking* important? My mind? My body? Or my *genes*? Am I still just a breeder to you?"

"No, of course not," Roland shouted. "You were always more than just a breeder."

"You're damn right." I practically snarled as I glowered at him, stepping around my chair and touching the door knob. "I'm the mother fucking Matriarch, and don't you forget it."

I yanked the door open and stomped out of the room, leaving the two men behind with their jaws in their laps.

****

"Layla!" Roland called. "Layla!" I could hear his footsteps padding against the hallway carpet as he caught up to me.

I didn't look at him, I just kept walking with my head down, and my fists at my sides.

"What the hell was that back there?" he asked. "You just walked out on a Clan Leader."

"So?"

"You weren't excused," he explained as we came up on two women talking over coffee. They watched us as we passed, but I ignored them, too hell-bent on finding my way out of there. "You're supposed to wait until you're dismissed by a Leader."

"Forgive me for my ignorance in Clan etiquette. It wasn't taught in school," I said drily as I rolled my eyes.

He grabbed my wrist and pulled me into him, catching my hips with both hands. Our personal space overlapped, and I became trapped within it, the heat of his body keeping me there.

I lightly pounded my fists on his chest, and gave the half-hearted demand, "Let me go."

His fingers dug deeper, and he lowered his face to meet mine. "You just cussed out a well-respected Clan Leader, and then walked out on him."

My stomach twisted a little, wondering if I just burned a bridge that someday I may need to cross. *Damnit, Layla. You really screwed up this time.*

His lips lifted into a smile. "It was awesome," he said laughing.

I watched him for a moment, relishing the sparkle in his eyes and the sound of his laughter before I smiled back, my frustration evaporating.

"Layla Carson," Roland said, his voice turning husky as he stared deep into my eyes. Gold searing into green. "You cannot be tamed." He sank his fingers into my hair, raking them over my ears. "And that is exactly why I'm crazy about you."

Everything around us faded until it was just the two of us, and I became intoxicated by his scent. It called to me, luring me closer and closer until our noses nearly touched.

"I only want to protect you," he said, his warm breath ghosting across my face as he spoke. "You're so damn important."

I sighed. I hated hearing how important I was, and I hated even more how fragile Roland thought I was. He treated me like a porcelain doll, delicate and easily broken.

He lifted my chin with his fingers. "And not because you're the Matriarch." His intense eyes searched mine, trying to relay the weight of his words.

"Because I love you."

My mouth parted, and my heart felt light with happiness.

The sound of heavy footfalls slowly approached us. "Okay, you two, save your Claiming for behind closed doors," Wade said, winking and slapping Roland on the shoulder.

Claiming? Startled, I stepped back, breaking the trance I was in, and leaving the intimate embrace I had shared with Roland. I felt empty, and Roland seemed too far away. As if sensing my mood, Roland reached out and entwined his fingers with mine.

"I have set up for two trackers to accompany you. They will also serve as Rangers," Wade informed as he looped his thumbs into his belt. He wore a shiny buckle with three interlocking 'W's' forged into the silver. It was easy to surmise what they stood for. Wade Walker, and Wanderlust.

"Rangers?" I asked, not understanding how the term was defined within the Clan society. I pictured park rangers in hunger green uniforms, wearing Smokey the Bear'esque campaign hats.

"Rangers are used as enforcement officials," Wade went on. "They seize, or 'arrest' individuals and bring them in to the governing Clan." He turned to Roland. "You too, will act as a Ranger. Bring him and put him in a cell. I'll hold a Council meeting to decide his penalty." He turned his blue eyes to me. "You should sit on the Judgment Panel."

"And what is that?" I asked, curious about Clan government.

"It's similar to a jury in human courtrooms."

"But I was the victim," I pointed out. Victims don't

sit in on the jury. That would be a sure-fire way to fast conviction.

"Human laws differ from Shifter's, Layla," Roland said, giving my hand a squeeze. "We don't follow the same rules."

As I thought about that, a man and a woman strolled leisurely up to us. The man was slim, with long red hair, parted down the center. His pointed features and beady eyes gave him a sly appearance. The woman was petite, with thick bangs grazing her wide eyes. Her face was long, but she was uniquely pretty.

"This is Tristan and Karla," Wade introduced. "Fine trackers, and Shifters." He nodded at the man. "Tristan is a fox-Shifter, and Karla here is the only mustang-Shifter in the Clan." He gave her a dazzling smile, and she seemed proud.

"Mustang-Shifters rarely pledge to a Clan," Roland said in a low voice. "They are free spirits who tend to stay away from organized groups."

The woman's eyes drifted to me, and then to Roland. "Are we going to go get the scumbag, or are we going to sit around and exchange each other's bios?" Karla wore frayed jeans and a fitted leather jacket. Her sharp features intimated me, and her abrasive tone did little to soften her persona.

Tristan's mouth twitched into a tiny smile, but he didn't speak.

"Lead the way," Roland said to Karla, waving his arm out. "You *are* the tracker, are you not?"

Karla rolled her eyes, and set off to lead us, walking several feet ahead. She looked over her shoulder as we filed behind her. "Can she keep up?"

"Of course she can keep up," Roland said, his tone

a little gruff.

"Oh right, my apologies, she's the all-powerful Matriarch. She sneezes sparkles and shits gold."

Everyone else held me in high regard because of my status as Matriarch, but Karla was clearly not impressed. Considering her wild nature as a mustang, and her seemingly less than trusting attitude to outsiders, I tried not to let her cutting remark affect me.

Wade stood on the front porch, watching us as we climbed into a huge black Hummer. With Tristan behind the wheel, we turned onto the main highway and drove through town, no one saying a word as we pulled into Greater Hope Hospital parking lot.

"Do you know what the doctor drives?" Tristan finally asked, flicking his eyes to the rearview mirror.

"Silver BMW," I answered, returning his gaze. His eyes were like polished sapphires, beautiful, but piercing.

We circled the parking lot, searching for his vehicle. It wasn't hard to find. It was parked in its usual spot, beneath the security lights and close to the staff entrance.

"That's it," I pointed out, leaning forward in my seat.

"Let me out," Karla instructed as she pushed open the car door. Not bothering to wait for Tristan to stop the vehicle, she leapt out, landing gracefully on her feet. She moved quickly, circling the car once as she inhaled deeply, trying to trace his scent. Her brows pinched tightly together before she slid back into the passenger seat.

"It's been awhile since he's been here," she said, mostly to Tristan.

"He works twelve-hour shifts," I replied, looking at my watch. "He should be getting off in about an hour."

"Do you know where he lives?" Tristan asked, turning slightly in his seat to look at me.

I shook my head. "I only know he lives somewhere in Marsh Landing," I answered.

"Of course," Karla said dryly.

Marsh Landing was home to the wealthy. Each house had a beautiful view of the marsh, and was connected to a sprawling, private golf course. Dr. Moore moved there about two years ago, and though my father had been there, I had never visited myself.

"His scent would be easy to track there," Tristan offered, looking back at Roland.

"We know he's here," Karla said, her tone a bit agitated. "Let's just wait and seize him when he comes out."

"In the parking lot?" I questioned, stunned they would do it so openly. "Won't someone see?"

"Human eyes cannot keep up with me," Karla said, almost smirking.

"I agree," Roland said. "We know he's coming out soon, let's just wait for him here."

Tristan pulled into a nearby parking spot and killed the engine. Karla looked impatient, staring out the window, and thrumming her fingers on the dashboard. Tristan crossed his arms over his chest and watched the parking lot. His gaze jumped around quickly, taking in everything.

Roland settled into his seat, but he appeared anxious. I knew he was worried about my reaction to seeing Dr. Moore seized. What exactly did that mean anyway? Would they use brute force, or would they simply ask him to come with us? I shuddered to think what Karla would do if he refused.

I leaned across the space between us and touched Roland's knee. His honey colored eyes held mine, and he gave me a small smile before covering my hand with his. His warm touch quickly spread through me, calming my nerves and frazzled thoughts.

Almost two hours later, Dr. Moore finally emerged from the hospital, toting a leather briefcase. He was still in his lab coat. The security lights reflected off his shiny oxfords, and his balding head. My stomach churned at seeing him again. I could still see his sick smile as he loomed over me with the gleaming needle. I shivered and forced myself to focus on the here and now.

Karla sat straighter, her eyes honing in on Moore like crosshairs over a target. As he drew closer, she touched the door handle. I gnawed anxiously at my lip, my eyes darting from her to Dr. Moore.

Karla quietly pushed open the car door and slid out. Pressing her body to the vehicle, she waited as Dr. Moore unlocked his BMW. Like a cat preparing to pounce, she crouched forward, ready to tackle him at any moment. Roland and Tristan slipped out of the car. As I watched from the backseat, my heartbeat pounded painfully against my eardrums.

Out of the corner of my eye, I caught movement. *Father?* He was strolling across the parking lot, calling to Dr. Moore. Karla stilled, but her eyes remained fixated on the doctor, who stood with one hand on his car door. Tristan and Roland dissolved into the shadows, leaving me alone in the car, wondering what I should do next. I didn't want my father to get hurt, but I also knew that it was imperative that we take Dr. Moore in.

My father walked up to the doctor, his eyes sharply scanning the empty cars around him. I ducked, sinking low into my seat. *Shit!* The two men engaged in conversation, though I could not make out anything they said. The longer they talked, the more compressed my lungs felt. I slid to the floorboards, flattening my body against the floor as best I could. My limbs trembled with adrenaline, readying itself to Turn. I tried steadying my breathing, willing myself to relax as not to trigger an unwanted change. I could hear my father's muffled voice giving Dr. Moore instructions of some sort, and then the clipped retreat of footsteps.

I chanced a peek out of the window. Dr. Moore was pulling away. I spotted my father quickly crossing the parking lot, heading back toward the hospital.

The SUV door jerked opened, causing me to jump and clutch frantically at my chest. *Shit!*

Karla easily slid in and started the Hummer.

"What's going on?" I asked, panic swelling within my gut.

"He got away," she answered simply, putting the car into drive and stomping the gas. I whirled around, looking out the windows as we flew past parked cars.

"Wait, where's Roland?"

"He and Tristan are following him. We're going to Marsh Landing, to see if we can head him off. If he's not going straight home, then Tristan and Roland will call us."

I gripped the seat beneath me as we pulled onto the main road, changing lanes as though we were in a race, our pace never slowing, even as we veered onto the interstate.

The bright lights of town whirled past as us we accelerated, passing Dr. Moore's BMW with ease and eventually taking the Marsh Landing exit. Karla's dark eyes kept flicking to the rearview mirror. I twisted in my seat, watching and waiting for the doctor to follow, but he didn't.

"Fuck!" Karla shouted, banging on the steering wheel with the heel of her hand.

"Where's he going?" I said aloud, though I knew she wouldn't have the answer.

Karla pulled a cell phone from her jacket pocket. Fisting it, she kept it in her hand as she drove, maneuvering the oversized SUV into a secluded lot outside the Marsh Landing limits. The Hummer's headlights shone on the tree line, revealing towering pine trees and sprawling privet. She parked, and then we just sat there, in total silence, waiting for the phone to ring.

Finally, it did. *This is it,* I thought as Karla quickly answered it. *That's Roland or Tristan on the other end with information on where Dr. Moore is.* Karla's eyes narrowed, and she frowned into the phone.

"Damn," she said, pinching the bridge of her nose. "Yes. We'll circle the perimeter until we locate either him or you." She snapped the phone shut and looked at me.

"So obviously, he's not on his way home," she explained. "He's heading somewhere near the outskirts of town."

I thought about that. *Why would he be going out there?* There wasn't much in Yemassee, and even less on the outskirts.

She started the engine once more, righting the vehicle to head to the edge of town. We traveled in absolute silence. I watched the scenery change outside my window from the populated, building-crowded town, to the more secluded and forest lush outskirts.

Eventually Karla slowed the Hummer, easing the vehicle off the road and sliding into a shadowed nook in the woods. Killing the engine, she wordlessly pushed open the door, and climbed out, slamming it hard behind her. She walked around to the rear of the Hummer and opened the back hatch.

I waited for instructions. *What was happening?* I wished I had my phone right then, needing to hear Roland's soothing voice on the other end of the line. Karla reached in the back, and withdrew a lightweight satchel, slinging it across her chest.

Squinting through the tinted glass, she rapped on the window. "Come on, Princess, we have some hiking to do," she said.

Stifling the urge to scowl, I opened the door and stepped down into the grass. The sound of chirping crickets stopped. The stillness of the night around me seemed eerie, but I tried not to let it show. The moon was full, casting a pale glow on everything beneath it. Even Karla's dark hair shined with silvery highlights.

"Tristan has him tracked near the old Abernathy Plantation. We are only a few miles away, so we will close in the perimeter until we find them."

"What's in the bag?" I asked.

"Clothes. Shifters always travel with extra. Maybe someday you'll get the memo," she said, treading through the underbrush.

I watched as she sank into the darkness of the

forest, my stomach gnawing at itself with worry. Something felt wrong about this—very wrong. *Why was Moore out here? What could possibly be out here, in the middle of nowhere?* Karla moved stealthily, her footfalls silent as we trudged our way through the trees. My toes caught occasionally on downed limbs and overgrown weeds, but for the most part, I had no problem keeping up with her. Perspiration began to collect along my hairline, and after a while, my feet began to ache.

Do Shifters always have to travel on foot? I thought, frowning as I glared at the back of Karla's head. I envisioned her Turning into a beautiful mustang, with a flowing mane and strong, muscular legs. *An ass would have been more appropriate,* I thought, nearly chuckling.

Karla's phone rang, echoing off the canopy of leaves above us. She quickly snatched it open and pressed it to her ear.

"Yeah?" she answered. "About half a mile out." Her gaze shifted to me, and then she swallowed. "We will be there." She closed the phone and tucked it back into her jacket pocket.

"What?" I searched her face, trying to figure out what she was about to tell me. Something told me it wasn't good.

"They've located him." Her fingers twitched just slightly as she adjusted the strap of the satchel. *Something's wrong.* My stomach soured, and my head felt light. I wavered slightly, and unfortunately, Karla noticed. *This is not the time for a panic attack!* Feeling her eyes boring into me, I turned my back on her, needing a moment to compose myself.

"He's in an old carriage house." She paused before saying, "He's not alone."

I whirled around. "What do you mean?"

"They've caught the scent of a Shifter inside."

Chapter 20

I tried to determine what this meant. A Shifter from the Croix Clan? Where they expecting us? Would they attack? Then, my thoughts grew darker.

"What if he's experimenting on whoever's in there?" I asked, suddenly frightened for the stranger.

"There's no way to know," she replied, her face somber. "Tristan and Roland want to storm the house. We need to be there when they do."

I licked my dry lips and nodded. "Let's go."

We moved with a hurried pace, weaving our way through the shadowed forest. The vision of a Shifter imprisoned within that house pressed me forward. I had to stop that madman. Determined, I pushed my legs to pump faster. The urgency escalated with each step. The trees cleared, revealing an old carriage house dating back well into the nineteenth century.

Sure enough, parked in front of it was Dr. Moore's BMW. The ground beneath its tires well-worn with use. The house had been remodeled slightly to keep it functional, but the façade stayed true to its historic roots. The wood had been whitewashed and the shutters were painted black. Several lights were on inside.

Inhaling deeply, I sensed the bodies within. *A Shifter and a human.* I closed my eyes, homing in on Roland's distinct scent, realizing then how much I missed it, even in the short amount of time we had been apart.

By smell alone, I traced Roland to somewhere at the backside of the house. Feeling the undeniable need to be near him again, I followed Karla as she crept along the side of the building.

We found Roland and Tristan pressed against the house, their backs flat against the wooden panels. They were nude. I sucked in a sharp intake of air. *Of course, they'd be naked,* I thought. *They Shifted, in order to track him.* My eyes lingered on Roland's body. The moon's shimmery rays outlined the taut muscles in his shoulders and abs, illuminating him like a work of art in a museum.

Karla unzipped her satchel and reached inside. "What's the plan?" she asked, keeping her voice low as she tossed a bundle of clothes to Tristan.

He caught it with ease. "We only sense one Shifter, and the human," Tristan whispered. "We can overtake them easily." He handed a wad of clothes to Roland before quickly pulling on a T-shirt and jeans. He remained barefoot.

Karla's eyes flickered with what could only be described as exhilaration. She apparently lived for this. The thrill of the chase.

Roland dressed, yanking a black T-shirt over his broad chest. His hair was mussed, but somehow he made it look sexy. He looked over at me and mouthed, "You okay?"

I nodded, and tried my best to look confident, but I knew I was failing miserably. My heart ached for the person inside. Somehow, I just *knew* they were in danger. I remembered the terror I felt when Dr. Moore lifted the needle in the air above me. Knowing that he was inflicting the same fear into someone else, not only frightened me, but it enraged me.

My adrenaline started to spike, saturating my blood like steeping tea. I took in deep, cleansing breaths of night air, trying to repress the instinct to Turn. *Now is not the time.*

With Tristan behind her, Karla snuck around the side of the house to the front door. They moved quietly and smoothly, like a scent on a breeze. Roland and I followed behind them, and like the small army we were, we bravely took our positions at the front door.

With a quick glance at us, Roland and Tristan readied themselves, and then hurled their bodies against the thick wood. The door thumped but did not open. They reared back and again they charged, striking the door with their shoulders. This time, it gave, and the two Shifters stormed the house. The smell of dander was strong, but not offensive. Dr. Moore looked stunned standing in the hallway. His eyes were big and round, staring at us from behind a pair of black spectacles.

Karla sprinted toward him. Seizing his arms, she restrained him easily. He resisted for a moment, but when Tristan pinned his arms behind his back, the doctor relented. His eyes lifted, and for a moment my heart tugged for the man I once knew. Like a worn rag doll, he looked battered and old.

"Wade Walker sends his regards," Tristan hissed against Dr. Moore's ear.

Karla wrenched his wrists tighter, causing him to wince. "And the Clan can't wait to personally send theirs," she said through gritted teeth.

They pushed him forward, causing him to stumble.

They didn't go easy on him, shoving and snarling the entire way outside. Roland was already on the phone, alerting Wade of Moore's capture.

With Moore gone, I finally took in the rest of the house. It resembled a clinic, which made my stomach turn. It had all the typical equipment you would find at your doctor's office. Thermometers, a blood pressure cuff, and otoscope. There was even a height chart and scale. Dread pressed upon me like a weight. *What went on here?* I slowly turned around myself, taking everything in.

A bricked fireplace in the center of the room seemed to section off the house into two parts. An almost-friendly clinic in the front, and a sterile make-shift laboratory in the back. White cabinets lined the back walls, and there was shiny technical equipment everywhere.

My gaze drifted farther, noticing the loft upstairs. *The Shifter.* I ran to the staircase, quickly climbing it, though my chest felt as it was crushing into pieces. *Please let them be okay, I thought. Please don't let me be too late.* I skidded to a halt when I faced a closed door. I inhaled, and again caught the scent of bird dander. *The person inside must be bird-Shifter,* I thought as I touched the doorknob.

I felt Roland come up behind me. We exchanged a nervous glance before I twisted the doorknob, only to find resistance. I pulled harder.

"It's locked," I said, looking at Roland. My stomach knotted. *I was right.* The Shifter was being used as a test experiment-against their will.

Roland threw his shoulder into the door, snapping the hinges easily. He barged into the room, with me right behind him. I peered over his shoulder, finding a petite woman shivering in the corner. I stared at her. The eyes that looked back at me were my own—green, and wide with fear. Her ebony hair shorn shockingly short. The edges shaggy as though they had been hacked with common kitchen shears.

Though our hair length was different, it was as though I were looking in a mirror. Sadly, though, the version of me across the room was emaciated and pale.

The room suddenly lurched, as did my stomach. I leaned into my knees, willing myself steady. Roland gaped at the woman, his mouth hanging open as he slowly shifted his eyes to me. He touched my back gently, rubbing soothing circles between my shoulder blades.

I finally stood upright, clasping Roland's hand to keep me sound. Sweat saturated my shirt, and I felt woozy on my feet. The edges of my vision, and not to mention, my sanity wavered. *No,* I thought. *It can't be her.* I studied her bright green eyes and pitch-black hair. *Could it?*

Roland's hand tightened around mine, anchoring me back to reality. "Who are you?" Roland questioned the woman.

The woman retreated farther into the corner, but her jade eyes never strayed from us. She hugged herself, rubbing her hands over her elbows in a sort of comforting self-embrace. I continued to stare at her, enthralled by our similarities. The curve of her chin matched mine, the slope of her nose, and even the way she fidgeted nervously on her feet mimicked my own movements.

"We can help you," Roland persisted.

In the distance, I heard the sound of tires crunching across the ground. Roland must have heard it too. His nostrils flared, and I knew he was capturing the scent of someone, or something.

Karla peered into the room. "Someone is approaching. We cannot place the scent." Her eyes moved to the woman, rounding slightly before switching back to Roland. "We need to go," she urged. "Now."

"What about her?" I asked, looking from Roland to the woman cowering in the corner.

His golden eyes looked resigned, but he gave a deep sigh of defeat. Looking at Karla, he said, "Deliver Moore to Walker. We'll be there soon."

Karla's brow creased as she frowned.

"Go," Roland growled.

Her frown deepened, but she backed out of the room and disappeared.

Roland turned to the woman. "We can't force you to come with us, but if you need help, we can give it to you."

The woman scoffed.

"Are you being held prisoner here?" I asked, taking a step forward.

The woman's eyes darted to me, watching my movement like a frightened animal.

"I serve a greater purpose," she said, her tone firm and unapologetic.

Roland arched an interested eyebrow. "A greater purpose?"

We exchanged a tense look, before the woman spoke again.

"One day, Shifters will emerge from the shadows

and become the majority, rather than the minority."

"Great." Roland threw up his hands in disgust. "A disciple of Victor Rizzo."

The woman's face remained stone-like, though I could have sworn I caught a trace of confusion briefly color her face.

"You don't know of him?" I asked, desperately searching her face.

Her eyes locked onto mine, and I knew she hadn't. I could read her as well as I knew my own thoughts. I wanted to touch her, to feel her skin, to be near her. I moved slowly across the floor. She backed away, her body tensing as I drew closer.

"Who's forcing you to do this?" I asked her gently.

"She's not being forced. She's supporting an effort," a voice said from behind me.

I turned, my hand flying to my mouth to smother a scream, because there, looking back at me...was my father.

Chapter 21

I stared at him, breathing through my fingers, too afraid to drop my hand for fear that the shriek building within my stomach would escape, and with it all of my strength would disappear.

He stood tall, framed by the doorway, but his face looked terribly saddened.

"What the hell is going on here?" Roland demanded.

My father's gaze moved around the entire room before landing on Roland. His eyes were like ice, and his features just as sharp.

"You," he spat, pulling a gun from his belt and aiming it at Roland. "Don't get to ask any questions." He fired the gun to the left of Roland, blowing a hole in the wall just over his shoulder. "Now, be a nice little pussycat and step outside so I can have a chat with my daughters."

My heart squeezed. So it was true. She was my sister. *My twin sister.* The woman's eyes widened, and her mouth went slack as she stared at me, our similarities finally connecting within her brain.

"How did you know—" Roland blurted out, his face full of bewilderment.

"That you're a Shifter?" my father finished. His expression was deadpan as he said, "You reek of it."

Roland looked confused. "You have Shifter

blood?"

"Unfortunately," Father shot, his eyes looking lethal as he repositioned the gun. It pointed straight at Roland's heart.

The walls of the room felt as if they were shrinking in on me. My throat on the verge of collapse as I pieced everything together. *My father is a Shifter?*

"But I can't make out your scent," Roland said, holding his hands up in surrender, his eyes locked on the barrel of the gun.

My father let out an eerie laugh. One that I had never heard before now. "Would you like to know why?" He smiled, but it was far from pleasant.

I shuddered. My father had taken over a whole new persona, and it was downright frightening. He had always been a gruff individual, but this side of him was far more dangerous than the demanding tyrant I experienced growing up. This side was pure evil.

The muscles in his face began to twitch. My stomach knotted as I watched his normally handsome features twisted into something sinister. His mouth opened and out came a chilling, gargled scream. His body convulsed wildly. With the gun still trained on Roland's chest, my father Turned into a creature so vile, it made my skin crawl and the bile rise in my throat.

I clamped my eyes shut for a moment, wanting so badly to blot out the image that was now permanently tattooed across my memory.

A hissing sound slashed fear into my gut. Snapping my eyes back open, I stared down at the thing that was once my father. His arms and legs were still undeniably human, but black, slick as oil, scales crept up his neck and face as though attempting to suffocate him. A flared cobra hood fanned out behind his ears. One eye had a dark pupil, like a chunk of hard obsidian, while his other eye remained his usual steely gray.

A forked tongue flicked out of his scaly lips. His mismatched eyes narrowed, and something menacing flashed behind them. "This is why." He dragged out his words, like a hissing serpent, sending a shiver down my spine.

"What are you?" Roland asked, his caramel eyes openly repulsed by the hideous creature in front of us.

"I'm a Shifter, just like you," he said, his tongue slipping out again to taste the air. "But unlike you, I wasn't satisfied with being a freak of nature. I hate what I am. For years, I've been trying to isolate the gene, getting closer and closer to the day I could reverse it. Until Shandy was born, I had been testing serums on myself, and as you can see, they have been *marginally* successful.

Shandy. My gaze leapt to my sister. *Her name is Shandy.* For a moment I grew lost in the what-ifs. What if my father didn't have Shifter blood? What if my mother knew Shandy was still alive? What if she discovered what my father has been doing the past twenty-seven years…?

"Her blood has given me a fresh, untampered gene pool to research," my father continued, nearly gloating now,"thus enabling me to create a serum that will eradicate the Shifting gene with just one injection."

My vison glowed red with anger. "How could you make your own daughter a test subject?" I questioned in disbelief. "How could you take away my sister?"

"She isn't your sister. She's an animal." His voice

flat and unapologetic.

"What would killing your own race prove?" Roland asked.

My father's reptilian face darkened with anger, and his lips pulled into a sneer. "Foolish felis-Shifter. Haven't you ever heard the saying, 'curiosity killed the cat'?" He stalked toward Roland, his movements lissome, and almost hypnotic.

I became suddenly aware and alarmed at how comfortable he was in this atrocious form. With my stomach fisting violently at the thought, I watched the graceful flow of his body, and the way his hooded serpent-like head flared with his movements like second nature.

Roland backed up until his back hit the wall, his eyes trained on the gun still gripped within my father's hand.

I wanted to Turn, but there was no time. I rushed my father, adrenaline pumping through me like boiling water. A squawk echoed the small room, and for a moment, I was distracted. A hawk circled the room overhead.

My father used the distraction to his advantage. Dripping with venom, his pointed fangs sank deep into Roland's shoulder.

Time slowed.

My heartbeat pulsed loudly within my ears, nearly caused me to double over, but I pushed on. *Roland!* I lunged at my father, digging my nails across his face, careful to aim for his human flesh and not the tough reptile skin. He let out a snarl, backhanding me with the butt of the gun. Pain shot through me like a speeding bullet. My mouth throbbed from the impact of metal on bone. My body ached everywhere from the hard landing on the floor. My vision began to grow spotty and the sounds around me grew muffled. I fought against the approaching darkness, struggling to sit up.

I blinked several times, distantly aware of the screeching hawk above. The tangy bite of copper filled my mouth. I choked on it, spitting it out, but instantly regretting it as I caught sight of the bright red spot against the wood grain floor. Ignoring a pounding headache, I forced myself onto swaying feet, only to nearly collapse where I stood.

I sought out Roland.

He was lying in a heap, his body unnaturally still and lifeless as my father loomed over him. His forked tongue ran over his sharp fangs, the look of sick satisfaction across his smug face. Sensing my stare, he whipped around to look me straight on. "The venom is disabling his nervous system." With the toe of his shoe, he prodded Roland's motionless body. It didn't move.

My heart crushed. A broken wail broke from my lips as I crumbled to the floor. Completely wrecked, I lay there defeated. Something inside me felt lost, and empty. Completely consumed by emotions, my breath hitched, and my shoulders shook with each sob.

"Disgusting," my father growled. "Crying over a pathetic house cat." He stepped over Roland's body. His footfalls were unnaturally heavy as he stalked toward me. Forced to acknowledge him, I wiped my face, peering up at him through stinging eyelids. When he drew too close, I shrank away from him, terrified of this twisted version of my father.

"Get away from me." I scrambled to Roland's side. "You're a lunatic." I took Roland's hand, and lifted it to my mouth. I kissed it, inhaling the scent of him. His skin was still warm. I held his fingers against my cheek. *Oh Roland.* I wept openly, not giving a damn about my father, or my own life to be frank. All that mattered right now was Roland.

Carefully, I brushed the hair from his forehead. He looked peaceful. If it wasn't for the twin punctures in his shoulder, both livid and oozing, then I could have believed he was merely sleeping. Overcome by the weight of guilt on my shoulders, I collapsed onto Roland's chest, heaving with a hard sob that wracked my entire body.

I sensed movement behind me. I snapped upright to find my father advancing on me.

"Get up, girl. It's time you understand your place in all of this."

"*My* place?"

"You think I didn't notice your eyes?" His words were cutting—like it was my fault they had Turned. Like it was my fault he had Shifter blood running rampant through his veins. The leathery scent of him grew stronger as he drew closer. This time, I caught traces of something stale, and burnt.

"Why are you doing this?" I demanded.

With his scaly lips drawn back, he gave me a mocking smile. "Our kind is on this Earth by a series of unfortunate biological mistakes." He pointed the gun to the ceiling and fired.

I jumped in my skin, my heart nearly exploding in my chest. Plaster and splintered wood rained down on the floor. My stomach churned violently, and I realized it was from the fierce loathing I felt. I dug my fingernails into my palms to keep myself grounded.

"I don't want to be a biological mistake!" he shouted, anger vibrating off him like an eerie aura.

"Thanks to evolution," he continued. "the gene has manifested into what we have today. A superhuman, if you will, with the abnormal ability to take on a second skin. This is totally unnatural and unethical. The only being that can take on another form is Satan. The fucking Devil himself, Layla." His hood flared wide, sending all of my instincts into flight mode. I wanted to run. Every fiber in me was alarming: DANGER! RUN!

Instead, I squared my shoulders. "Satan, huh? Well, isn't it ironic that you take the form of the serpent," I said, glaring at him, willing him to feel my immense hatred.

"We're animals, for Christ's sake, Layla," he continued, seemingly oblivious to my heated stare. "And animals are impulsive creatures with no boundaries or morals."

My father tossed the gun to the floor. It landed heavily and slid across the wood. I eyed it, wondering if I should reach for it. Would I have the nerve to aim it at my own father? Would I be able to pull the trigger? He began pacing the floor, the same way he always did whenever I was on the receiving end of one of his pompous rants.

"Shifters should not be walking this Earth, Layla. I want to weed out the impetuous gene," he said. "And return the world back to the order for which is was intended. Simple human genetics. No anomalies. No Shifters."

"You are not God," I said through grounded teeth.

"*God* has nothing to do with this, child," he laughed. "You think God intended for a race of mongrels to spawn?"

"Mongrels? That's a harsh word for something that runs through your very own blood."

"Unfortunately, Layla, that's the hand I've been dealt." He clasped his hands behind his back as he strolled across the floor. "But fate chose me, so in turn, I am giving the world a gift. An antidote to this illegitimate race. With help from Shandy, I've finally discovered a reversing serum."

"How do you even know it works?" I asked, cringing a little as he whipped his head to look at me. The cobra hood opened wide like a cape, pulsating with each breath he took.

"My dear child, you know me well enough to know that I have researched each and every DNA strand within my body until the point of obsession. Devouring each chromosome and dissecting every double helix until I found the abnormality."

"You're crazy," I blurted out.

He merely smirked, stalking forward until he was looming over me. Glossy scales blotted out much of his face. The wide flare of his hood was intimating. I felt much like prey, and he was preparing to strike.

Father let out a deep, chilling laugh. In all my childhood, I had never seen the man smile, or laugh, but here he was, doing both in a maniacal way.

Like the serpent he was, he lashed out with his arm, snatching me by my hair. I tried to fight against him, but his strength was much more powerful than usual. Pain splintered its way across my scalp as his fingers gripped tighter.

With his free hand, he pointed behind his left ear. "Do you see that?"

I had seen it. I had seen it countless times growing up. It was a patch of rough, scarred skin. When I was a child, he told me the scar had come from boiling grease that had splattered from a frying pan when he was a young boy. Confused and frightened, I nodded woodenly and mumbled, "Yes."

"It's my Mark."

His Mark? I squinted at it. The small spot was disfigured, and thick with bumpy scars. Faintly, I could make out the tiny scales, which matched the snakeskin that covered most of his body.

"I burned it myself in high school, trying to rid myself of the blasted Mark, promising myself that I would one day be free of the gene that Turned me into a monster."

He seized my arm, squeezing painfully tight. He yanked me down the staircase and through the house, back toward the makeshift laboratory.

"No," I cried, struggling against him. He only clamped down harder, the pressure practically snapping my bones.

With a shove, he sent me sailing into the lab table. My hip smarted as it connected with the corner. I thought about Turning—willing all of my anger into Shifting me into something fierce. But nothing happened. My mind was far too rampant to focus on channeling anything except fear and confusion.

Father rounded the workstation and snatched open a cabinet door. He reached in and removed something. With a face frozen in a perpetual grimace, he lifted a syringe into the air. Light refracted off the thick liquid inside. "This serum will rid the receiver of the vexing anomaly." The horrific way he hissed out the words like a snake caused me pause.

My father is not only a lunatic. He is also a predator. A cunning, feels no remorse, predator.

Regarding me with disgust, he said, "As Matriarch, you'll need to be dealt with first, of course. Can't have you trying to fuck up everything I have worked so hard for all these years."

I swallowed back a scream.

The color of rust water, the serum promised normality to my father, but to me, it meant erasing my newfound identity. I had to destroy it.

Movement caught my eye. *The hawk.* It circled once, then screeched loudly as it sank its talons into my father's shoulder. He expelled a pained hiss, but before the bird could fly off, he wrapped his hands around the bird's neck, smothering a squawk.

The corners of Father's mouth quirked into a deranged version of a smile as he brought the bird to eye level.

His forked tongue slipped out, flicking across the hawk's beak. "You dare defy me?" He gave a mocking laugh, then drove the syringe down, piercing the bird's wing. Without a hint of hesitation, he pushed the plunger down, administering the honey-like substance into the bird's system. The hawk thrashed and screamed. Father held it for a moment, seemingly enjoying its torture. "You're seeing firsthand the effects of the serum, Layla."

He released his cage-like grip, allowing the bird to drop heavily to the floor.

"What did you do?" I stared at the poor animal as it writhed in agony. My heart ached for it. I ran to it, sinking to my knees, and cupping it gently with my hands.

"At this very moment the Shifting gene is dissipating, unwinding its disgusting barbs from her chromosomes."

"Her?" My gaze tore from the bird in my hands to my father. "What do you mean her? This isn't…"

He arched an eyebrow, a sadistic smile touching his lips. "Who else could it be?"

Shandy. Tears welled in my eyes as I watched her beautiful, sleek feathers break off, falling lightly to the floor like snowflakes. Her beak retracted and took the shape of a human nose. Bones snapped and stretched until the naked body of my sister lay before me. Her green eyes opened and blinked wearily. She licked her lips, and coughed haggardly before her gaze went from foggy, to fierce, zeroing in on me as if I were a target.

Her nostrils flared, taking in my scent. Her sweet face paled, and she cinched her eyes tight for a moment, holding in either a whimper or maybe a scream. I wouldn't blame her if she did both.

A loud crash at the front door caused me to start. The door splintered and smashed inward as if blown apart by a bomb. In poured an army of Wanderlust Shifters.

"Seize him!" shouted Wade Walker, his white hair standing out among the crowd of men. "And kill him on the spot."

My heart compressed painfully in my chest. *Kill him?* I stood on shaky legs, blocking my father from the oncoming Shifters. I stood there, torn, the ache in my heart unbearable as I weighed the situation. My Mate is lying dead in the other room at the hands, or more pointedly, the fangs of my father. My sister's Shifting ability has been stolen, literally *ripped* away from her, again, by the cruel hands of my father, and yet here I stand, shielding him as the Wanderlust Clan converge to complete their orders to take his life. Why? He deserved whatever fate awaited him, but still I guarded him.

"Wait," I cried, with hands out before me, trying to calm the quickly escalating tension in the air. "What about the Judgment Panel?"

"Assholes like him don't get a fair trial," snarled a thin man whom I'd never met. "Swift justice comes to those who fuck with our race." He quickly Shifted into a huge alligator, his massive jaws wasting no time to clamp on my father's leg like a steel trap. Blood slickened the floorboards. Seeing the pain on my father's face was too much for me. This man, though sick and delusional, was still my father. He deserved punishment, but not an outright execution.

Without a plan, I simply reacted. Kicking at the alligator until he loosened his hold, I was out of breath when I ordered my father, "Go!".

I watched him limp away, disappearing out the backdoor before I turned back to Wade and the rest of the advancing men. "By my orders, Harvey Carson will be tried according to Shifter Laws and will face the Judgment Panel to receive his sentence." I kept my voice strong and level, demanding respect as the Matriarch.

Wade lifted a white eyebrow, his face full of apprehension and budding anger. Through tight lips, he said. "Very well, Matriarch, but know that even your intervention will not keep him from receiving the strictest penalty allowed by Shifter Laws." He turned to the awaiting men. "Seize him and bring him back to the compound."

The Shifters flew into action, their stampede of feet thundering through the carriage house, and out the backdoor in pursuit of my father.

"I'm not asking for leniency," I said to Wade. "I'm asking for fairness." We met each other's gaze, neither of us willing to yield or show weakness. Pushing my shoulders back, I made a vow to myself that I would not relent. *Wade Walker will respect my decision. He will respect me.* Holding him in my insistent stare, I held my posture as rigid as possible. *I will not back down.*

Wade averted his eyes first, signaling my power and my triumph.

My shoulder began to tighten, and itch. I reached up, touching it lightly with my fingertips. A small patch of skin, just below my shoulder blade felt oddly warm, and scaly.

"Your scaled-creature Mark," Wade informed me. His eyes held mine and his friendly smile returned to his face. "You saved your father, whose true nature was reptilian." He studied my eyes. "Your eyes indicate that you've saved a furry already."

I thought back to the rhesus macaque and nodded.

"Looks like all you got left is a winged animal, and you've earned all your Matriarchal Marks."

Feathered, furred and scaled. Then I gasped, remembering my sister. I ran to her.

She was lying on the floor, eyes closed, and mouth parted. My chest squeezed. *Oh no! Did the serum kill her?* I fell to my knees beside her.

"Shandy?" I said quietly. She didn't stir. The rush of hot tears rose behind my eyes. *No!* I felt as though my throat was closing in. "Shandy," I repeated, shaking her. *I can't lose you! I just found you! Please wake up!*

Shandy's eyes fluttered open.

Relief flooded through me. "Oh thank God." A hospital gown hung on a hook nearby. I leapt up, snagging it off the hook for her. I laid it over Shandy, trying to warm her ice-cold body.

"I was so worried," I said, taking her hand into both of mine. "Are you all right?"

Our matching green eyes touched, and I smiled. She didn't return it, in fact, her lips pulled into a tight grimace before she whispered, "Kill me now."

"What?"

Her voice was so faint, I wasn't sure if I heard her right, or if I even heard her small voice at all.

"Kill me now! I'm weak and helpless without the Shifting gene," she said, her tone clearer now. She jerked her hand away and pulled herself into a sitting position. "My own father stripped me of the only thing that made me strong." She began to cry, and I cried with her, feeling my heart break for my twin sister. How horrible it must have been growing up alone. Used as a test subject.

"Don't you see?" she continued, slipping into the hospital gown. "In this world, all I'll ever be, is weak and helpless." She tied the strings at her neck. In the gown she looked sicker. Like an actual patient with pallid skin pulled taut across sharp cheekbones.

She brought her knees up to her chest and locked her thin arms around them.

"You're not weak, or helpless." I touched her shoulder. "You're human." I sniffed. "What's wrong with being human?" I asked, searching her face, wishing I could erase her pain.

She laughed through her sobs. "I'd rather die." She shook free of me, startling me back onto my heels. She darted out of the room, taking the stairs two at time as she ran.

I jumped to my feet and went after her. My boots clunked their way up the solid steps, my adrenaline pumping through my blood.

I skidded to a stop when I reached the top of the stairs. She stood stock-still, gripping Father's gun tightly with both hands. My stomach twisted as I glanced down at Roland, still lying where I left him. I closed my eyes for a beat, composing myself before I shattered right on the spot. *There is nothing you can do for him now...but you can save Shandy...*

When I opened my eyes, I said, "Shandy", holding my hands outward in order to calm the building tension in the air. "Put the gun down."

"No," she shouted, clutching the gun tighter. "You don't understand. Shifting is all I know." Tears streamed down her face, leaving wet trails along her dirty cheeks. "He made me feel that I was doing something important, something significant with my life." Her eyes slowly moved around the small room, her face getting increasingly rigid with anger. "He kept me cooped up here, filling my head with lies!" Her shouts echoed off the walls, making it feel tiny and empty. I tried to imagine living here but couldn't.

The isolation and loneliness she must have felt all those years surely had scarred her. I wondered if my father intimidated her, like he did me, and I instantly knew the answer. Of course he did. He used her like a lab rat, and deep inside, the small part of me that still cared for him, died. *The bastard deserves whatever the Clan does to him*, I thought.

"Did you know about me?" I asked, trying to distract her. "Did you know that you had a twin?"

She stared at me, her lips trembling as she said, "No."

"What about Mom?"

For the first time, a hint of uncertainty colored her face, the gun lowered a fraction as she considered it. Her bare feet shifted nervously.

"She thinks you're dead," I told her, my voice cracking. It pained me to say it, but she had to know. She had to know that she had a mother who mourned her, who loved her, who would be thrilled to know she was alive.

Shandy paled, and I thought her knees were about to buckle as several emotions passed across her features. And just as suddenly, she steeled, her expression hardened as she lifted the gun to her head, pressing the barrel against her temple.

"I should be," she said icily. Her eyes closed, and her fingers shook as she held the gun against her head.

"Shandy," I began. "You deserve a new beginning." I resisted the urge to fling myself at her, instead evenly pacing my steps, moving quietly and slowly, trying not to provoke her to do anything rash. "We can fix this. We can put our lives back together. You want to know why? Because this time, all the pieces are here." I pointed at her and said, "You" before motioning to myself and saying, "Me. Us."

"No," she said, shaking her head roughly. "I can't be a human. It's what *he* wanted." She opened her eyes, locking them straight onto mine. "Don't you see that?"

Her voice rose. Tears streamed down her cheeks as her tortured eyes flashed with anger. "He won."

Luckily, my Shifter genes didn't fail me. I easily sensed the twitch in her finger just before she squeezed the trigger. I leapt at her, slamming my body into hers, knocking the breath from her lungs as I fell against her. The deafening sound of a gunshot rang through the air.

She slapped at me. "Leave me alone!"

I fastened my hands on her shoulders, holding firm as she struggled against me. "Shandy! Stop it. Please."

She thrashed a moment longer, then latched her wild green eyes onto mine. Bloodshot, and anguished, I read them like a beloved book. She was enraged, dejected, overwhelmed and above all, bewildered. Her life was a clusterfuck to begin with, but in the past half-hour, her reality, the very reason for her existence had been ripped away from her.

Her shoulders sagged beneath my grip, and she began shaking as she cried. She lowered her head, leaning into my chest as she openly wept.

I smoothed her hair, shushing her as I patted her back consolingly. "It's all right. We will figure this out, together."

I held her for a long time, refusing to let go until she was ready. If all I had to give her right now was my strength, then damnit that was what I was going to give her.

Eventually the tears subsided, and she finally lifted her head from my shoulder. I wiped her cheeks and gave her an encouraging smile. Her gaze swept over me, her eyes growing round with surprise.

"What?" I asked, recoiling slightly under her bold stare.

She reached out, her fingers touching my hair lightly. "A feather," she explained, sifting through the strands.

I looked down and saw a beautiful turquoise feather. I lifted my hand, tracking the feather down to my hair roots. It was slender and dainty, easily concealable, should I wish to hide it within my thick hair. I ran my fingertips over the soft wisps. *My winged Mark.* My heart swelled with pride, and overwhelming happiness. *I saved Shandy.*

I pulled her close and hugged her tight. Emotion started to overtake me when I heard a low groan nearby. I whirled around, my breath hitching in my throat when I noticed Roland starting to stir…

Chapter 22

Roland moaned and pressed the heels of his hands to his forehead. Unable to take the distance, I hurled myself at him, folding into his body. I wept into the tender crook of his neck. I inhaled his distinct, heavenly scent, and I wanted nothing more than to lose myself in it. *Thank you, God, for giving him back to me.*

His fingers sought out my chin, lifting it gently, urging me to look at him. His eyes fixed onto mine, and a strained smile pulled at his lips.

"Hey," he said, touching his hand clumsily to my face. His fingers traced my cheek, the warmth of them soothing me, just as they always had.

I leaned into his palm as a flood of different emotions ran through me. Relief. Elation. Love. "How are you not..."

"Dead?" he said, with a soft snicker. "Sheer will and defiance, I suppose."

"Here I thought it was because you had nine lives." I smiled.

He tried to chuckle, but the way his eyes tightened let me know he was still in deep pain.

With my help, and a lot of effort from Roland, he sat up. He winced when he adjusted his shoulders. I pulled aside the collar of his shirt, getting a good look at the two puncture wounds left by my father's fangs. Swollen, the area was an angry shade of red, the holes glistening an odd shade of green.

"His venom isn't potent anymore," Shandy offered somewhere behind me. "A side effect of all the testing he did on himself."

I thought about that. Not only was he unable to fully Shift into a cobra anymore, but he'd diluted his venom to the point it was no longer lethal. Regarding the sweat that dotted Roland's hairline, and the ashen hue to his normally tanned skin tone, it was obvious it still packed a powerful punch.

"So he'd been testing on himself as well," Roland said, trying to put together what had transpired since he lost consciousness. "That explains the partial Shift." Slowly, his eyes tracked the distance to Shandy. "And her?"

I swallowed on a dry throat. "She's my sister. *Twin* sister."

Roland expression smoothed.

I pressed on, "He's been testing on her all these years, trying to find a reversing agent." I glanced at Shandy, my voice growing smaller as I said, "He's created a serum…and it works."

Roland studied her for a moment. "What do you mean, it works?"

The words were hard to form. "It removed her Shifter gene. She's human now."

Shandy shuddered, and bitterly wiped away the tears that slipped down her chin.

Roland's gaze moved back to me. "Where is Carson now?"

I lifted a shoulder. "I'm guessing the Clan has caught up to him by now. They're taking him to the compound."

"We'd better go," he said. "The Clan is not going to wait to set his Judgment."

I nodded and turned to Shandy. "You don't have to come, but I need to be there when he receives his sentence."

Shandy climbed to her feet, her face tear-streaked and swollen. "I want to be there."

I walked to her and wrapped an arm protectively around her shoulder. "Are you sure?"

She gave me a stiff nod, before wiggling out of my grip. Her feet padded across the floorboards to a small oak armoire.

"We'll wait outside," I told her.

I helped Roland to his feet, and together we descended the staircase, leaving Shandy to change out of the depressing hospital gown.

Moving through the laboratory, my stomach soured at the sight of all the tools and shiny equipment. My imagination went wild, considering all the horrors Shandy must have seen. The trials and unsuccessful attempts. The anger from my father when he failed.

Roland stopped me in mid-step, pulling me into him and enfolding me into a strong embrace. I laid my cheek against his chest. His wounds smelled faintly of copper and sulfur. I held him, the crushing thought of almost losing him overwhelmed me until I began to sob. He smoothed my hair, clutching me tighter as he whispered, "I've got you. I won't let go until you're ready. You say when."

Oh, those tender words. He had been saying them since the day we met. It seemed like a lifetime ago. Zbornies, Kurt's assault, Roland rescuing me.

I lifted my face from his chest and gazed into his

beautiful, golden eyes. As sure as the sun would rise in the morning, I knew I loved him. Deeply. Almost innately, as if it were predetermined by Mother Nature herself.

"Roland." I licked my lips, not knowing where to start. His eyes were soft, gazing at me with a gentleness that relaxed me into spilling every thought that was dancing in my head. "In my lifetime, I have only been sure of one thing. The choices you make guide you to your destiny. And now, looking at you, I can say I was actually right. Every decision I've made from the day I was born, led me to this point. They led me straight to you, straight into your arms. I know, without a doubt, there is no other place I'd rather be. I love you, Roland Stone.

"Layla," he said, his voice raspy and raw with emotion. "You should already know my feelings. I don't think I've done a good job hiding them." He smiled and took my face into his warm palms. "My heart beats for you, and you only. There was no one before you, and there could never be anyone after you. I belong to you. The moment I laid eyes on you, I was Claimed—mind, body and soul." He covered my mouth with his, kissing me deeply. When we finally parted, he murmured, "I love you."

My heart nearly imploded. Roland was mine. The label "boyfriend" was definitely inadequate—almost laughable really. Roland was so much more. He was my Mate. Our love, and our bond, was strong, and permanent.

I felt a presence come up behind us. Untangling myself from Roland, I sought his hand and took my place beside him. Shandy stood at the foot of the stairwell. Sharp knees peeked through the holes in her jeans and a loose sweater hung well past her fingertips.

"Are you ready for this?" I asked her.

She gave me a curt nod. Her gazed floated across the span of the lab, and then with a swallow, she shuffled out the front door. Roland and I exchanged an incredulous look before following her outside. We were surprised to find Wade waiting outside in a four-door pickup truck. He waved at us from behind the steering wheel.

Roland broke off first, meeting Wade at the driver's side window. Shandy stood alone, her head rotating in every direction, taking everything in. I took another glance at the carriage house. I wondered if it was the first time Shandy had left it? Would she want to return to it?

Roland's voice interrupted my thinking. "Layla."

I acknowledged him with a nod and went to Shandy. "We should go," I said quietly.

She gave the thick woods surrounding the house one last, long look, and then followed me to Wade's truck.

Roland and Wade were deep in conversation. Though I was curious what happened to my father, I was thankful their hushed voices were undistinguishable to the human ear. Shandy didn't need to hear any gory details on his takedown.

I opened the truck door and waited for Shandy to climb inside before I slid in beside her. The leather seats squeaked beneath us as we made ourselves comfortable behind Wade. Roland sank into the passenger seat, clicking his seatbelt into place as he questioned Wade.

"When's Judgment?" he asked.

Wade put the truck into drive and pulled onto the worn dirt path. "Tonight," he said, flicking his eyes to the rearview mirror. Our gazes met, and I held firm, letting him know that I was not weak, nor was I concerned about the approaching Judgment of my father. What little love I had salvaged for him from my childhood, was now dead and gone. Forever.

He tore his gaze from me, turning his attention back to the road. Wade kept his window down, his arm leaning out of it, the other casually gripping the steering wheel. The pickup bounced its way down the unpaved road, until finally we pulled onto the main highway.

Watching his white hair whip in the wind, I couldn't take it anymore. I had to know what he Turned into. "Wade, what's your true nature?" I asked.

His blue eyes lifted to the rearview mirror again. "Bison," he answered with a laugh.

I sank back into my seat. *Of course,* I thought with a smile. His broad back and massive stature should have been an indication. "Fitting," I said with a smile.

"Oh give me a home, where the buffalo roam..." he sang in a twang that only a true southerner could manage.

Roland and I laughed, but Shandy just stared out the window. Her fingers dug into the seat beneath her, her skin stretched tight over her knuckles. I wanted to ask her so many things. Have you ever been away from the carriage house? Have you ever driven a car before? Have you ever been *in* a car before? The strained look on her face told me now was not the time to ask.

Reacting on pure instinct, I slowly reached across the space between us and touched her hand. Her head whipped around, and her emerald eyes bore into mine. Her nostrils flared, and she seemed to be battling something internally.

I gave her an encouraging smile.

We stared at one another for a while. I tried to relay through the silence that I was there for her, and always would be. She looked away first, pursing her lips and turning her back to me.

We rode in silence the rest of the way. The Wanderlust compound eventually came into view like a daydream. Small and distant at first, then sharpening into the sprawling complex it was. The truck bumped along the dirt road, passing several rows of well-kept horse stables.

The property looked deserted. Not a single Shifter was outside.

Wade threw the truck into park, jerking my thoughts into focus. "Looks like most everybody is already waiting at the Judgment Quarters," he told Roland.

Roland's eyes scanned the property. "They're eager for retribution."

"They're eager for blood," Wade replied, getting out of the truck. Roland followed behind him, slamming the door, leaving me alone with Shandy.

"You can wait here, if you want," I said to her.

Her gaze swung to me, her green eyes direct and unflinching. "I will not."

In that moment, with her rigid back, and daring eyes, she fit the image of 'Matriarch' more than I ever could.

Roland tapped on my window, so I got out of the truck, my senses immediately assaulted when I did. The scents in the air ran the gambit of every possible Shifter in the Clan, from the clawed, hooved, and winged to the cold-blooded. *The entire Clan is here to ensure he receives proper Judgment,* I thought with a sudden dip in my gut. *Everyone wants him to pay for what he's done.*

Needing support, I took Roland firmly by the hand. Shandy slipped out of the truck quietly, lingering close by to ensure she was not left behind.

Wade led the way, his broad shoulders cutting a path through the scent-thick air in front of us. His boots clomped heavily on the cabin's wooden porch steps. Tristan met us at the door. "Sir, we've arranged a list of possible participants for the Judgment Panel." He handed Wade a sheet of paper. "After you've reviewed it, I'll make the proper arrangements."

Wade scanned the list, his blue eyes narrowing as he considered each name. "This list is fine, except I want one of his kin on the Panel."

My breath caught, and my mouth went dry. *How could one of us help decide his fate?* I looked over my shoulder. Shandy was standing awkwardly near the front door, her eyes darting madly around the room as she picked at the frayed cuffs of her sweater. It was painfully obvious that she was uncomfortable being outside of the carriage house, and that resonated deep within me. *That house is all she knows. She knows nothing of the outside world.* I knew then, that I must protect my sister. She was vulnerable, and not to mention unstable, so sitting in on her father's sentencing could easily put her over the edge.

"I'll do it." My voice was not as strong as I had hoped, breaking just slightly.

"Excellent," Wade said, thrusting the paper into Tristan's chest. "We got ourselves a Panel." He strolled to his office, with Tristan in tow. The door slammed shut behind them, leaving us alone with the quiet of the room, and our thoughts.

We all remained silent for a long time. It wasn't until Wade's office door opened, and Tristan came out that we finally spoke.

"What's going on?" Roland asked.

"The Panel has been summoned. Judgment is set to begin in one hour." He shifted his eyes to me. "The Clan is calling for immediate action. The Panel is assembling now. Come, I'll accompany you to the Judgment Quarters." He started down an alternate hallway.

I hesitated, turning to Roland.

"It's all right," he assured me. "It's customary for The Panel to be seated first. The rest of the Clan will be allowed in the Quarters soon." He squeezed my hand and gave me a smile. "I'll be right there with you."

I looked over at Shandy. She was sitting in an oversized leather chair, her legs pulled up to her chest. Her eyes shifted to mine, but only hold them for a second before casting them down to the floor. I wanted to hug her but didn't. *Poor Shandy. She's been through so much.*

"I'll have someone watch her while Judgment is in session," Roland said.

I nodded before hurrying after Tristan. With his long legs, he was able to move quickly, briskly rounding corners and turning down adjacent halls. Finally, he stopped at a closed door. Indicating it, he said, "This is it. There are nine members of the Panel.

After the crimes have been read, you will convene and conclude a proper punishment. The offender will have a chance to make a plea, though don't expect Wade to consider it."

Without saying another word, Tristan pushed open the door. Poorly lit and without windows, the Quarters seemed cavernous and dreary. Each corner of the room was illuminated with tall iron lamps, which cast a dull glow across the dark-washed walls and floor.

Some members of the Panel were already seated, while others meandered around the room, drinking coffee or talking quietly. My stomach knotted as I scanned all the faces. The only person I recognized was Karla. *She's on the Panel? Might as well fit him for the electric chair now,* I thought.

Tristan nudged me. The room fell silent the moment I walked in. I swallowed, and kept going, my footsteps echoing as I made my way across the floor. A grand leather chair dominated the head of the room. Nine seats, designated for The Panel, lined the far wall. The weight of everyone's stare clung to me as I took the last seat on the end. As the murmuring started again, I shifted uncomfortably in my chair. *Will I be able to do this?* I thought, staring down at my hands in my lap. *Can I really help sentence my own father?*

The chair beside me scrapped across the floor as someone sat down. I glanced up. Karla jerked her chin as a greeting but said nothing.

The doors to the Chamber suddenly swept open. Clan members began to file in, filling the room with dozens of bodies, quickly warming the temperature to an uncomfortable degree. The mingling scent of bird, mammals and other odors of the wild wafted through the air.

My eyes quickly found Roland. He winked and gave me a supportive smile.

I mouthed, "Where's Shandy?"

He pointed to the back corner, and though I couldn't see her, I felt her presence.

Since there weren't any chairs for the Clan members, they stood shoulder to shoulder, like an army on the front line ready to march into battle.

Like a flash of bright light, Wade burst into the Quarters. He wore a crisp white shirt, starched stiff across his barrel of a chest. White boots and shiny spurs clicked across the floor as he made his way to his chair. If not for the solemn setting, I would have laughed. Over-dressed and polished, Wade shone like a star in the bleak room. He settled his big frame into the plush leather, removing a well-worn cowboy hat and setting it on his knee.

A whiff of oiled leather crept through the room. Father was near. *What will he think of me being on The Panel?* I thought with a crushing wave of guilt.

My father stalked through the room. He was in his human form, bound in clinking handcuffs. He moved a bit slower, likely from the wound caused by the alligator-Shifter. His eyes were downcast, and his jaw set firmly. He radiated all things dark, like hatred, disgust and anger.

"Attention," Wade called out, stomping the heel of his boot into the wooden floor. "Order in the Quarters."

The room quieted.

Wade addressed the Clan. "You are witnessing the trial of cobra-Shifter, Harvey Carson. Former member, and registered deserter of the Courier Palm Clan. Any member who wishes to make a statement in defense or opposition of Carson, please do so only when I ask for statements. Any member who rushes the culprit whether in aid or aggression will be held accountable by Clan laws as well." His gaze moved across the throng of Shifters. "We will now begin."

I drew in a sudden intake of breath. Father's head lifted, and his eyes met mine in an exchange so bitter, I felt my stomach sour at the sight of him. A hint of a smile pulled at his lips, and I wanted to scream. To shake him and ask him, *why?* Surely, he couldn't find pleasure in any of this. He was about to be sentenced for a sick plot to eradicate an entire population of Shifters, morphing them into what he felt was *normal*, what he felt was *natural*.

"Harvey Carson," Wade went on. "The Wanderlust Clan is seeking a swift trial for your cruel intentions of exterminating the very core of what makes our race exceptional. This is a travesty and a malicious act of violence against your brothers and sisters. The Panel before you will select the appropriate punishment that they deem just for your crimes against the Shifting community. Do you understand these conditions?"

My father slowly tore his gaze from me and looked to Wade. He remained stoic, seemingly unnerved by Wade's words.

Tristan took position next to Wade, his hands clasped behind his back. He looked professional with his long auburn hair slicked into a low ponytail. He cleared his throat and said with a strong voice, "Harvey Carson has been generating a serum designed with the sole purpose of eliminating the distinguishing gene that makes us who we are. Shifters. Through experimentations on himself, and his daughter, Shandy Carson, he has created a serum that has been proven to be successful in eliminating the gene. He verbally relayed his desire to eradicate all Shifters with the serum, to his daughter, Layla Carson."

All eyes briefly moved to me. I tried to meet each stare with dignity.

"Harvey Carson, do you deny any of these charges?" Wade asked pointedly.

My father scoffed. "No," he said simply.

The room erupted into conversation. I tried to ignore it, choosing to keep my focus on my father. He looked arrogant, with his smug smile, and the way he held his shoulders loose, with a relaxed posture that appeared almost bored.

"Do you have any words for the Panel?"

My father's lips inched upward, curving into a sneer. "I will not plead my case, nor will I explain my actions to a bunch of mongrels. I wish each and every one of you grueling death, or impotence as not to be able to reproduce, bringing forth a new generation of mutants."

That threw the room into a tizzy. The murmurs were now raised, obviously outraged at his callousness. Tristan looked surprised, his mouth parted as he stared in bewilderment at my father. Wade's normally pleasant expression fell, and his jowl lines deepened into an angry scowl.

"Are there any statements from the Panel or the Clan?"

"Hang him high," yelled someone in the back of the room.

An unsettling number of eyes fell on me, expecting

me to argue. I pursed my lips tight. I had nothing to say. I knew my father was wrong. Dead wrong. He deserved whatever the Clan did to him.

"Members of the Clan, please excuse us while the Panel convenes," Wade said with a booming voice. "Tristan will collect you for the verdict reading." He threaded his fingers together on the desk.

As everyone filtered through the doorway, the Panel members immediately started conversing. It appeared unanimous. My father was guilty, and the highest punishment was to be inflicted. Eventually the conversation trickled down to whispers as they discussed a suitable sentence. As tense glances were being tossed in my direction, my urge to contribute to the decision grew. *This is my father, damn it. The pain he inflicted was on MY family. The innocence lost was MY sister's. I will decide his fate.*

I sat up a little straighter and squared my shoulders. "He doesn't deserve to die," I said firmly, interrupting all conversations. The eight Shifters on the Panel turned to face me. Some looked surprised, others appeared irritated, but I pushed on anyway. "Although his intentions were ultimately to humanize the entire Shifting community, his actual damage was minimal."

"That doesn't make it any less of a crime," someone pointed out.

I considered that, and they were right. If he wasn't stopped, he would have injected the reversing serum into every Clan member across the state. And beyond.

"My father essentially kidnapped his own daughter, lied to his wife, a Shifter gene-carrier. He told her their daughter had died, and instead locked her up in the woods and used her like a lab rat. He deserves punishment, and I think the greatest punishment there is, is not his own death, but the death of his movement." I held each Panel member's gaze, waiting for them think about that.

"What are you proposing?" asked an elder-Shifter.

Karla's eyes looked calculating, and I knew she had figured it out.

"Destroy the serum," I said. "All of it."

Karla smiled, and then turned to the other Panel members. "It's perfect. We'll burn his lab to the ground and make him watch."

The Shifters started talking all at once. I held my hand up to interrupt. "Afterward, he should be imprisoned so he cannot replicate the serum."

This seemed to please them. Each Panel member nodded, until everyone agreed that we had finally come to a suitable sentence for Doctor Harvey Carson.

Karla waved to Tristan, who stood waiting at the Chamber doors. "We're ready," she called.

Tristan gave a terse nod, and opened the doors, letting the Clan back in. One by one, each Clan member took their place inside the room. They seemed anxious, the tension in air thick as their eyes lingered on me.

"So, have you come to a decision?" Wade asked the Panel.

"Yes sir," answered the elder-Shifter.

Tristan collected the hand-written verdict and delivered it to Wade. I bit my lip as I watched his gaze skim across the paper, then swing to my father.

"Harvey Carson, the Wanderlust Judgment Panel has determined a fair punishment for your crimes against the Shifting community."

My father lowered his chin and stared at his bound

wrists.

"You will witness your laboratory and all the contents within in it burn to the ground until all that remains is ash—"

"No!" my father shouted, his handcuffs rattling as he rushed forward. Tristan easily restrained him, holding him back as my father yelled, "I've spent *years* developing that serum!"

"It will be destroyed, as will your plot to use it against your own kind," Wade continued. "You will be imprisoned within the Wanderlust compound, never to have the opportunity to replicate the serum. Your sentence is a life-term, so you will live and ultimately die within our territory."

The veins in Father's forehead bulged as he glowered at Wade. His lifted his lips from his teeth, which had transitioned to cobra fangs. Venom dripped from the serrated tips, dripping onto his lip and chin. "You better kill me, because if I'm given the chance, I *will* kill you." He turned his fearsome gaze on the Panel. "*All* of you." His eyes settled on me, and I could feel the hatred behind his words.

I gripped the armrests of my chair as I stared back at him. *Who was this man?* This was a mere shadow of the insensitive man I knew. This version was pure evil.

Tristan grabbed something from his waistband. When he lifted it to my father's neck, I realized it was a Taser.

"Quiet, Carson," Wade snapped. "Your words mean nothing. You heard your Judgment, and it begins immediately. Take him away and set that serum ablaze."

Tristan ushered my father out of the Judgment

Quarters. I moved to stand, but Wade's booming voice startled me, sinking me back into the chair. "We now have the matter of Sid McCarty to discuss. Trackers have traced him across the borders, well into the Jerrico Clan territory," Wade explained.

I had nearly forgotten about Sid. The fiasco at the Croix Compound felt like an eternity ago in light of the atrocity my father committed.

"Well, he's as good as dead then. Jerrico's leader doesn't take kindly to fugitives squatting on his land," said the elder member. He gave a smug smile, as if chuckling from an inside joke that the rest of us were not privy to. Perhaps he was. I knew nothing of the Jerrico Clan, or how their society was governed. "I say call Angelo, the Clan leader, inform him of McCarty's treachery and allow his men to flush him out and impose their jurisdiction upon him."

Several members nodded in agreement.

"What if McCarty is granted leniency, or is allowed to devote his loyalty to Jerrico?" I asked, not certain I like the idea of allowing another Clan the authority to punish McCarty.

"Believe me," the elder started, his dark eyes narrowing as he said, "The Jerrico Clan does *not* impose leniency in their lands. He may be given the option to redirect his loyalty, but it will come with sacrifices on McCarty's part. The Jerricos are ruthless, and their Laws are governed with an iron fist."

No one said anything else, for everyone must have agreed that that fate seemed fair, and just. All eyes turned to their leader, awaiting his final ruling.

Wade looked thoughtful as he considered this, stroking his beard. Finally, he said, "Let the Jerricos have him. I will contact Angelo and fill him in on McCarty's alliance with Rizzo. I am certain if McCarty's life is spared, he will be praying for death soon after he announces his loyalty to Angelo."

The Panel seemed thrilled with that plan of action, each smiling, some broader than others. It was those grins that make me wonder what exactly they know about the Jerrico Clan to make them so eager to see McCarty at their mercy.

"And Moore?" I questioned. "What about him?"

"He sits behind bars at the moment," Wade said. "His judgement is approaching." He glanced at the Panel. "And it won't be kind. He worked with Victor Rizzo. He worked with your father. The man has a bitter end awaiting him." I swallowed.

"I call closure to this Judgment Panel Session, and thank each of you for your time, loyalty and commitment to keep harmony within our Clan." Wade looked at me directly. "Especially to you, Matriarch. You saved our race." He stood and clapped me on the back. "You're tough as nails, kid. Be proud of yourself." He smiled down at me, and gave me a wink before strolling away, his spurs clicking on the floor as he went.

As the rest of the room emptied, I continued to sit there, lost in a stupor of confusion, relief and sadness. My father as I knew him was gone. Now replaced with a vile man, full of so much hatred for Shifters he'd go to extremes to remove them from society. My blood ran cold at the thought.

A gentle touch roused me, and I jerked my head up, meeting the smoldering gaze of Roland. His fingertips grazed my temple as he pushed my hair from my face.

"You okay?" he asked.

I leaned forward, burying my head into his stomach. I wrapped my arms around his waist and sobbed. The emotion of the Judgment was too much. He let me cry in peace, offering only his comforting presence and a gentle massage on my neck.

I mumbled into his shirt, "Where did they take him?"

"They're accompanying him back to the carriage house."

I lifted my face, unable to hide my surprise. "Now?" I quickly stood, wiping my cheeks dry. My eyes felt swollen, and my head ached from crying. "We have to go, I want to be there."

"What?" Roland stared at me, his golden eyes round. "No, Layla, you've done enough. No one expects you to be there."

"I want to. I *have* to." I crossed the room, glad to be leaving the shadowed room, now full of painful memories. "Where's Shandy? She may want some things out of the house before they burn it."

"She's in the lobby."

I picked up my pace, but Roland caught my elbow, pulling me back.

"Layla, you can be weak, you know" he said. "You don't have to be the Matriarch all the time. You can be *just* Layla." I shook my head. "I haven't been *just* Layla since the rhesus macaque at the hospital begged me for help. I have to see this to the end Roland, not just because it's my father, but because it's my duty. I was chosen to protect, and I'm going to do just that." I refused to back down, my eyes securely on his, waiting for him to say something.

He sighed. "I should learn to just follow you, because I'll be damned if I'll ever be able to hold you back."

I smiled and gave him a quick peck on the cheek. "My mom always said that my will is strong, and my head is just as hard." *Mom.* My stomach sank. Amid all the chaos I somehow forgotten about her. How was she? How was she going to handle everything? How would she take the news of Father being sentenced to life in prison, and Shandy being alive?

My heart felt as though it was shrinking, but I didn't have time to dwell on that. I had to get to the carriage house, and watch it perish. Hopefully it would bring some closure. Or at least solace that the serum was finally destroyed, never to be used viciously against another Shifter again.

****

My father was still heavily bound with shiny restraints, held back by two Shifters. He fought against them, seemingly never tiring. His wrists were raw and bloodied from the biting metal, but he didn't seem to notice. He continuously screamed and cussed until his voice grew hoarse.

Members of the Clan poured gas throughout the house. The smell of it was overwhelming. Stone-faced and somber, Shifters gathered around the carriage house, ready to watch my father receive punishment for his crimes.

Soon, the laboratory will be set ablaze, destroying decades worth of work and torture.

Shandy didn't want anything from the house, in fact, she insisted that everything within it remain, and face the flames along with Father's beloved serum. She stood with slumped shoulders, the rings beneath her eyes deeply shadowed, and her face drawn. I went to her, standing at her side quietly until I gathered the courage to reach for her hand.

She let me take it, and together we watched as Wade lit a match.

"And so it begins," Wade said directly to my father. "The end of your reign of terror and devilish intentions." He flicked the match into a puddle of gasoline, and it ignited into a furious bundle of fire, spreading quickly across the porch and into the laboratory. The deafening whoosh of flames and shattering glass echoed throughout the quiet forest. I shrank back, feeling the heat across my face as the house became engulfed in flames. The wooden floorboards snapped, and the whizzing sound of flammable chemicals shot into the air.

Father let out a furious scream.

Then something awful happened. Father broke free from the Shifters and charged straight into the carriage house.

No! I ripped my hand free from Shandy and found myself running to him on instinct and adrenaline alone.

Two strong arms caught me by the waist.

"Let me go!" I shouted.

Roland held me tight. "You can't save him, Layla!"

A loud hiss came from inside the burning house, sending a shudder through me. Was it from the fire? Or was it my father?

My knees gave out, crumbling me to the ground. Roland sank to the grass with me, holding me as I sobbed. Why was I even crying? My father was a sick man. He caused my family nothing but heartache. Still...I didn't want him dead. It took me a long time to realize I was crying for the man I wished he was, not the man he had become.

I felt a light touch at my shoulder. I turned, surprised to find Shandy standing there. Her lips quivered just before she dropped to her knees beside me and threw her arms around my neck. Together we wept. The nightmare was over, but the memories of it would be real and long lasting.

Chapter 23

My father's body burned with the carriage house. His remains a part of the crispy ashes that lay strewn across the charred grass. Shandy and I mourned the father that he could have been, leaning on one another for support as we departed the forest, vowing never to return there.

"I want to introduce you to someone," I said to Shandy as we hauled ourselves inside Roland's SUV.

Her jade eyes darted to me, her face full of worry. She began fumbling with her sleeves, picking at a loose string.

"You deserve to have a parent who will love you unconditionally," I continued. "And Mom will do just that."

She bit at her bottom lip. I smiled at the nervous gesture we shared. I couldn't wait to learn all of our similarities, and our differences. Did we have twin telepathy? Dawning hit me quick as I thought about my panic attacks. They were from Shandy—they were from her fear—not mine.

Roland started the engine, reached across the console and laid a hand on my knee. Looking at the two of them, my heart swelled. I may have lost my father but look at what I had gained.

****

Shandy stood outside the door to our mother's

hospital room, fidgeting with her sweater. I took her hands, squeezing them as I said, "Take a deep breath."

Her expectant eyes locked onto mine. She inhaled, expelling it through her mouth as she was told. I waited until her shoulders relaxed before I led her inside. Roland waited just outside the door as Shandy and I entered, hand in hand.

Mom no longer needed to be connected to the monitor, so the room was quiet without the steady clicks and beeps of the machinery. The light over her bed was still on, casting a buttery glow across her face as she slept. Her hair spilled across the pillow and her hands were resting lightly on her chest.

Shandy shot me a worried look.

"It's okay. She's just sleeping."

Her eyes swept across Mother's body.

"Komodo-Shifters," I said, answering her unspoken question.

Her footfalls were silent as she padded slowly, crossing the room, her eyes never leaving Mom.

Together we stood at the foot of the bed, watching her chest rise and fall as she peacefully slept.

"She's beautiful," Shandy whispered.

Mother stirred, her eyes fluttering open sleepily before she finally focused on the two matching faces before her. She sat up with a start.

I reached out and touched her foot, and said softly, "Mom. Do you know who this is?"

Her breaths came out like frightened pants, her brown eyes wild as she touched her temple. "Am I dreaming?"

I shook my head.

Her eyes were wide, and disbelieving. "I have to

be, Layla. This can't be real. Shandy is dead." Her lips began to tremble, and her eyes shone with a sadness that I had never seen before.

"Mom," I began carefully. "I have to tell you something." I rounded the foot of her bed and took her hand into mine. Biting my lip, I struggled to form the right words, then finally just said it. "Did you know Fatber was a Shifter?"

Her jaw locked and her eyes steeled. "Yes."

A flash of anger struck through me. Another secret.

"He told me after we married." Her hands slowly clenched into fists. "After I saw him Turn."

The memory of him as a disfigured cobra had me shaking. How could that monster be my father?

"I was thrilled," she continued, her eyes far-away. "I could tell him about my blood-lines without worry of being judged. I was just about to tell him when he confessed how he despised what he was. How much he hated Shifters, and wished he wasn't one. I decided then, and there, to never tell him the truth about me." She cast her eyes to her fists.

That's why she was adamant about me wearing sunglasses around him when my eyes changed. She knew Father would realize what I was and hate me for it. My heart felt too heavy in my chest. I never had a chance. Father hated me when I was a human, and he hated me even more as a Shifter.

"Did you know the lengths he went through to *not* be a Shifter?"

Mother raised her head, questioning me quietly.

"With Dr. Moore's help, they created a serum that could reverse the Shifting gene. He tested it on himself, and on Shandy."

Mom's eyes shot to my twin. "He told me you died."

"He took the baby that bore the Mark," I continued. "Raised her in the woods outside of town and used her as a test subject."

Sadness welled in my mother's eyes as she held me in her gaze. "You were spared only because you didn't have a Mark." She squeezed my fingers, and closed her eyes, tears running down her cheeks.

I watched her, unsure if I should continue.

"That bastard," she said through gritted teeth, as she pounded a fist against the mattress.

"Mom." I glanced at Shandy fleetingly, then back at my mother. "The Wanderlust Clan set his Judgment." My lips suddenly felt brittle, like autumn leaves. I wet them before saying, "He was sentenced to lifetime imprisonment and the serum destroyed."

"Good," she spat.

"But," I said, my voice cracking.

She looked at me sharply. "But? But what?"

"But…he died himself before they could return him to the compound." I felt the impending tears building up, but they just would not fall, as if refusing to release for the man who overtook my father's soul. "As part of his punishment, his lab was set on fire, and he was forced to watch." A lump formed in my throat. "He ran straight into it. He died with his serum."

She stared at me for a long time, her face unreadable. I wished badly I could see her thoughts. With our fingers still intertwined, she began to weep. Shandy looked lost as she watched us from a distance.

"Mom, I know you're hurting, but we are here to help you. Together, we will get through this. We will heal each other."

Her pained eyes lifted to mine. "You are incredibly strong. It's no wonder you've been chosen." She sniffed and motioned for Shandy to come closer. Slowly, my sister made her way to the bedside. Mother raised a hand toward her, but Shandy's face was just out of reach. I was surprised when she bent forward, allowing Mom to run her fingers across her cheek and chin.

"Shandy, I never stopped loving you. I've been mourning you for twenty-seven years, but in that time, I've also been celebrating your life. In my head, I heard your laugh, your first word, saw your first day at school, your graduation, and each birthday. You had a life within my mind. I'm heartbroken that your actual life, didn't live up to what I envisioned for you."

Now my tears came. I cried for my sister's pain and I cried for my mother's grief.

"I don't know if I can live with the memories of what he did," Shandy whispered, anguish casting a darkness about her face. "I look at Layla, and I'm jealous. I can't help but think, why me? Why didn't he love me?" She angrily wiped her tears with the back of her hand. She spoke directly to Mother. "I don't know if you're enough to erase the memories." She covered her face with her hands, sobbing uncontrollably into her palms. "I wish he had just killed me. I wasn't born to be human." She suddenly pivoted her body and slammed both fists against the window, pounding on it ruthlessly as if trying to break out.

My heart broke for her. Fear gripped my stomach. Call it twin telepathy, or call it a hunch, but something deep inside my gut told me Shandy would rather die, than live with her memories.

She began beating her head against the glass, wailing.

I knew what I had to do. It was the only way to help her. I crossed the room, adrenaline starting to spike my blood as I watched her unlock the window.

"I can't be human," she cried. "I'd rather die!"

I steeled myself before grasping her shoulder. I fastened my fingers deep into her skin and closed my eyes. *Your memories of the past twenty-seven years will fade away. They will be replaced with fond memories of Mother, Father, and me. You know nothing of the Shifting world, and as you know it, we are visiting Mother at the hospital after a car accident took Father's life. You are sad now, but you know that you are deeply loved.*

Shandy's muscles began to relax, and her flailing body grew still. I released my grip, lowering my arm to my side as I watched her carefully. *Did it work?*

She turned around and tucked her hair behind her ears. She gave me a tender smile, then walked over to Mom. She took Mom's hand, then held out an open hand out toward me. I crossed the floor and grasped her outstretched hand.

It worked.

Of course, I realized I'd eventually have to lie to Shandy to cover up what I'd done. I'd have to figure out how to explain why there are no baby pictures of her, no high school diploma, no bedroom to call her own. But those were problems for another day. Right then I just wanted to soak in the moment of happiness.

"Layla and I are here for you, Mama. Though our hearts ache for Daddy, I know we can get through this together."

I could feel my mom's eyes on me. I pleaded with her silently. *I had to,* I thought.

Mom gave me a knowing nod and forced a tight smile as she turned her eyes to Shandy. A tiny hitch of breath caught in her throat as she collected herself. It was going to be a challenge, dealing with the truth in secret, but for Shandy's wellbeing, it would be worth it.

Roland cleared his throat from the hall. His silhouette was statuesque, filling most of the doorway. He stepped inside the room, his eyes roaming over our joined hands. He seemed pleased to see us like that, his mouth curving into a warm smile.

"How's it going in here?" he asked, his honey voice arrowing through my blood. A sudden need for him overwhelmed me—and not just physically. I needed to be just Layla for a while, and that was only possible when I was with Roland.

"Mom, I'm going to leave you with Shandy, is that all right?"

"Oh yes," she said. "I'll think we take a walk down memory lane for a while." She winked at me and mouthed 'thank you' as I bent to kiss her.

"I love you, Mom," I whispered against her cheek.

"I love you more," she replied, patting my hand consolingly.

I smiled at her and went to Shandy. "You up to staying with Mom awhile?"

"Of course. I'll snuggle up on the chair over here, and we'll be fine. Go and get some rest, Layla."

I gave her a hug, and she actually hugged me back. My heart felt full, and finally whole. I planned on fulfilling Shandy's memories of happiness and love, so what she felt was honest and real, not just false emotions that I planted within her head.

Linking my arm through Roland's, we departed, leaving my mom and Shandy to create their own memories. The task will help her cope with Father's passing, giving her a reason to recall tender moments, and forging a bond with the daughter she thought she lost.

As we drove to my house, I sat there quiet, lost in thoughts about the past twenty-four hours. How I gained a sister but lost a father. How I drove away the demons that haunted my sister's mind and brought peace to my mother's grieving heart.

The SUV's headlights finally swung across the front of the house as we turned into my driveway, and for the first time since discovering Shifters existed, I was not afraid to go in alone. As I looked back at Roland, I realized something. Although I wasn't scared, I wasn't ready to be alone. I needed him, even if he just held me through the night, I *needed* to be close to him.

"Will you stay with me?" I asked.

His brows lifted in surprise. "Of course," he said.

I smiled and stepped out into the crisp night air. Roland followed me across the lawn and up the porch steps. I could feel him behind me as I unlocked the door and pushed it open, and suddenly I felt anxious, and giddy all at once. Roland was going to stay with me, all night, and I just knew it was the first of many.

I led him to my room, where I kicked out of my shoes and padded to the bathroom.

"I'm in a desperate need of a shower," I said, unbuttoning my jeans. "You're welcome to it when I'm done."

Roland took a quick assessment of himself, saying,

and "I'll take that offer" as he sniffed his soiled shirt and wrinkled his nose.

I giggled and closed the door behind me. I quickly stripped out of my dingy clothes and left them in a heap on the floor. Humming to myself, I turned the dials on the shower and stepped in. I let the water run over me, drenching my hair and washing away the grit that layered my skin. In no time, steam fogged the glass on the shower door, filling the room with a dreamy haze. A rush of cool air sent a shiver through me. My gaze flickered to the bathroom door. Roland stood in the doorway, his arms folded in front of him with a sexy smirk on his lips.

Heat crept across my cheeks, and I felt the compulsion to shield myself. Then I remembered the night in the woods after I Shifted. He saw my naked body once already, why should I be shy? *Nudity is commonplace among Shifters, remember?*

I stared across the shower door at him, the sound of water trickling across the glass was the only sound other than our steady breathing.

He unhitched himself from the door jamb and sauntered across the floor. His fingers appeared over the edge of the door as he peeked inside the shower, saying in a husky voice, "Mind if I join you?"

I laughed. "I thought cats hate water."

His hooded eyes looked devilish as he said, "Total misconception. Let me prove it."

I bit my lip, considering it, my heart fluttering wildly within my chest.

He wet his lips, and that sent me over the edge. I slid the shower door open, sucking in a shocked breath as the cold air nipped at me, prickling my flesh with goose bumps.

Roland shed his clothes, and stepped inside, the water spraying off his broad shoulders, and misting his golden skin with sparkling water droplets. He looked amazing, like a statue of a Greek God in the center of a fountain. I admired him for a moment, gazing at him as the steam dampened his hair against his head, and a stream of water flowed over his chest and down his muscular abs. His hands cupped my hips, pulling me against him, his woodsy scent wafting around me, drawing me closer. I arched my back, looking up into his golden eyes.

He cocked his head just slightly, causing the water to trickle down his nose, and drip onto my chest. I felt as though I were going to explode from all of the sensations. The steam-filled air, the warm water slipping across my skin, and the feel of his hands. My body reacted, yearning to be touched all over. Pushing my hair back, Roland held my face as he pressed his lips against mine. I grew dizzy from the kiss, pulling away to meet his smoldering stare.

Without saying a word, he swooped me into his arms and carried me out of the shower and into the bedroom. Ever so gently, he placed me in the center of the bed. The comforter absorbed the moisture from my body, but my hair was still sopping wet. I lay back, spreading it out across the pillows. Roland ran his fingers through his hair, shaking off the excess water before crawling toward me, the bed dipping slightly from his weight.

His face hovered over my thighs, and I clenched them together, trying to relieve the thrumming that radiated from my core. He gently nudged them apart, his breath hot against my skin as he placed several lazy, worshipping kisses at the crease of my inner thighs. I should have felt self-conscious. I should have played coy, but nothing short of a tornado touching down on top of us would make me stop.

I gasped as his tongue ran across me. Warm, and wet, and sheet-clawing delicious as he trailed it up and over to my navel. Peering at me from across my abdomen, he said, "I've licked it. Now it's mine."

Those words were nearly my undoing. I envisioned a lean jungle cat licking the nape of its prey just before it sinks it teeth into it. I squirmed at the thought.

He let out a sensual growl, and slowly covered my body with his, bearing his own weight on his forearms. I fit within him perfectly. His fingers traced my hairline tenderly, before he planted kisses along my jaw. I watched the muscles within his shoulders flex, then something on his skin caught my eye. I stared at it, trying to make it out.

I clasped his fingers, stretching his arm out straight. There, beneath his bicep, was a splotch of spots peppering his skin. *His Mark*—a paw print. It was beautiful, and it made him who he was. A felis-Shifter. My Mate. I touched my lips to it, feeling him shudder as I lightly kissed it.

He purred, and something stirred within me that was more than just longing, more than just desire. It was stronger. It was instinct. My body knew it was made for Roland, and it cried out for him. This was my destiny. Not just being a hark-Shifter, or the Matriarch, but being in love with Roland Stone. Claiming him as mine, just as he Claimed me as his.

As we made love, I wept with happiness. I found

my Mate, the other half of me that made me stronger, safer, braver and utterly fulfilled. His love gave me everything I could possibly need as a woman, as a Shifter, as Layla Carson, as the Matriarch.

"I've got you, and I won't let go until you're ready," I murmured.

Smiling, he trailed a finger across my bottom lip. "You say when."

Epilogue

I traced my palm across my bulging belly. "I can't wait to meet them," I said with a smile to Roland. He covered my hand with his, the familiar warmth of his touch spreading across my skin like honey. "I wonder if they'll be Marked?"

"It doesn't matter whether they are or not. I'll love them, no matter what," he said before touching his lips to my temple.

My heart lifted, knowing that he would. Roland would love his Young, just as he loved me. Fiercely and wholly. I touched his chin and pressed a kiss to his lips just before the ceremony began.

The crowd hushed as Shandy and Gwen stepped forward, each taking their places before Wade. He greeted them both with a broad, teeth-flashing grin before saying, "Upon this Nurturing Ceremony, Roland and Layla Stone ask that each of you vow to protect their Young as you would your own should any unfortunate circumstances take place." Wade faced Shandy. "As twin sister to the Mother, your role as Aunt and Nurturer will be vital. I know you embrace this with open arms and heart."

Shandy nodded, reaching behind her to grip my hand, giving it a gentle squeeze. I smiled, happy I decided to tell Shandy about Shifters, though I never revealed that she had been one herself.

Wade turned to Gwen. She was practically bouncing. She was so excited about the twins. From the time she learned I was expecting a boy and a girl, she tried to convince me to name them either Donny and Marie or Jasper and Alice.

"Gwen Gibb," Wade began. "You have been appointed Nurturer because of your strong bond with Layla. It has been said that family is not just by blood, but also by those who display loyalty to others. Do you embrace this role with open arms and heart?"

"Absolutely," she stated in a loud, clear voice. She looked over at me and flashed her famous Gwen smile that deepened her dimples.

"Then I hereby declare that with the birth of the Stone twins, so begins the declared Nurturers charge of providing a secondary source of love, teaching, guidance, and support for this family."

There was an eruption of applause from the audience, which consisted of the entire Wanderlust Clan, and my mother.

As we faced them, I rested one hand on my stomach, waving to the crowd with the other, relishing the outpouring of love and support from my newly extended family.

Shandy smiled at me, her breezy dress floating lightly around her knees. Her face had filled out over the past year, and her frame didn't seem as fragile. She leaned over and rested her hand against my stomach. "Roland's side of the family sure do things differently. All of this hoopla, just to say I'm the god-mother." She rolled her eyes and gave a little laugh.

One of the babies kicked, and when Shandy's smile brightened, I knew she felt it too.

"This one is going to be feisty," she said. "Like her mama." She patted my arm, then walked away, and sat down beside Mother.

Roland draped an arm around my shoulder, pulling me into him, his eyes casting out to Shandy and Mom.

"They've come a long way, haven't they?" he said.

I nodded, emotion sneaking up on me and pricking my eyes with tears.

"They're strong women," I said. "I just hope I did the right thing by wiping Shandy's memory." I thought back to the day in the hospital. To when her rage overtook her senses to the point she thought the only way to escape was to die. Just like our father.

"You did what you had to do to protect her. You relied on your intuition, and if it told you to wipe her mind, then that's what you had to do. It's instincts over rationality now, Layla."

Looking out at the beautiful ceremony, I smiled, thankful my life led me to this moment. I had inherited a new family-the Wanderlust Clan. I loved my job as a zookeeper, and not once did I regret my decision to leave Greater Hope Hospital. Now more than ever, I knew my father could never have planned for this.

My destiny was already set. My destiny as a Shifter, who was in love with a Shifter, and who was chosen to protect all Shifters. I was no longer ashamed of my new identity, and in fact I embraced it. I was proud to let my true nature roar.

A word about the author…

I work full-time as a zoo curator, so when I'm not running a zoo, I'm trying to tame the one I live in! I have two kids, and a husband who sometimes acts their age.

I can usually be found jamming to Elvis Presley tunes or diligently chipping away at my never-ending "to be read" pile.

I tend to gravitate toward anything paranormal. I love creatures who fly and characters who sprout fur or fangs. Sprinkle some romance and magic into the mix, and I'm a happy girl!